NICKELODEON™

降 世 神 通

AVATAR

THE LAST AIRBENDER™

S0-CFQ-359

⊙ TOKYOPOP®

amburg • London • Los Angeles • Tokyo

Contributing Editor - Robert Langhorn
Associate Editor - Katherine Schilling
Cover Designer - Monalisa J. de Asis
Graphic Designer, Letterer - Tomás Montalvo-Lagos
Graphic Artist - Monalisa J. de Asis

Digital Imaging Manager - Chris Buford
Production Managers - Elisabeth Brizzi
Senior Designer - Louis Csontos
Art Director - Al-insan Lashley
Senior Editor - Luis Reyes
Managing Editor - Vy Nguyen
Editor in Chief - Rob Tokar
Creative Director - Anne Marie Horne
Publisher - Mike Kiley
President & C.O.O. - John Parker
C.E.O. & Chief Creative Officer - Stuart Levy

E-mail: info@TOKYOPOP.com
Come visit us online at www.TOKYOPOP.com

A **TOKYOPOP**® Cine-Manga® Book
TOKYOPOP Inc.
5900 Wilshire Blvd., Suite 2000
Los Angeles, CA 90036

Avatar: The Last Airbender Chapter 7

ISBN: 978-1-4278-1143-1

First TOKYOPOP® printing: June 2008

10 9 8 7 6 5 4 3 2 1

Printed in the USA

NICKELODEON™

降世神通

AVATAR
THE LAST AIRBENDER

Created By

Michael Dante DiMartino &

Bryan Konietzko

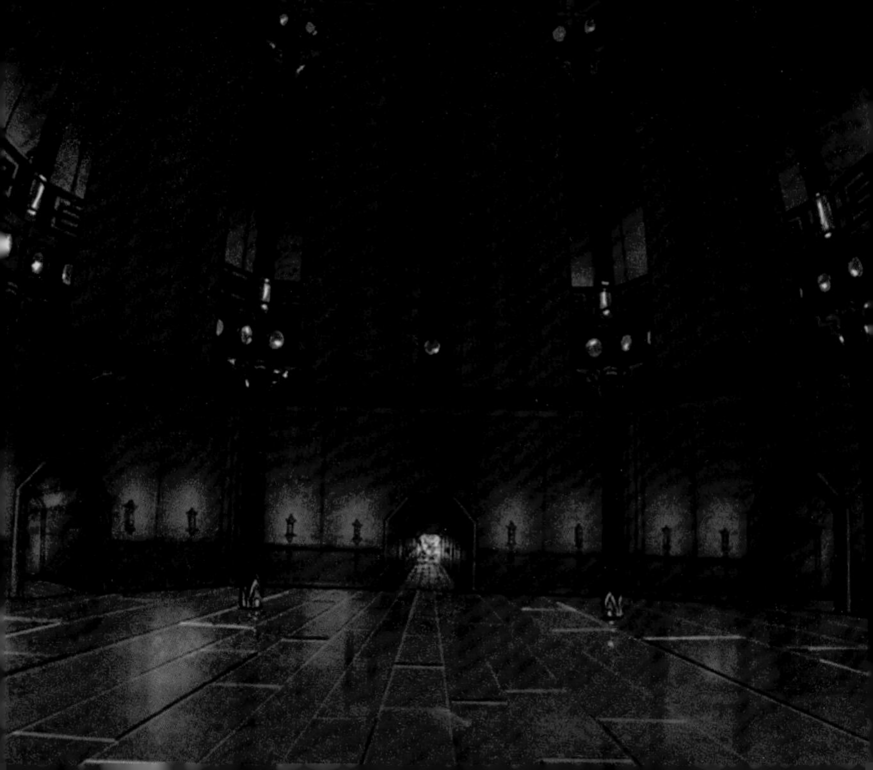

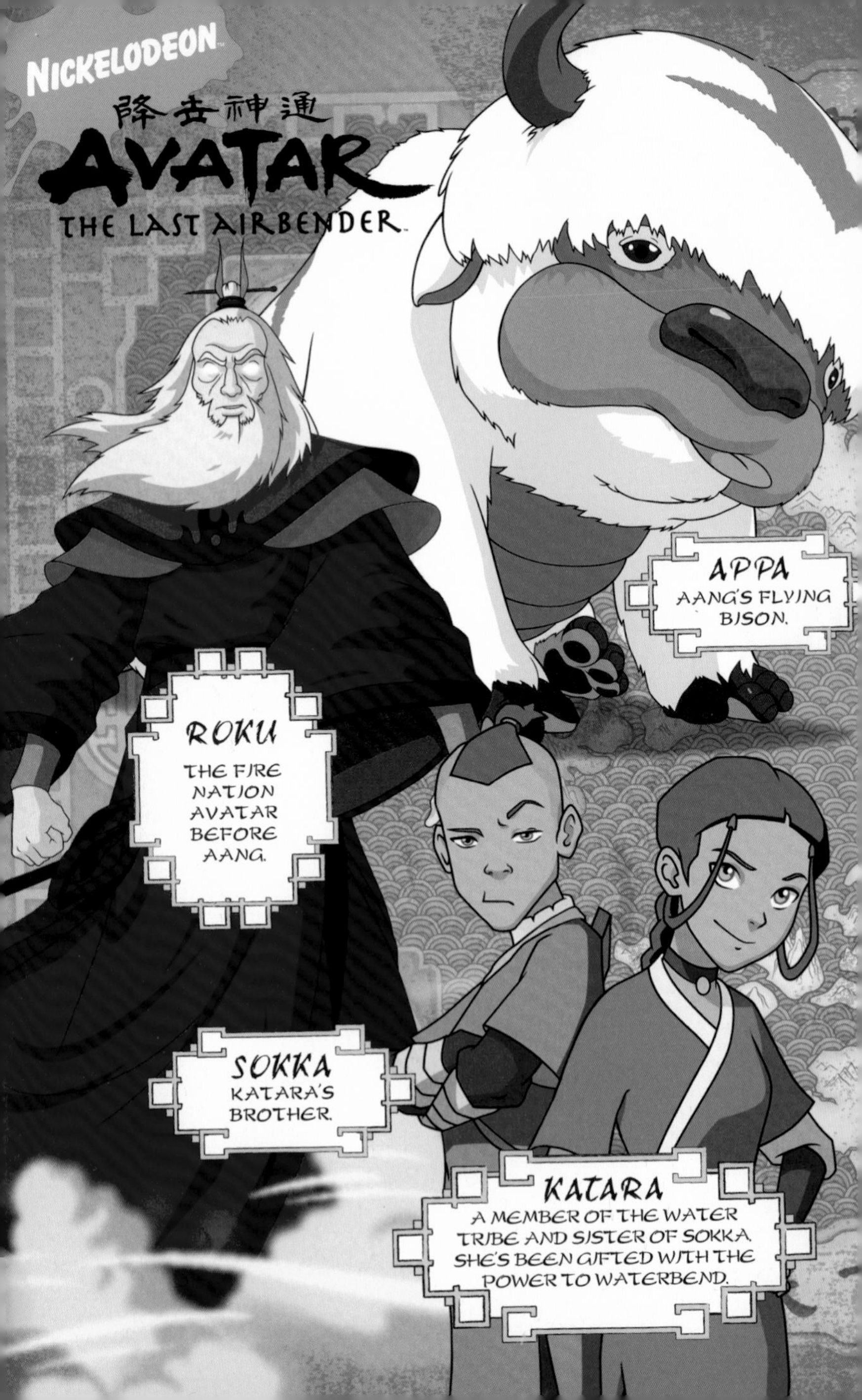
NICKELODEON
降世神通
AVATAR
THE LAST AIRBENDER
APPA
AANG'S FLYING BISON.
ROKU
THE FIRE NATION AVATAR BEFORE AANG.
SOKKA
KATARA'S BROTHER.
KATARA
A MEMBER OF THE WATER TRIBE AND SISTER OF SOKKA. SHE'S BEEN GIFTED WITH THE POWER TO WATERBEND.

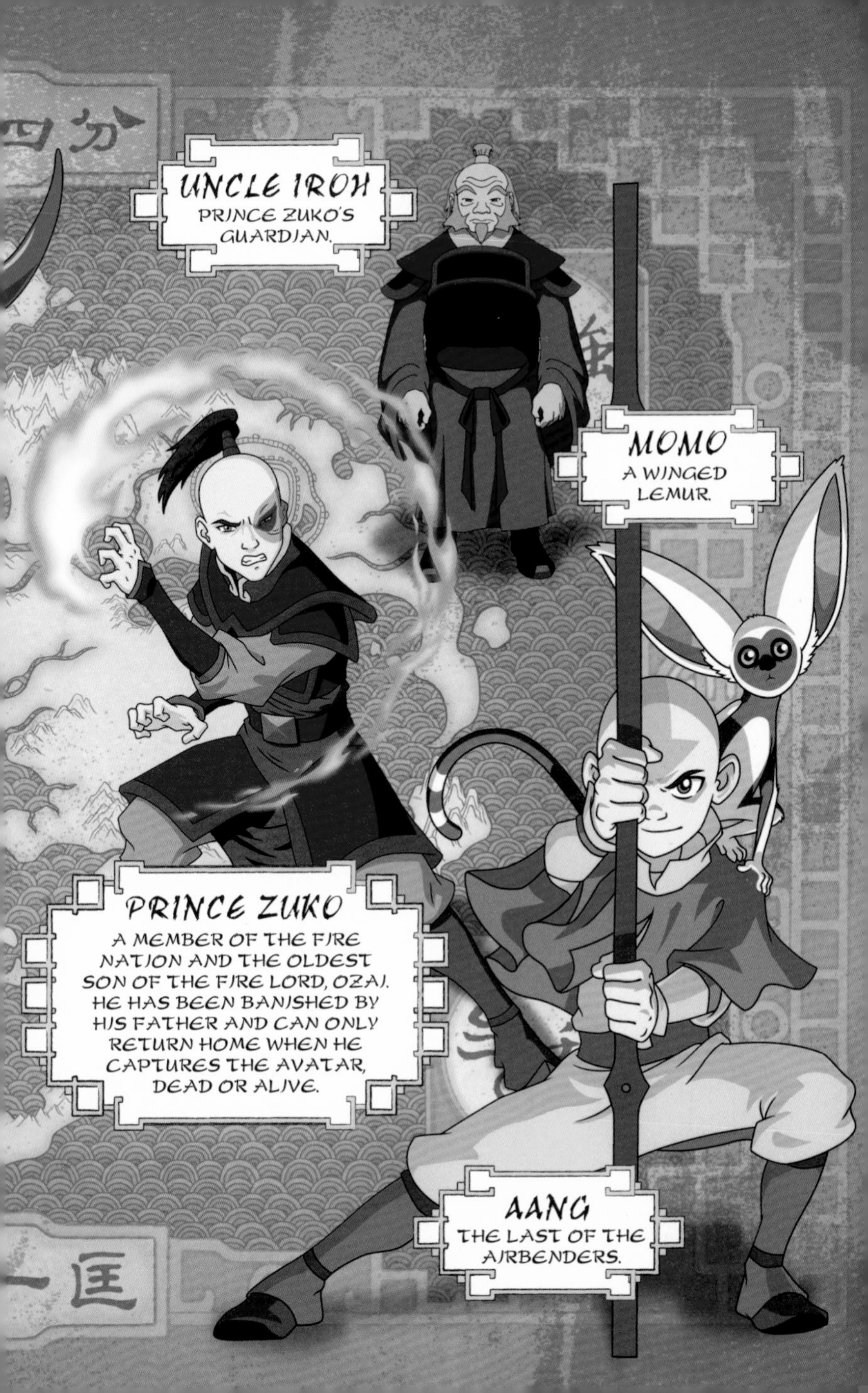

UNCLE IROH
PRINCE ZUKO'S GUARDIAN.
MOMO
A WINGED LEMUR.
PRINCE ZUKO
A MEMBER OF THE FIRE NATION AND THE OLDEST SON OF THE FIRE LORD, OZAI. HE HAS BEEN BANISHED BY HIS FATHER AND CAN ONLY RETURN HOME WHEN HE CAPTURES THE AVATAR, DEAD OR ALIVE.
AANG
THE LAST OF THE AIRBENDERS.

NICKELODEON™

降去神通

AVATAR
THE LAST AIRBENDER™

CHAPTER 7:
CONTENTS

THE STORY SO FAR...

BEING THE AVATAR ISN'T ALL FUN AND GAMES FOR AANG AND HIS TEAM. THE TITLE ALSO BRINGS GREAT RESPONSIBILITY, AND AANG HAS ALREADY FOUND HIMSELF BEING RELIED ON BY MANY IN NEED OF HIS HELP. AFTER RESCUING THE EARTHBENDERS FROM IMPRISONMENT, AANG AND HIS FRIENDS SOON FIND MORE EVIDENCE OF THE FIRE NATION'S DESCTRUCTIVE TYRANNY OVER THE LAND, AND THE DEFEATED PEOPLE LEFT IN ITS WAKE.

IS AANG READY TO FULFILL HIS ROLE AS AVATAR...?

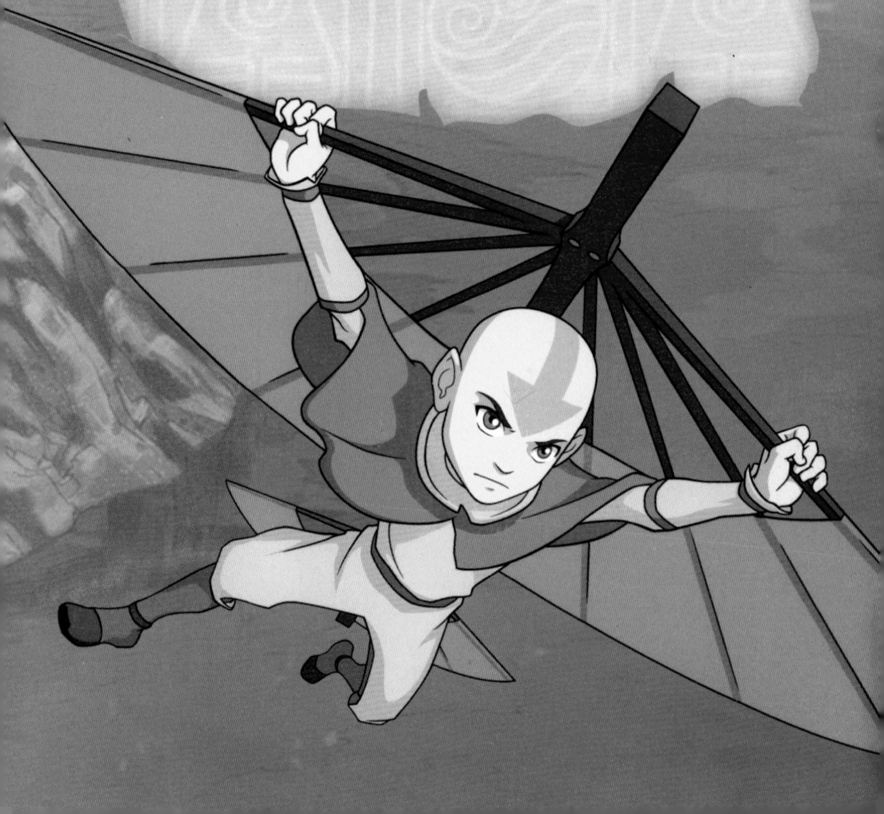

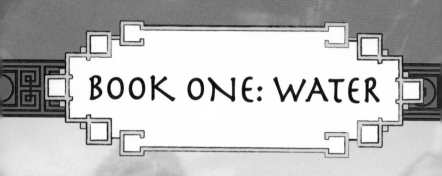

BOOK ONE: WATER

CHAPTER SEVEN:
THE SPIRIT WORLD:
WINTER SOLSTICE PART 1

WRITTEN BY
AARON EHASZ

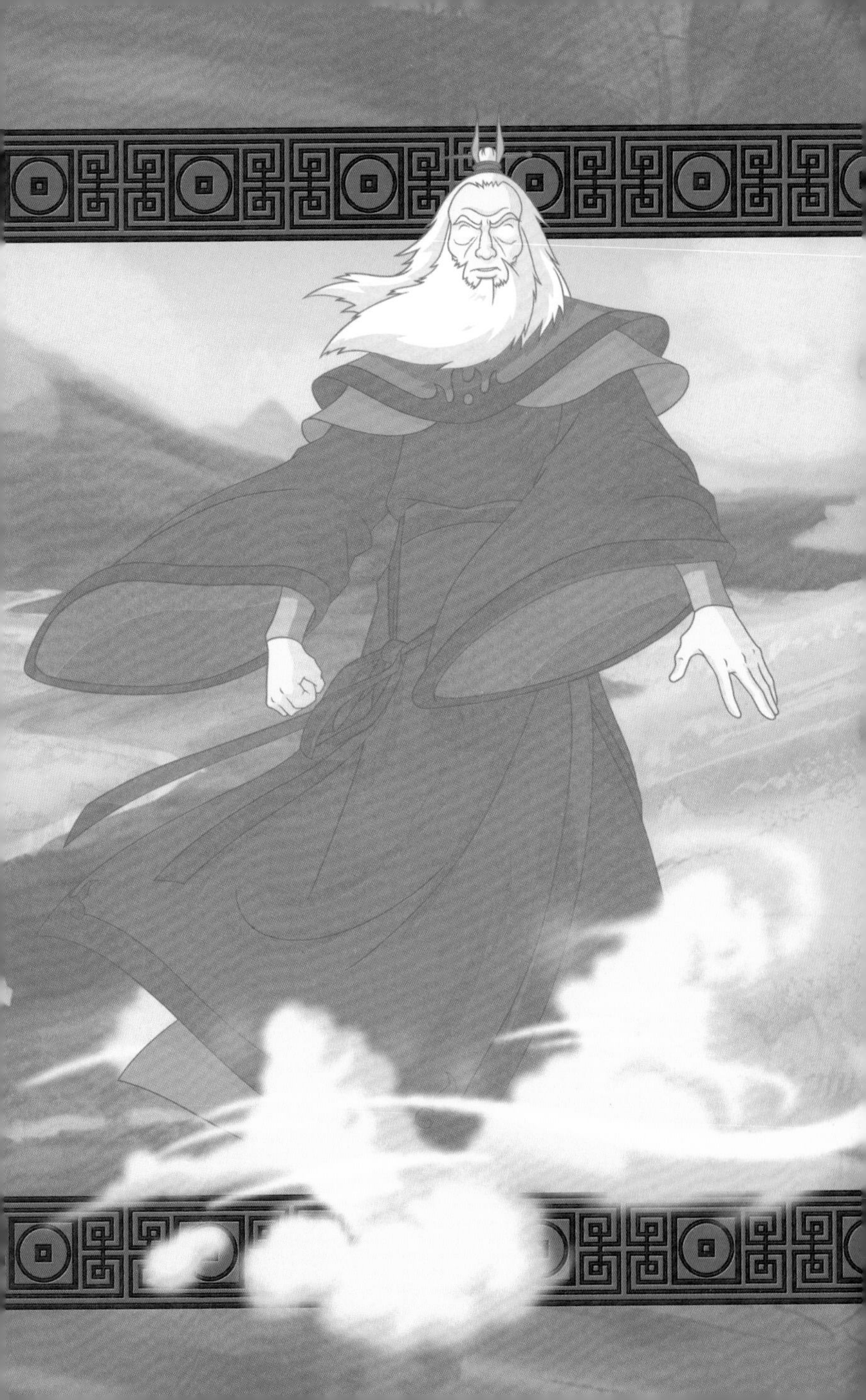

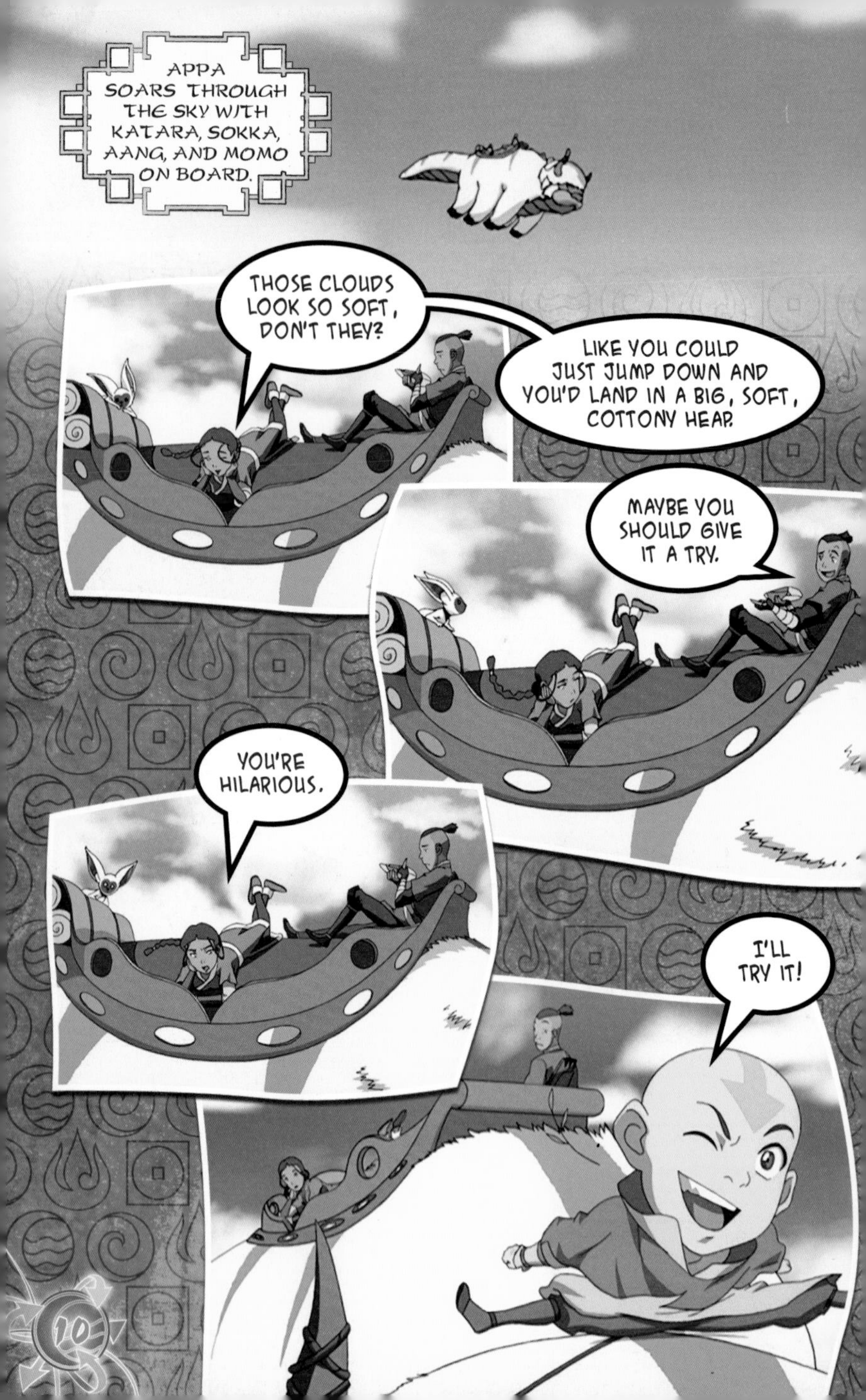
APPA SOARS THROUGH THE SKY WITH KATARA, SOKKA, AANG, AND MOMO ON BOARD.
THOSE CLOUDS LOOK SO SOFT, DON'T THEY?
LIKE YOU COULD JUST JUMP DOWN AND YOU'D LAND IN A BIG, SOFT, COTTONY HEAP.
MAYBE YOU SHOULD GIVE IT A TRY.
YOU'RE HILARIOUS.
I'LL TRY IT!
10

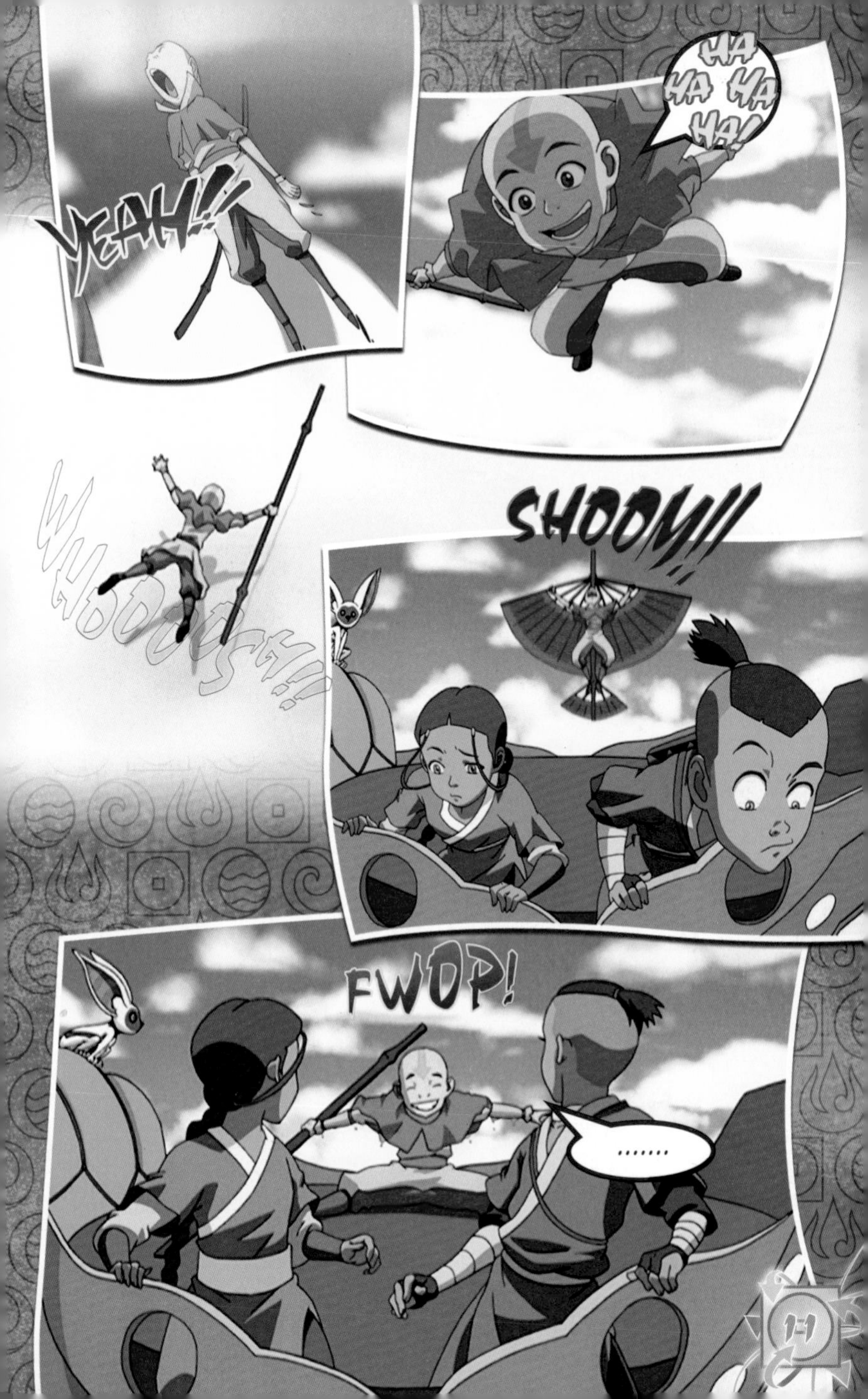
YEAH!!
HA HA HA HA!
WHOOOSH!!!
SHOOM!!
FWOP!
....

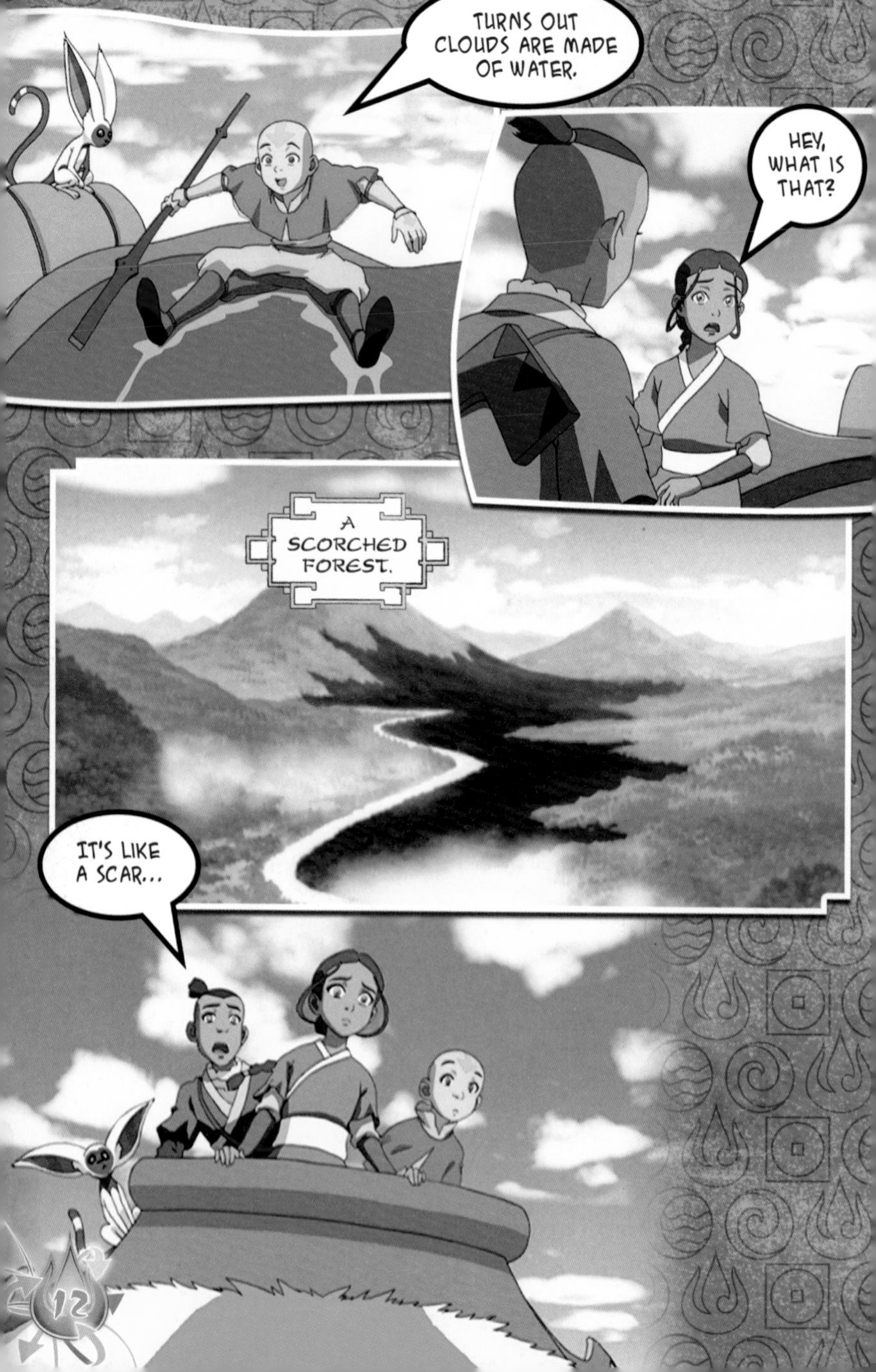
TURNS OUT CLOUDS ARE MADE OF WATER.
HEY, WHAT IS THAT?
A SCORCHED FOREST.
IT'S LIKE A SCAR...

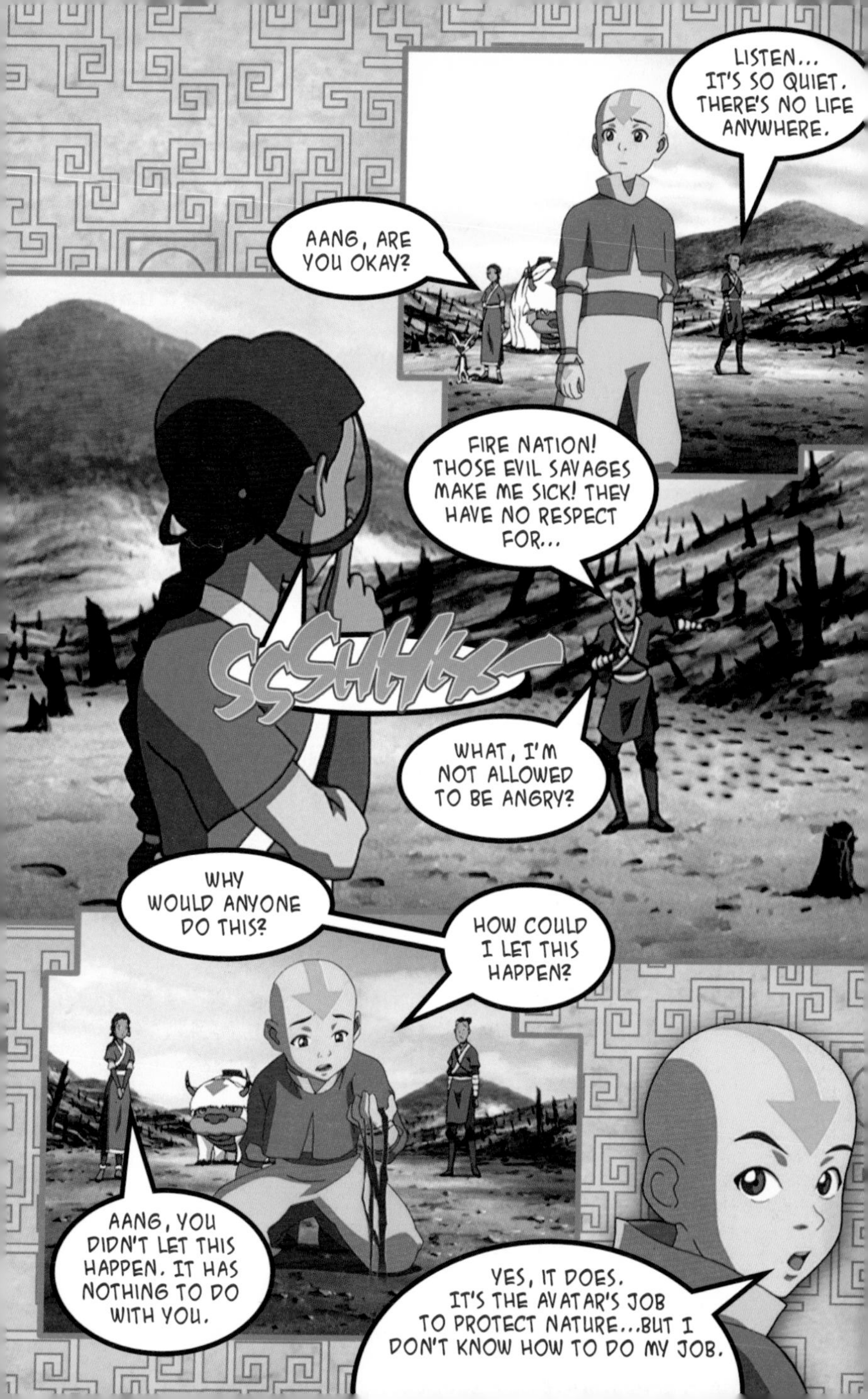
LISTEN... IT'S SO QUIET. THERE'S NO LIFE ANYWHERE.
AANG, ARE YOU OKAY?
FIRE NATION! THOSE EVIL SAVAGES MAKE ME SICK! THEY HAVE NO RESPECT FOR...
SSSHHHH-
WHAT, I'M NOT ALLOWED TO BE ANGRY?
WHY WOULD ANYONE DO THIS?
HOW COULD I LET THIS HAPPEN?
AANG, YOU DIDN'T LET THIS HAPPEN. IT HAS NOTHING TO DO WITH YOU.
YES, IT DOES. IT'S THE AVATAR'S JOB TO PROTECT NATURE...BUT I DON'T KNOW HOW TO DO MY JOB.

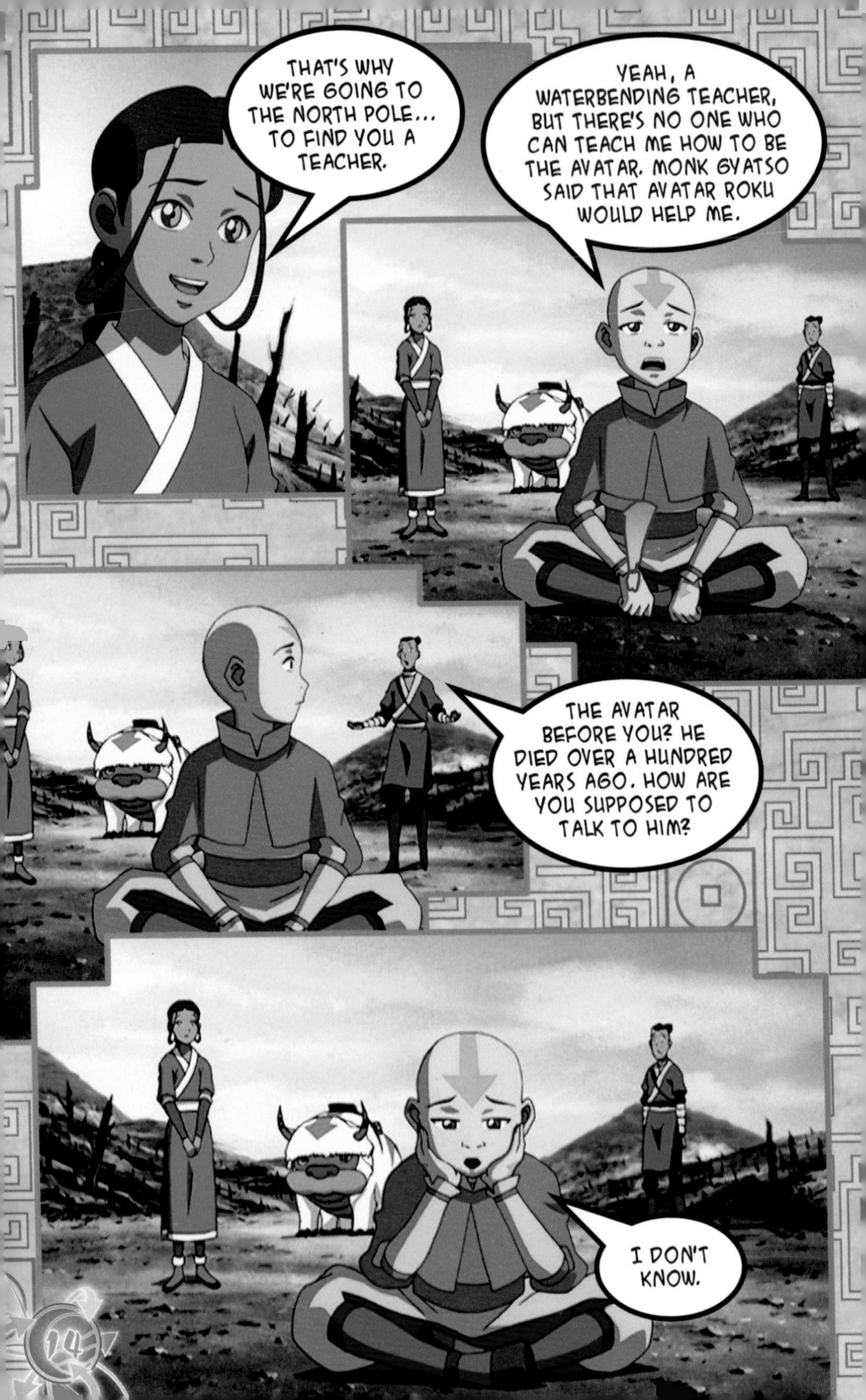
THAT'S WHY WE'RE GOING TO THE NORTH POLE... TO FIND YOU A TEACHER.
YEAH, A WATERBENDING TEACHER, BUT THERE'S NO ONE WHO CAN TEACH ME HOW TO BE THE AVATAR. MONK GYATSO SAID THAT AVATAR ROKU WOULD HELP ME.
THE AVATAR BEFORE YOU? HE DIED OVER A HUNDRED YEARS AGO. HOW ARE YOU SUPPOSED TO TALK TO HIM?
I DON'T KNOW.

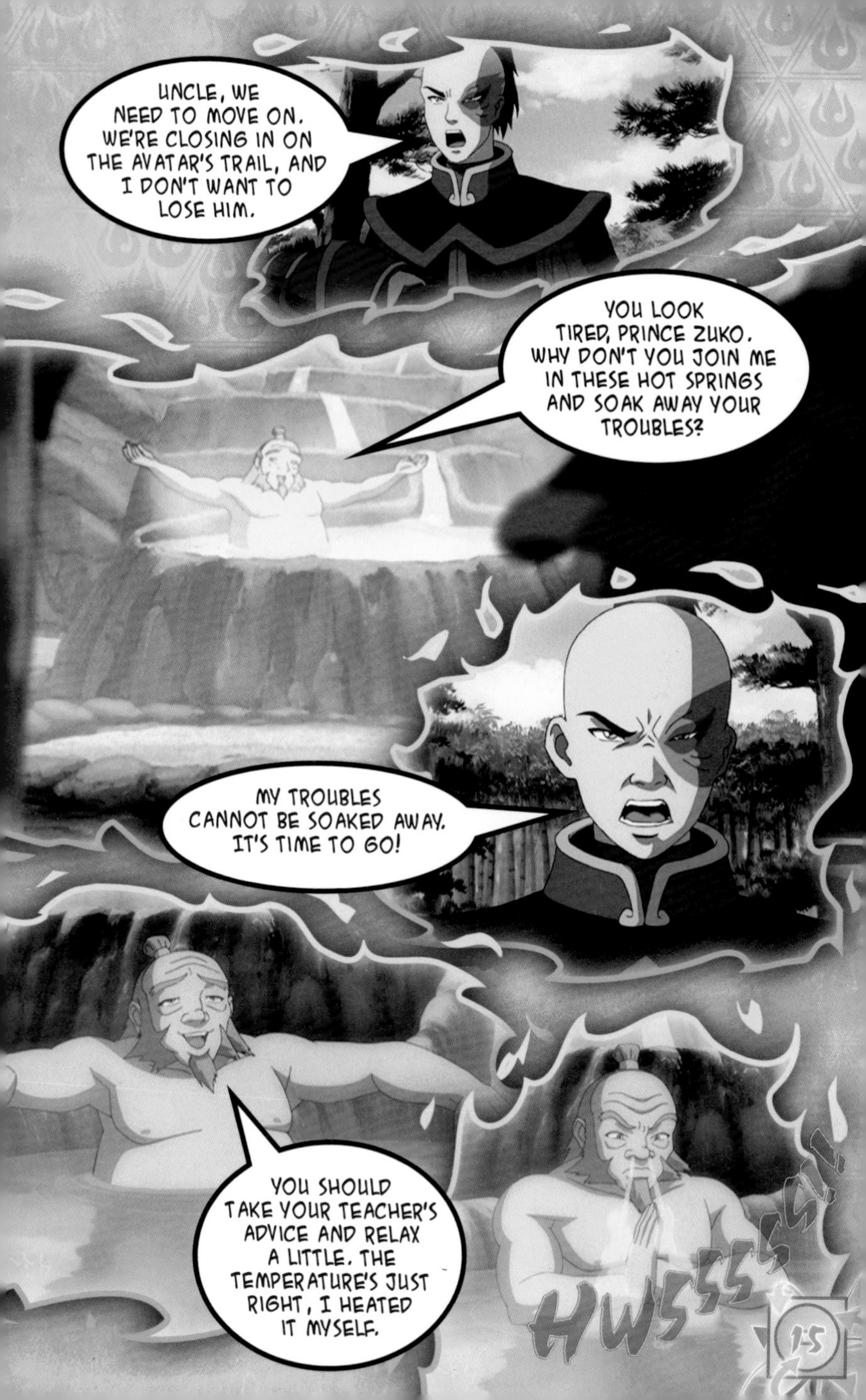
UNCLE, WE NEED TO MOVE ON. WE'RE CLOSING IN ON THE AVATAR'S TRAIL, AND I DON'T WANT TO LOSE HIM.
YOU LOOK TIRED, PRINCE ZUKO. WHY DON'T YOU JOIN ME IN THESE HOT SPRINGS AND SOAK AWAY YOUR TROUBLES?
MY TROUBLES CANNOT BE SOAKED AWAY. IT'S TIME TO GO!
YOU SHOULD TAKE YOUR TEACHER'S ADVICE AND RELAX A LITTLE. THE TEMPERATURE'S JUST RIGHT, I HEATED IT MYSELF.
HWSSSSS!

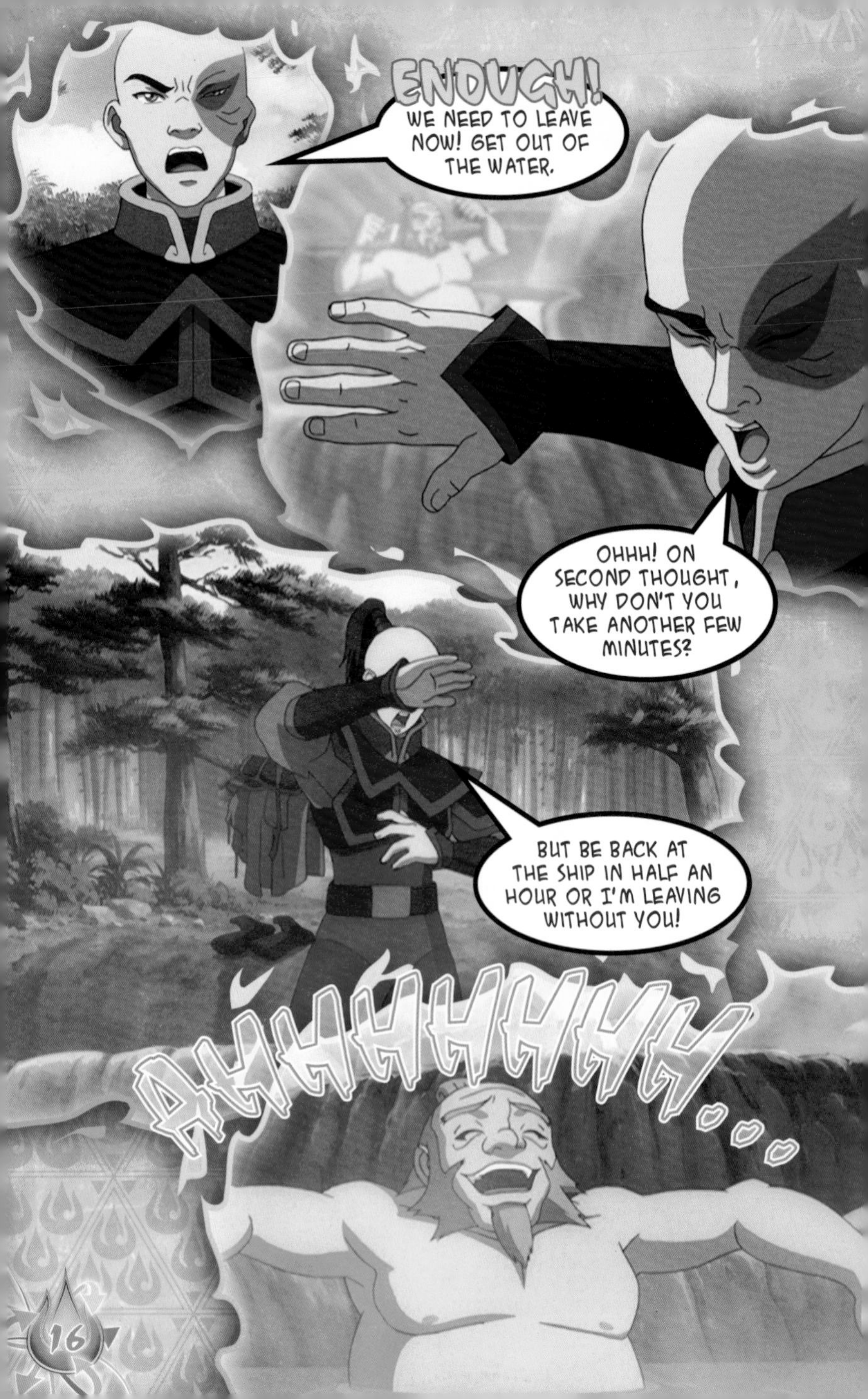
ENOUGH!
WE NEED TO LEAVE NOW! GET OUT OF THE WATER.
OHHH! ON SECOND THOUGHT, WHY DON'T YOU TAKE ANOTHER FEW MINUTES?
BUT BE BACK AT THE SHIP IN HALF AN HOUR OR I'M LEAVING WITHOUT YOU!
AHHHHHHH...

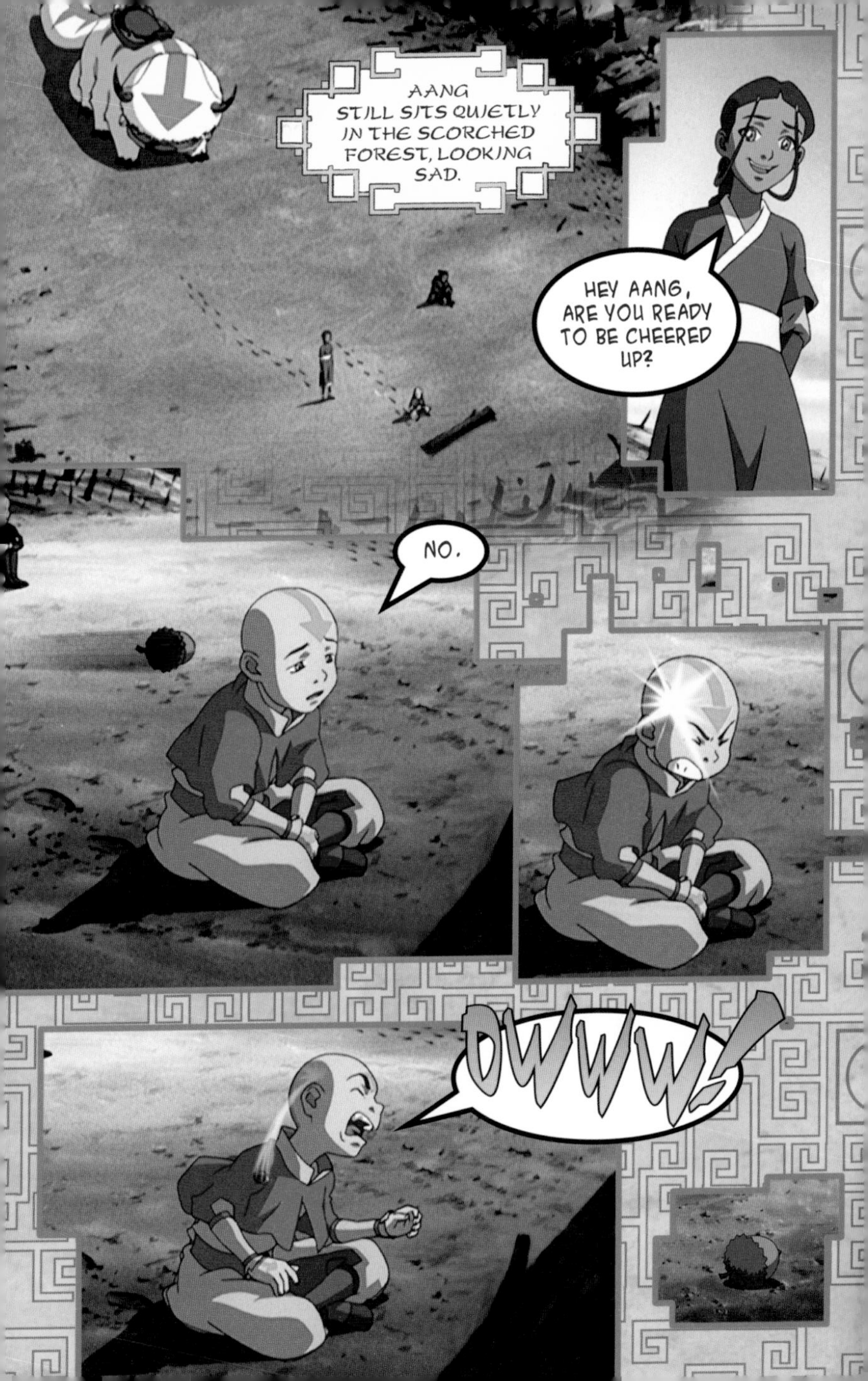
AANG STILL SITS QUIETLY IN THE SCORCHED FOREST, LOOKING SAD.
HEY AANG, ARE YOU READY TO BE CHEERED UP?
NO.
OWWW!

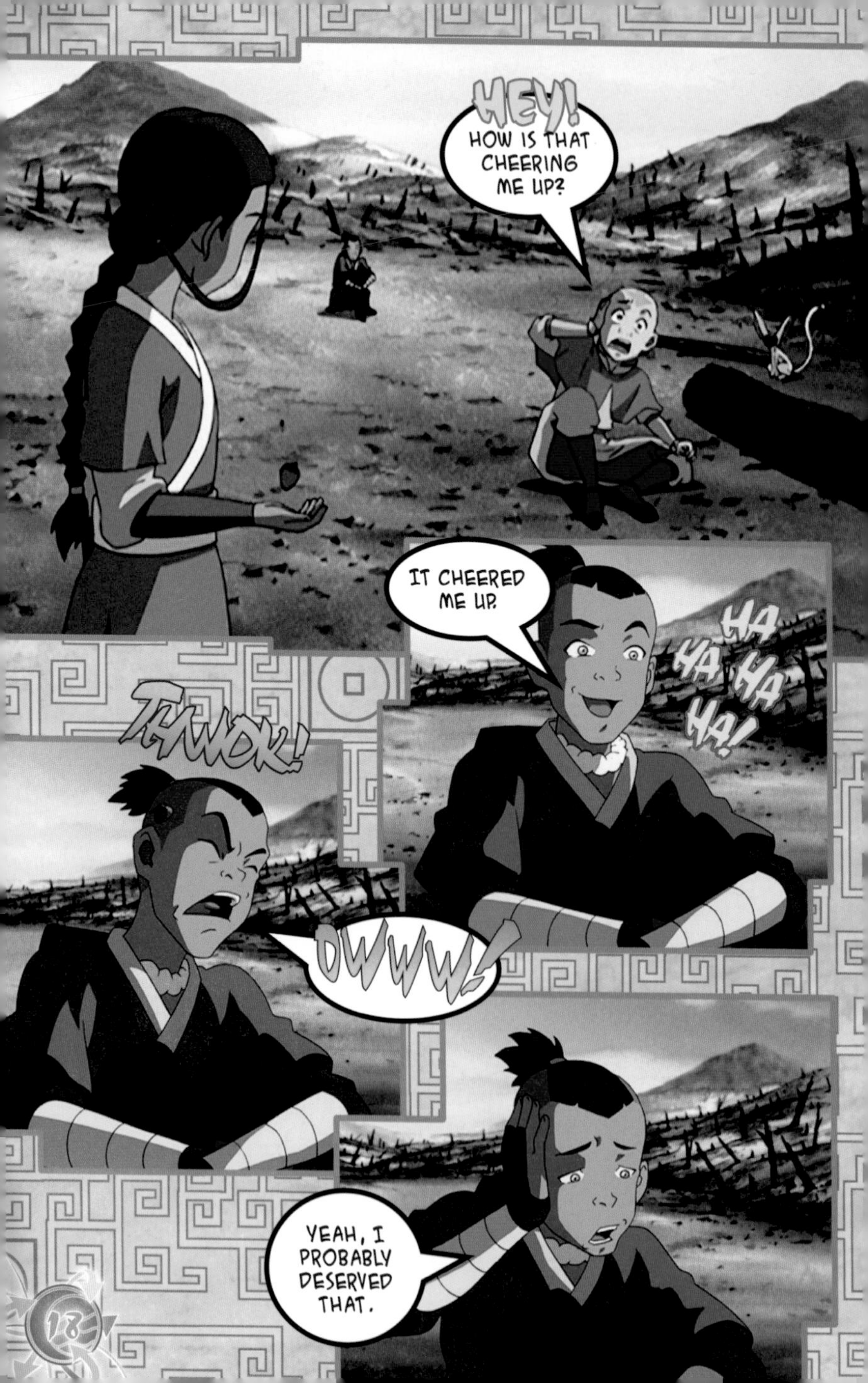
HEY!
HOW IS THAT CHEERING ME UP?
IT CHEERED ME UP.
HA HA HA HA HA!
THWOK!
OWWW!
YEAH, I PROBABLY DESERVED THAT.

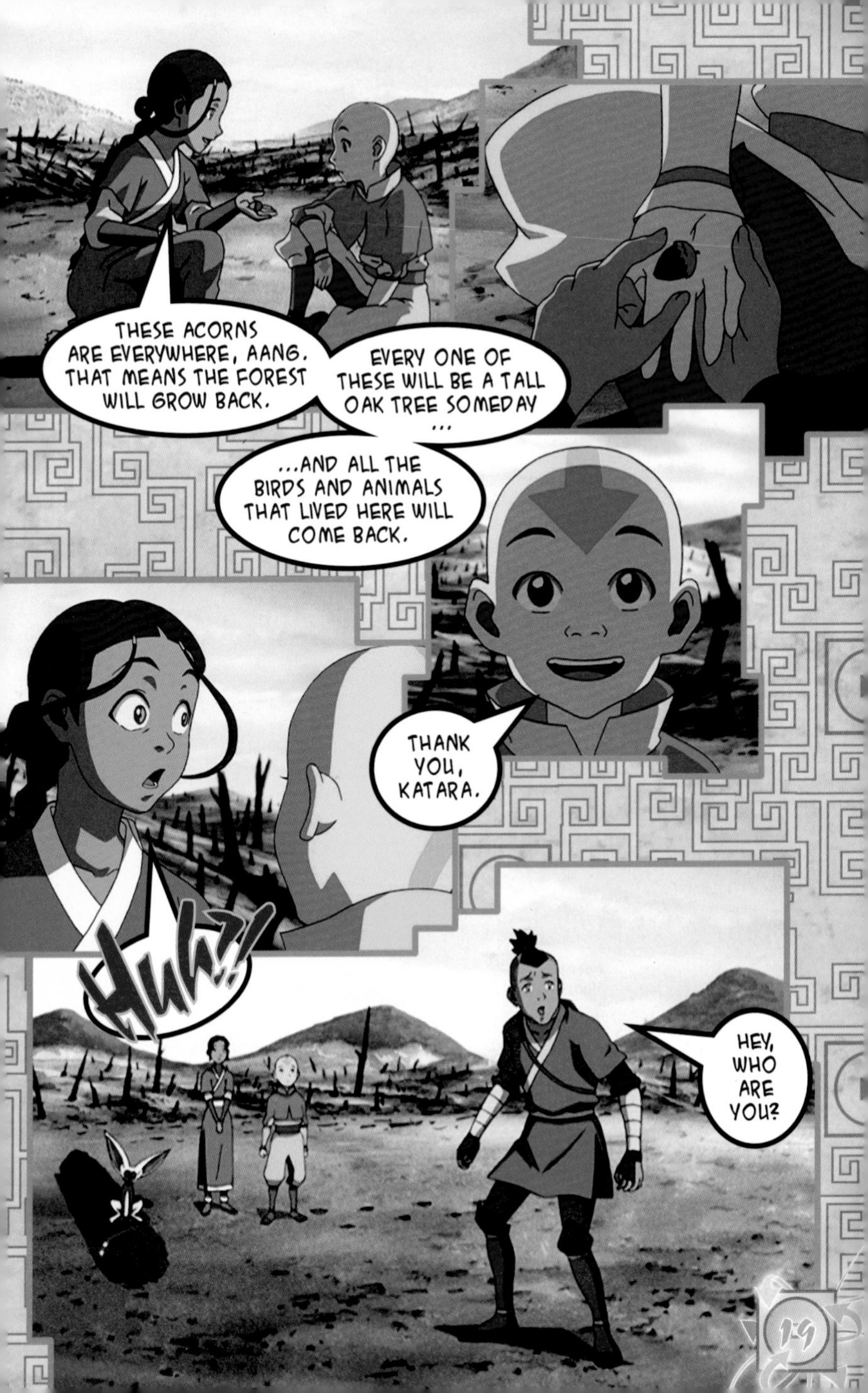

THESE ACORNS ARE EVERYWHERE, AANG. THAT MEANS THE FOREST WILL GROW BACK.
EVERY ONE OF THESE WILL BE A TALL OAK TREE SOMEDAY ...
...AND ALL THE BIRDS AND ANIMALS THAT LIVED HERE WILL COME BACK.
THANK YOU, KATARA.
HUH?!
HEY, WHO ARE YOU?

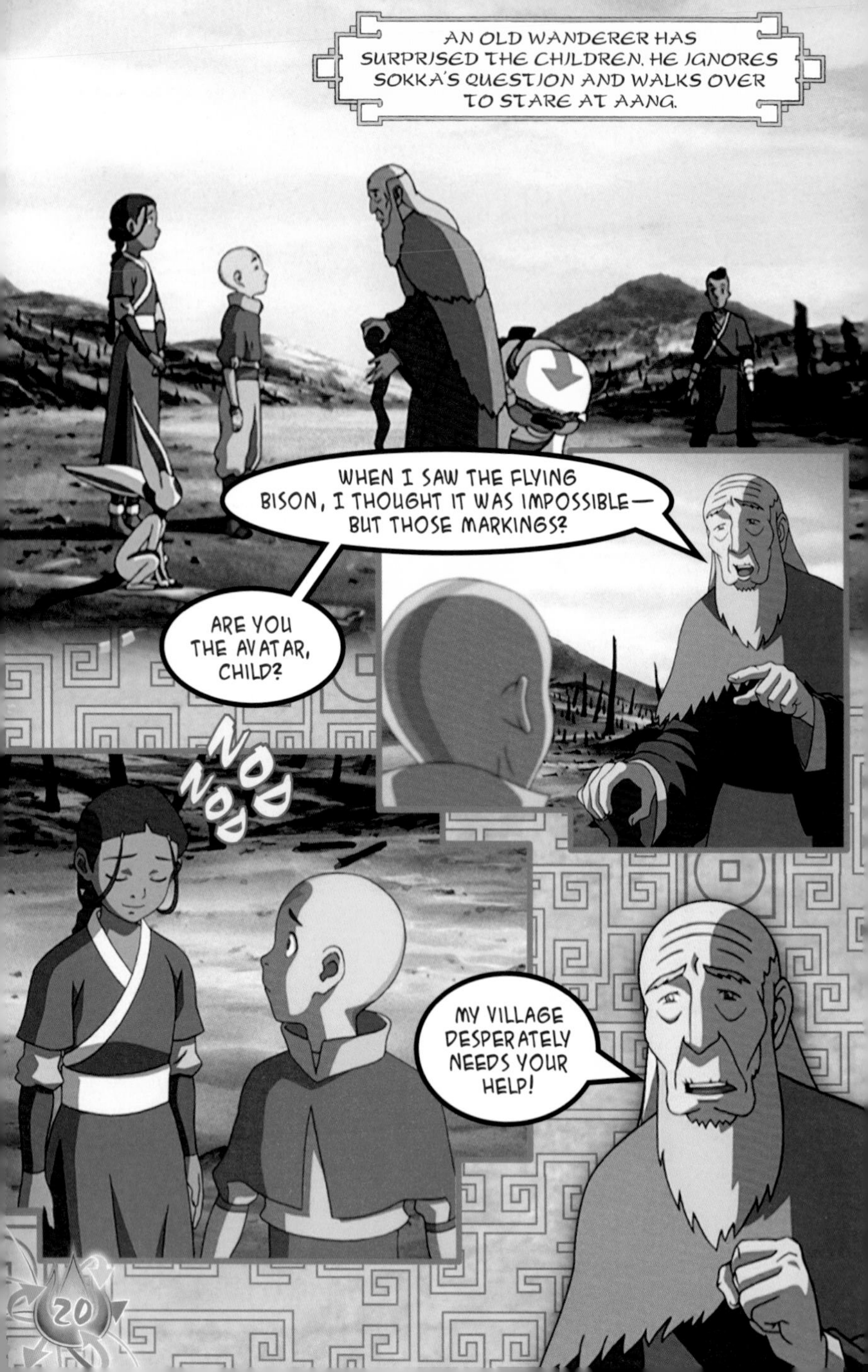
AN OLD WANDERER HAS SURPRISED THE CHILDREN. HE IGNORES SOKKA'S QUESTION AND WALKS OVER TO STARE AT AANG.
WHEN I SAW THE FLYING BISON, I THOUGHT IT WAS IMPOSSIBLE— BUT THOSE MARKINGS?
ARE YOU THE AVATAR, CHILD?
NOD NOD
MY VILLAGE DESPERATELY NEEDS YOUR HELP!

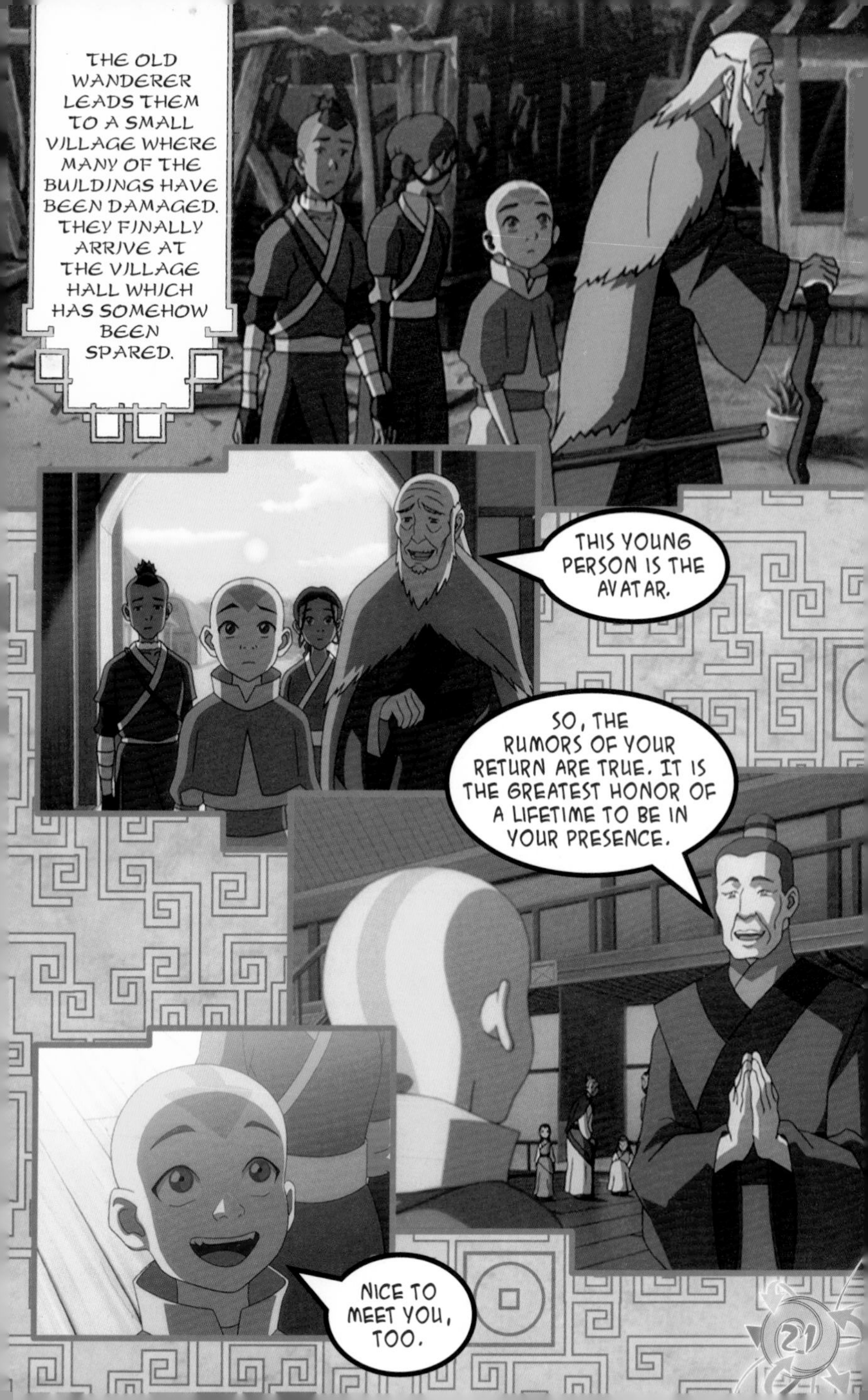
THE OLD WANDERER LEADS THEM TO A SMALL VILLAGE WHERE MANY OF THE BUILDINGS HAVE BEEN DAMAGED. THEY FINALLY ARRIVE AT THE VILLAGE HALL WHICH HAS SOMEHOW BEEN SPARED.
THIS YOUNG PERSON IS THE AVATAR.
SO, THE RUMORS OF YOUR RETURN ARE TRUE. IT IS THE GREATEST HONOR OF A LIFETIME TO BE IN YOUR PRESENCE.
NICE TO MEET YOU, TOO.

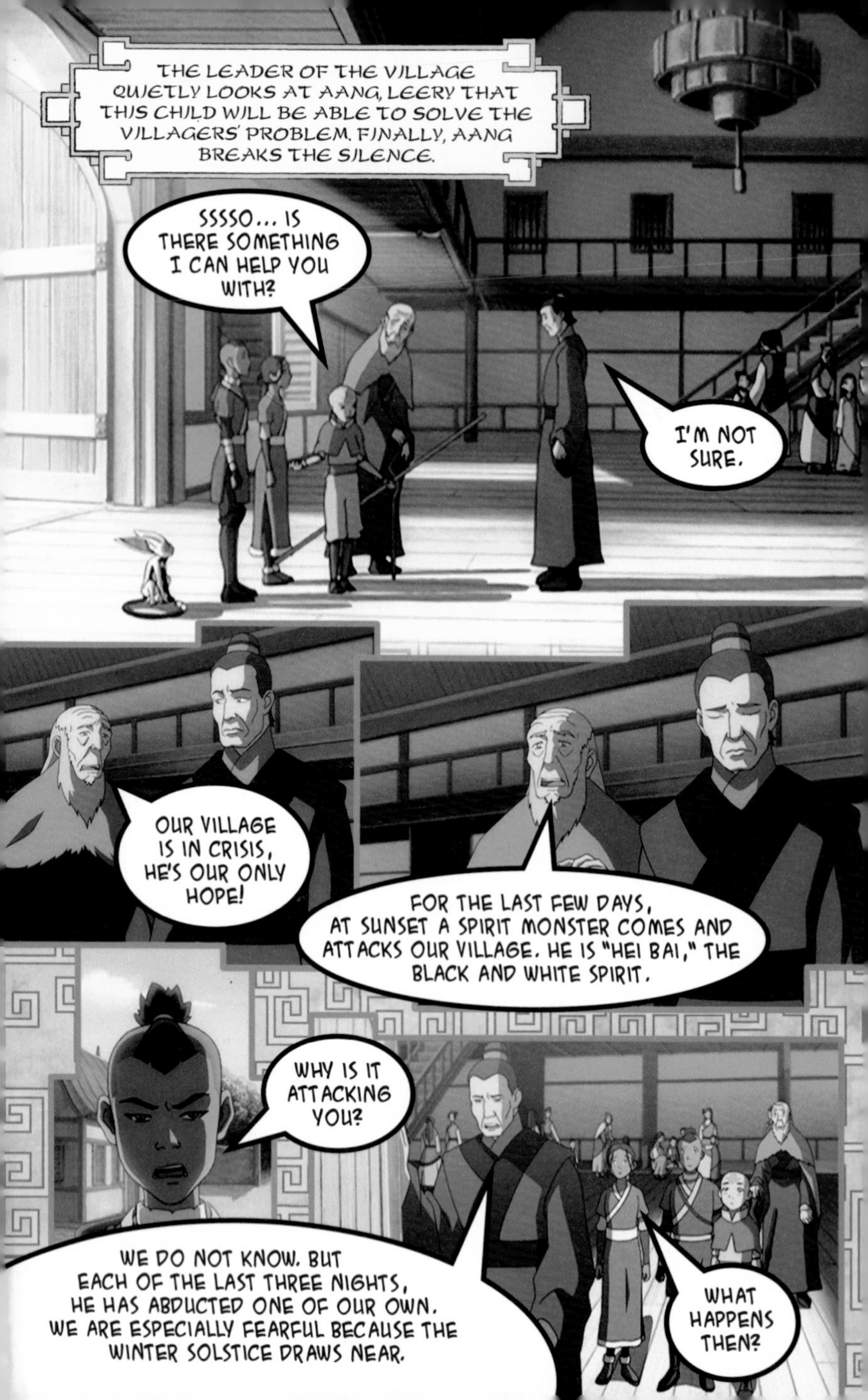
THE LEADER OF THE VILLAGE QUIETLY LOOKS AT AANG, LEERY THAT THIS CHILD WILL BE ABLE TO SOLVE THE VILLAGERS' PROBLEM. FINALLY, AANG BREAKS THE SILENCE.
SSSSO... IS THERE SOMETHING I CAN HELP YOU WITH?
I'M NOT SURE.
OUR VILLAGE IS IN CRISIS, HE'S OUR ONLY HOPE!
FOR THE LAST FEW DAYS, AT SUNSET A SPIRIT MONSTER COMES AND ATTACKS OUR VILLAGE. HE IS "HEI BAI," THE BLACK AND WHITE SPIRIT.
WHY IS IT ATTACKING YOU?
WE DO NOT KNOW. BUT EACH OF THE LAST THREE NIGHTS, HE HAS ABDUCTED ONE OF OUR OWN. WE ARE ESPECIALLY FEARFUL BECAUSE THE WINTER SOLSTICE DRAWS NEAR.
WHAT HAPPENS THEN?

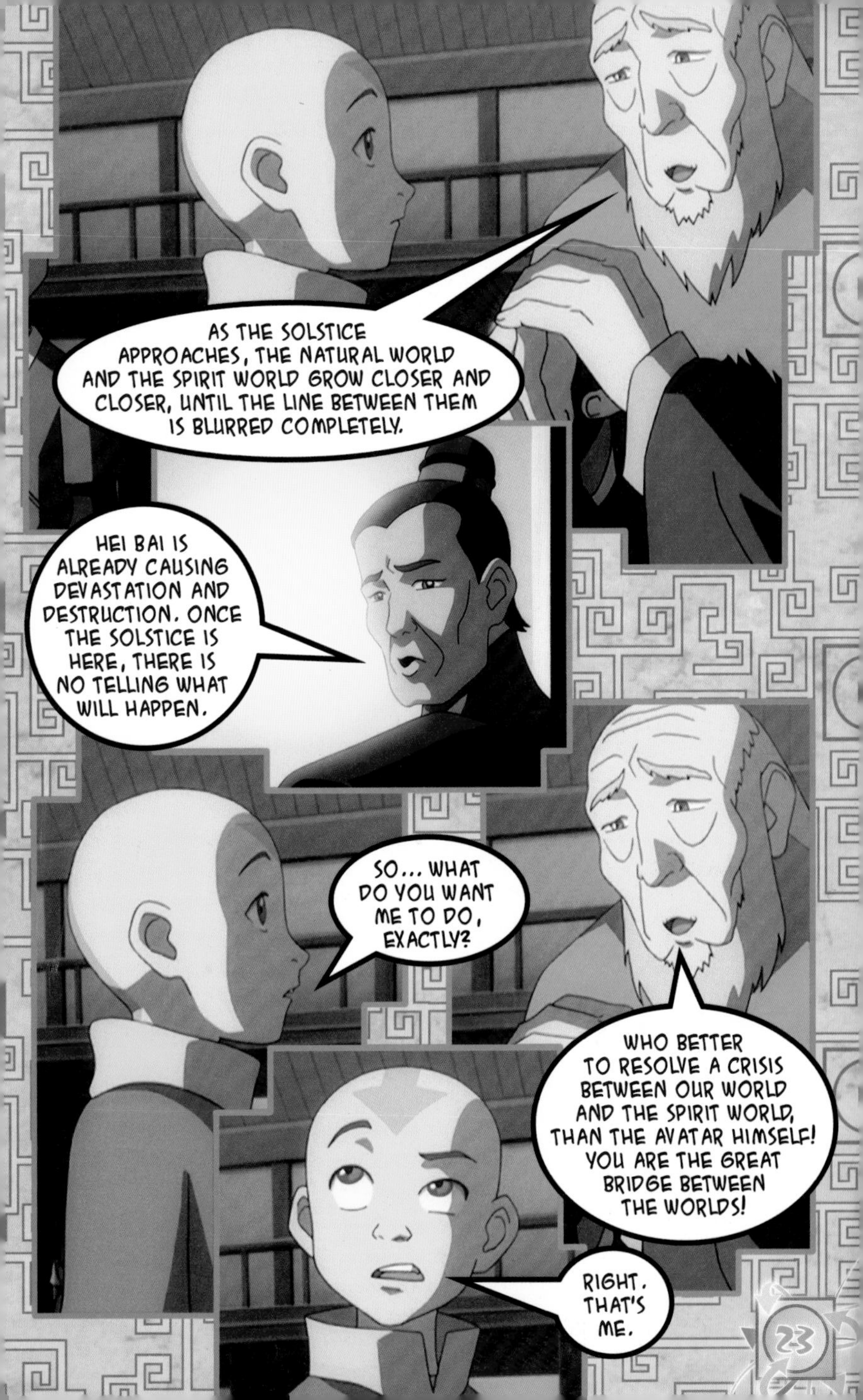

AS THE SOLSTICE APPROACHES, THE NATURAL WORLD AND THE SPIRIT WORLD GROW CLOSER AND CLOSER, UNTIL THE LINE BETWEEN THEM IS BLURRED COMPLETELY.
HEI BAI IS ALREADY CAUSING DEVASTATION AND DESTRUCTION. ONCE THE SOLSTICE IS HERE, THERE IS NO TELLING WHAT WILL HAPPEN.
SO... WHAT DO YOU WANT ME TO DO, EXACTLY?
WHO BETTER TO RESOLVE A CRISIS BETWEEN OUR WORLD AND THE SPIRIT WORLD, THAN THE AVATAR HIMSELF! YOU ARE THE GREAT BRIDGE BETWEEN THE WORLDS!
RIGHT. THAT'S ME.

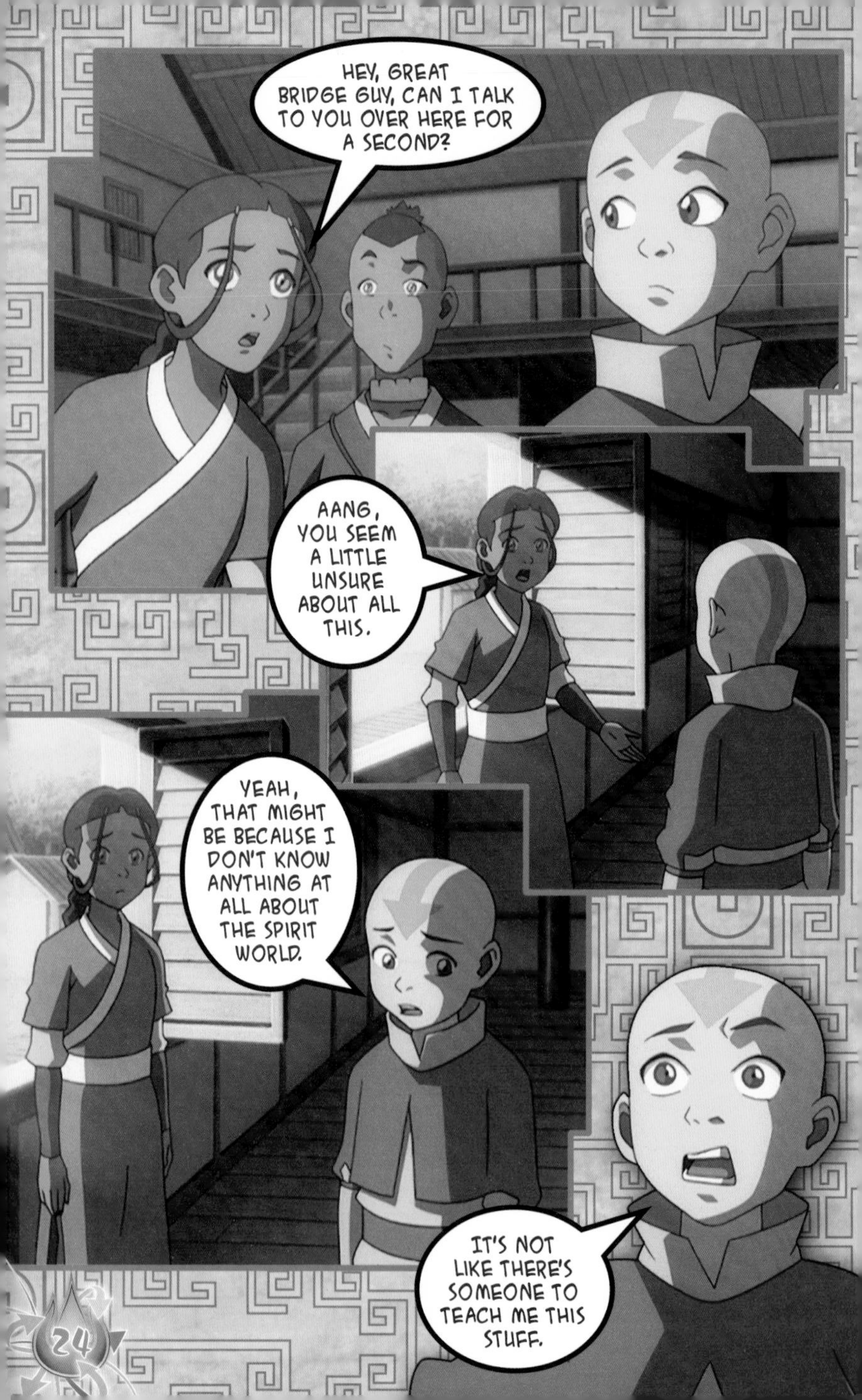
HEY, GREAT BRIDGE GUY, CAN I TALK TO YOU OVER HERE FOR A SECOND?
AANG, YOU SEEM A LITTLE UNSURE ABOUT ALL THIS.
YEAH, THAT MIGHT BE BECAUSE I DON'T KNOW ANYTHING AT ALL ABOUT THE SPIRIT WORLD.
IT'S NOT LIKE THERE'S SOMEONE TO TEACH ME THIS STUFF.

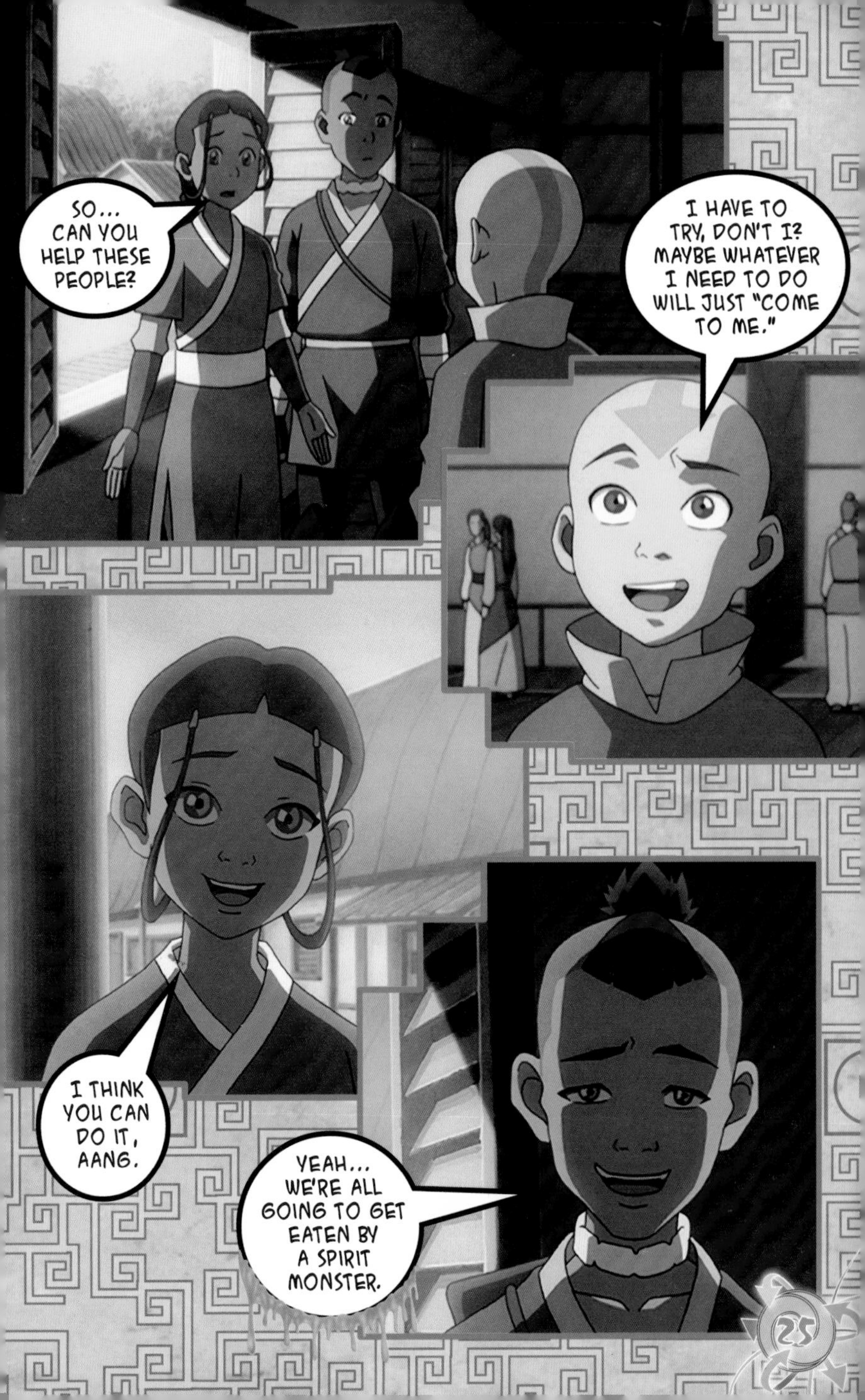
SO... CAN YOU HELP THESE PEOPLE?
I HAVE TO TRY, DON'T I? MAYBE WHATEVER I NEED TO DO WILL JUST "COME TO ME."
I THINK YOU CAN DO IT, AANG.
YEAH... WE'RE ALL GOING TO GET EATEN BY A SPIRIT MONSTER.

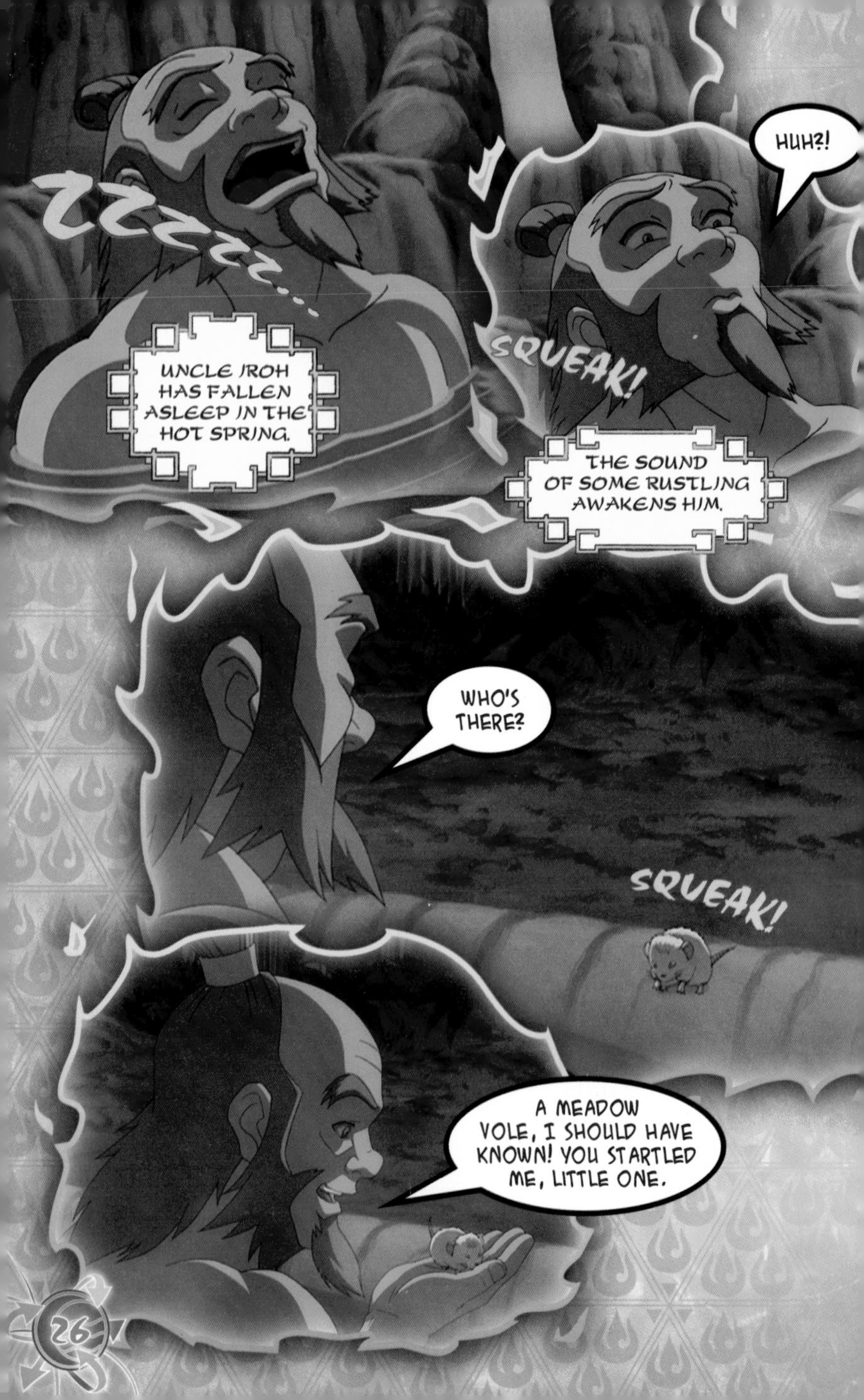
ZZZZZZ...
UNCLE IROH HAS FALLEN ASLEEP IN THE HOT SPRING.
HUH?!
SQUEAK!
THE SOUND OF SOME RUSTLING AWAKENS HIM.
WHO'S THERE?
SQUEAK!
A MEADOW VOLE, I SHOULD HAVE KNOWN! YOU STARTLED ME, LITTLE ONE.

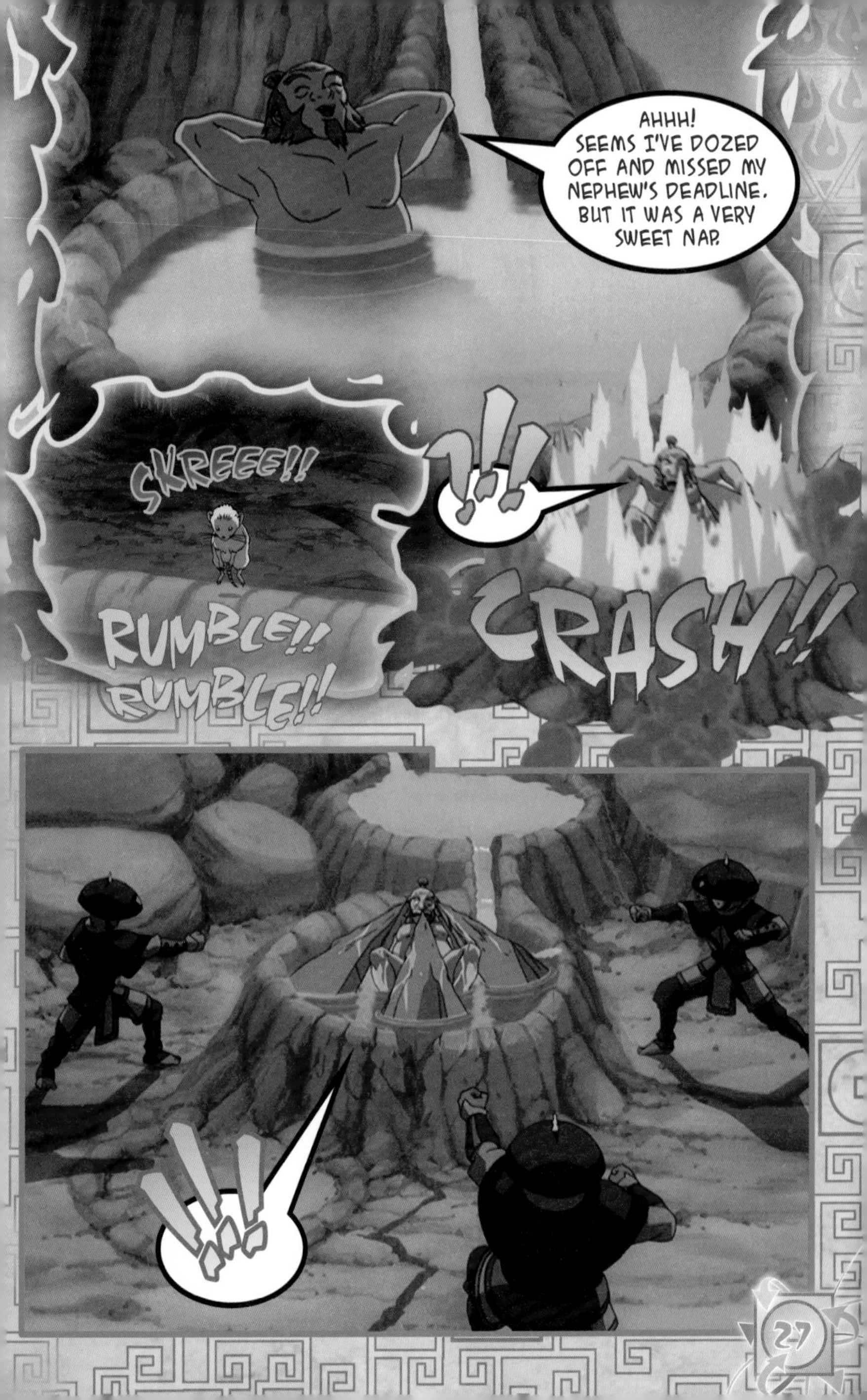
AHHH! SEEMS I'VE DOZED OFF AND MISSED MY NEPHEW'S DEADLINE. BUT IT WAS A VERY SWEET NAP.
SKREEEE!!
?!!
RUMBLE!! RUMBLE!!
CRASH!!
!!!

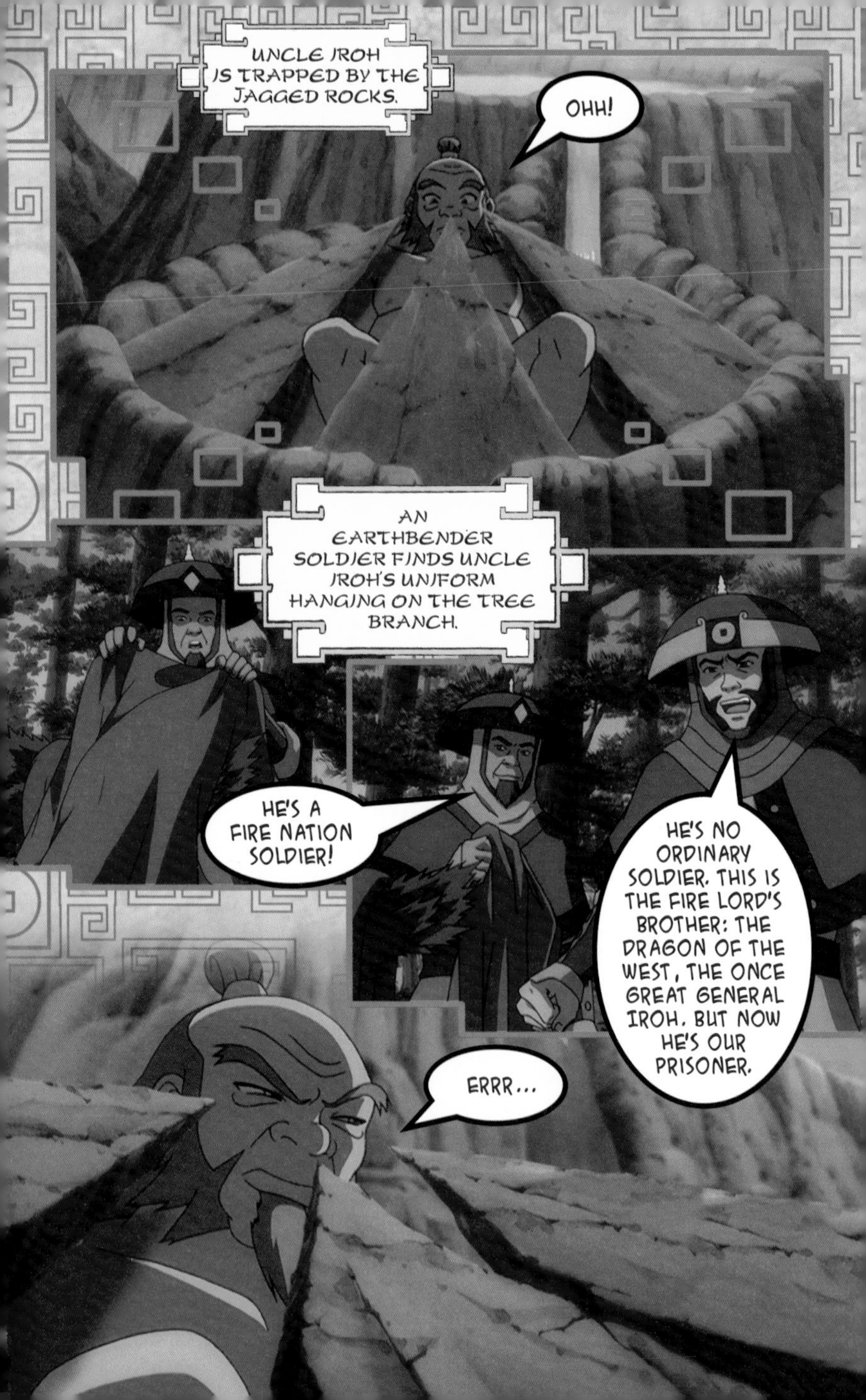
UNCLE IROH IS TRAPPED BY THE JAGGED ROCKS.
OHH!
AN EARTHBENDER SOLDIER FINDS UNCLE IROH'S UNIFORM HANGING ON THE TREE BRANCH.
HE'S A FIRE NATION SOLDIER!
HE'S NO ORDINARY SOLDIER. THIS IS THE FIRE LORD'S BROTHER: THE DRAGON OF THE WEST, THE ONCE GREAT GENERAL IROH. BUT NOW HE'S OUR PRISONER.
ERRR...

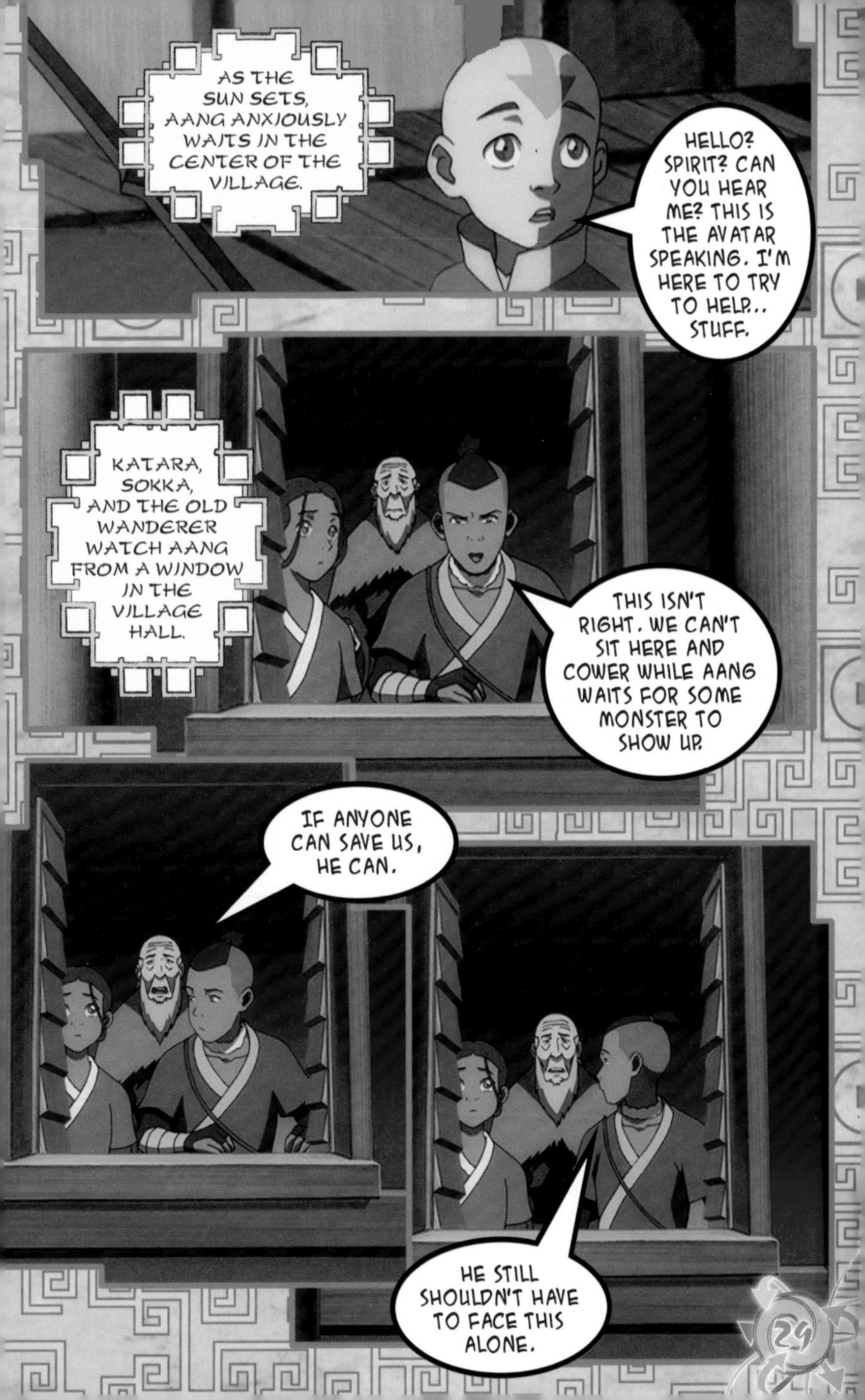
AS THE SUN SETS, AANG ANXIOUSLY WAITS IN THE CENTER OF THE VILLAGE.
HELLO? SPIRIT? CAN YOU HEAR ME? THIS IS THE AVATAR SPEAKING. I'M HERE TO TRY TO HELP... STUFF.
KATARA, SOKKA, AND THE OLD WANDERER WATCH AANG FROM A WINDOW IN THE VILLAGE HALL.
THIS ISN'T RIGHT. WE CAN'T SIT HERE AND COWER WHILE AANG WAITS FOR SOME MONSTER TO SHOW UP.
IF ANYONE CAN SAVE US, HE CAN.
HE STILL SHOULDN'T HAVE TO FACE THIS ALONE.
29

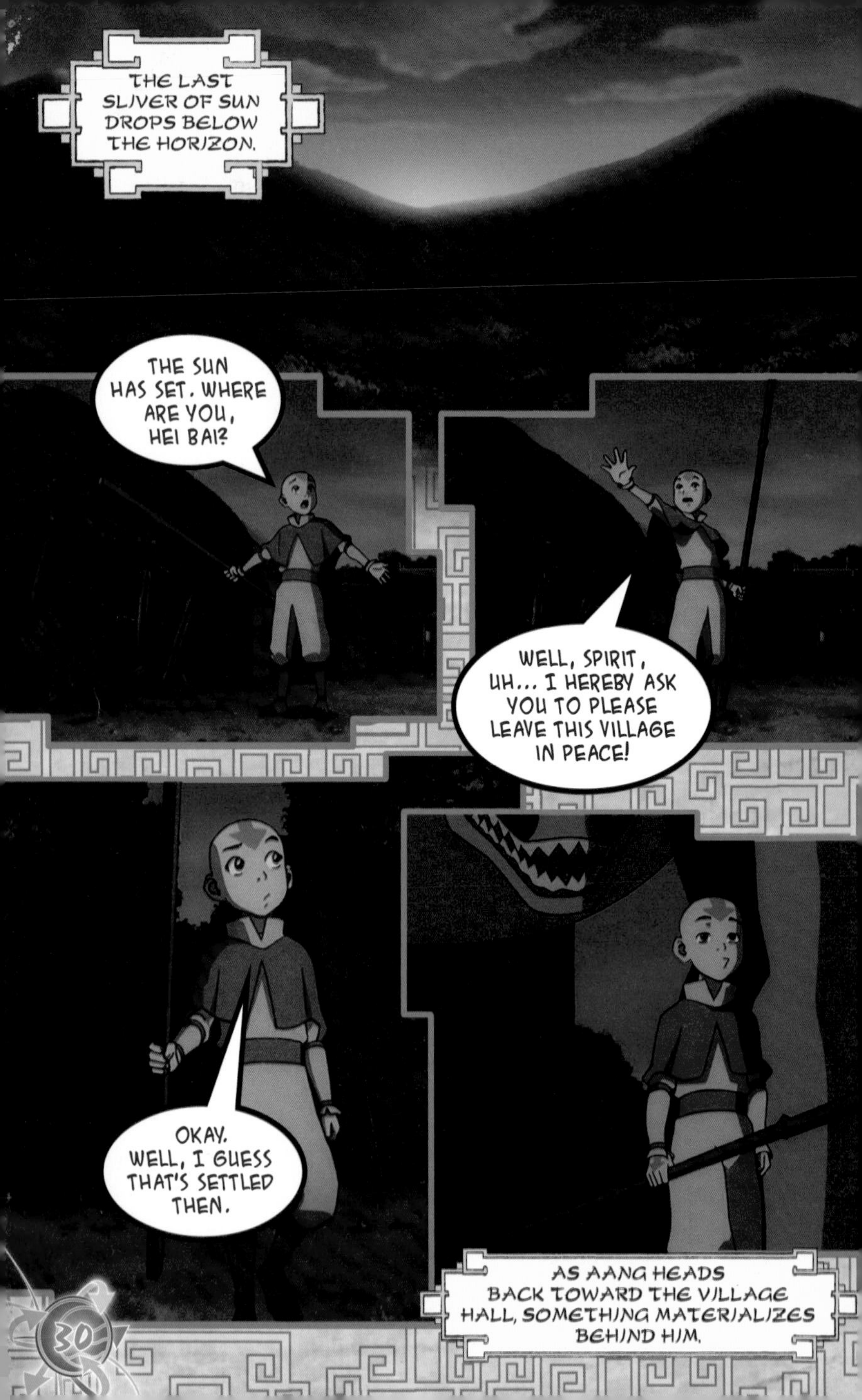

THE LAST SLIVER OF SUN DROPS BELOW THE HORIZON.
THE SUN HAS SET. WHERE ARE YOU, HEI BAI?
WELL, SPIRIT, UH... I HEREBY ASK YOU TO PLEASE LEAVE THIS VILLAGE IN PEACE!
OKAY. WELL, I GUESS THAT'S SETTLED THEN.
AS AANG HEADS BACK TOWARD THE VILLAGE HALL, SOMETHING MATERIALIZES BEHIND HIM.

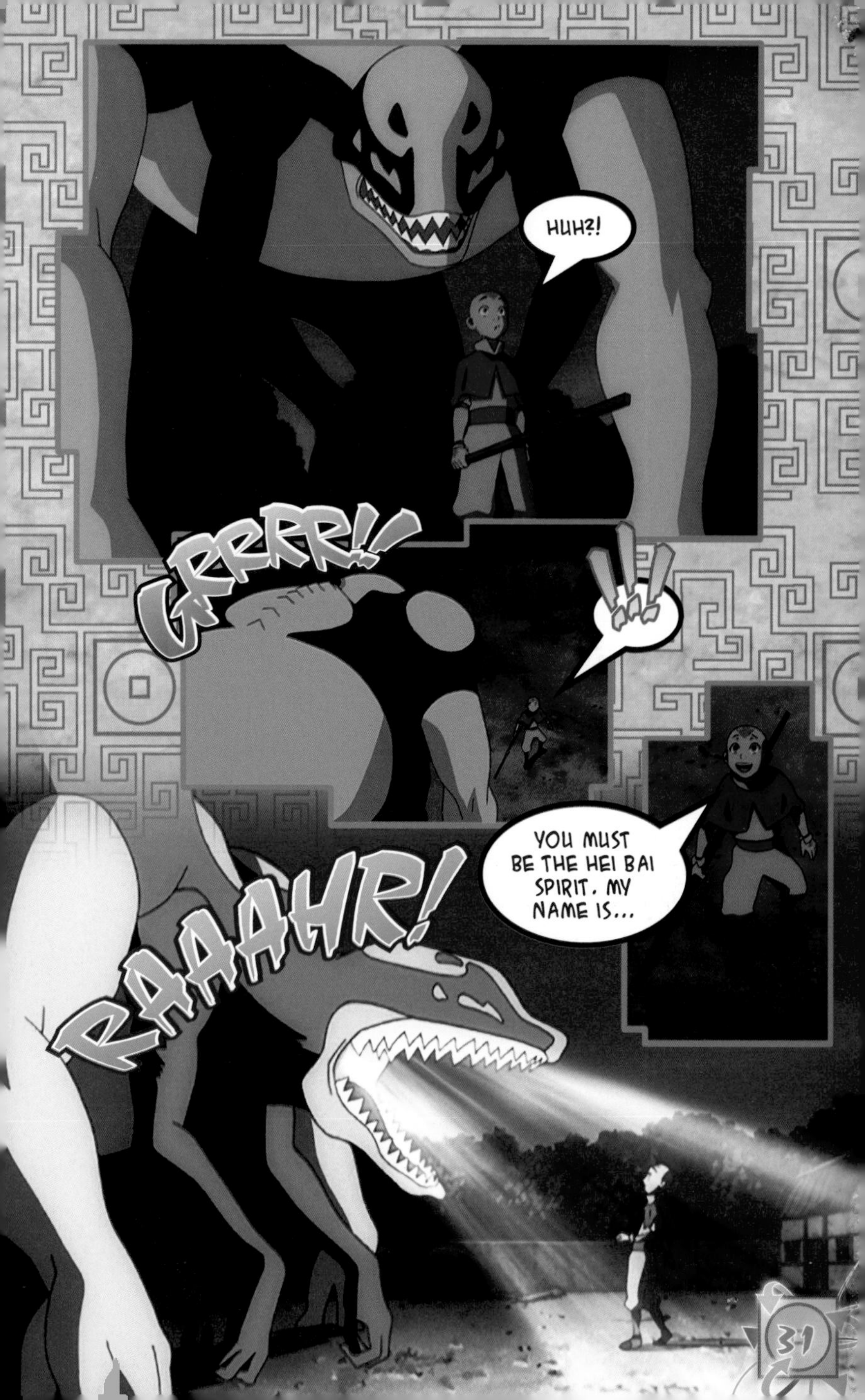
HUH?!
GRRRR!!
!!!
YOU MUST BE THE HEI BAI SPIRIT. MY NAME IS...
RAAAHR!
31

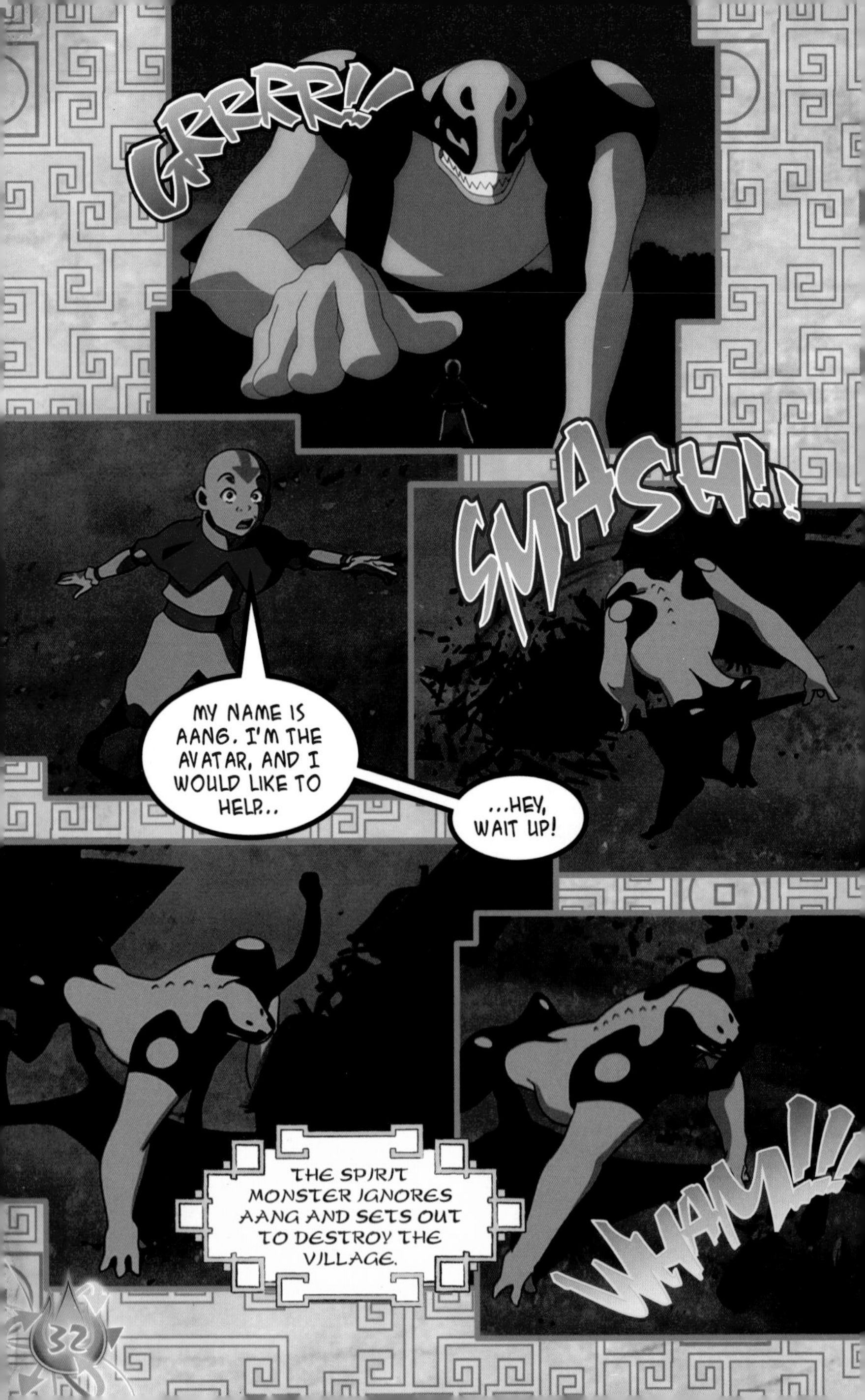
GRRRR!!
SMASH!!
MY NAME IS AANG. I'M THE AVATAR, AND I WOULD LIKE TO HELP...
...HEY, WAIT UP!
THE SPIRIT MONSTER IGNORES AANG AND SETS OUT TO DESTROY THE VILLAGE.
WHAM!!!

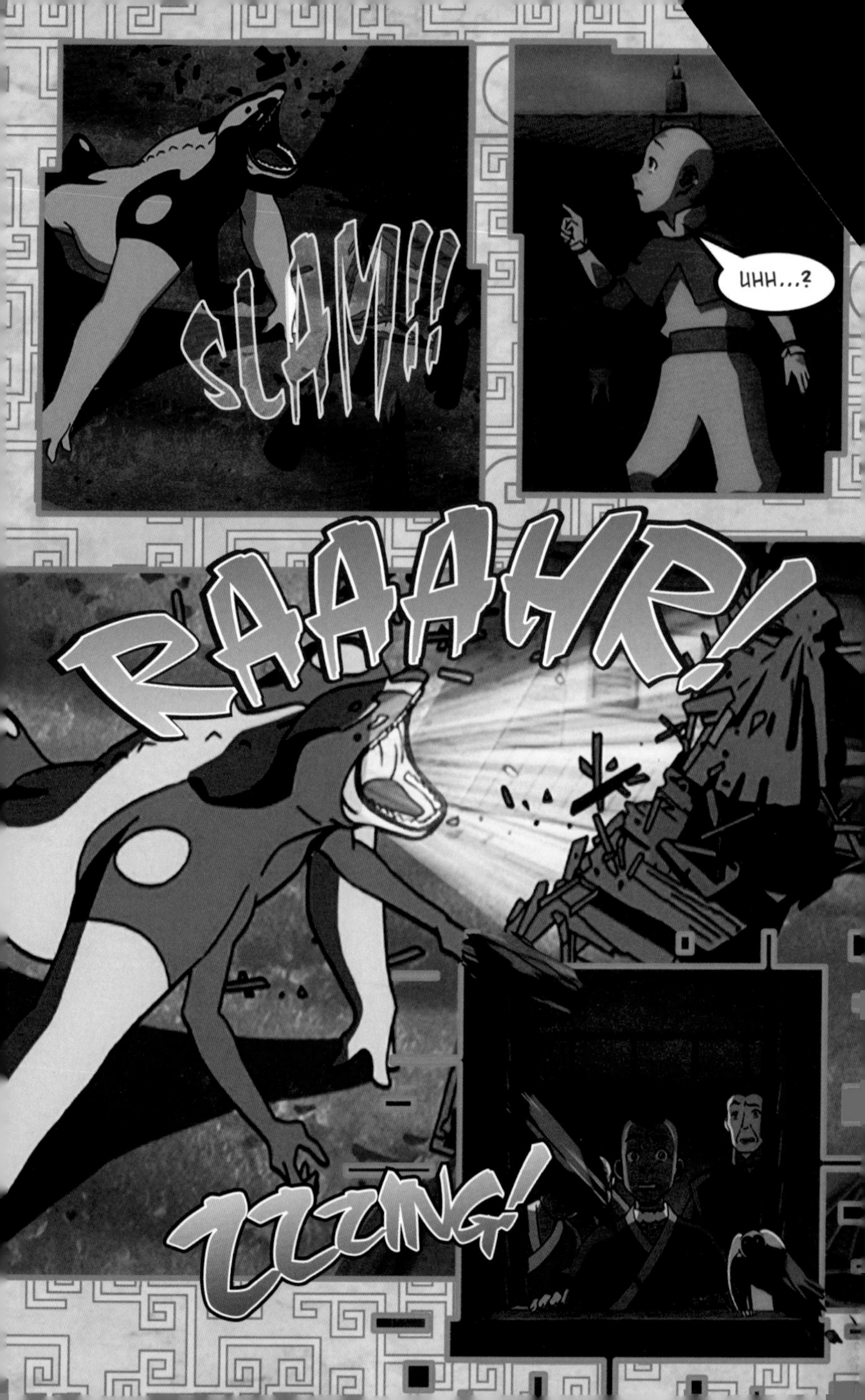
SLAM!!
UHH...?
RAAAHR!
ZZZING!

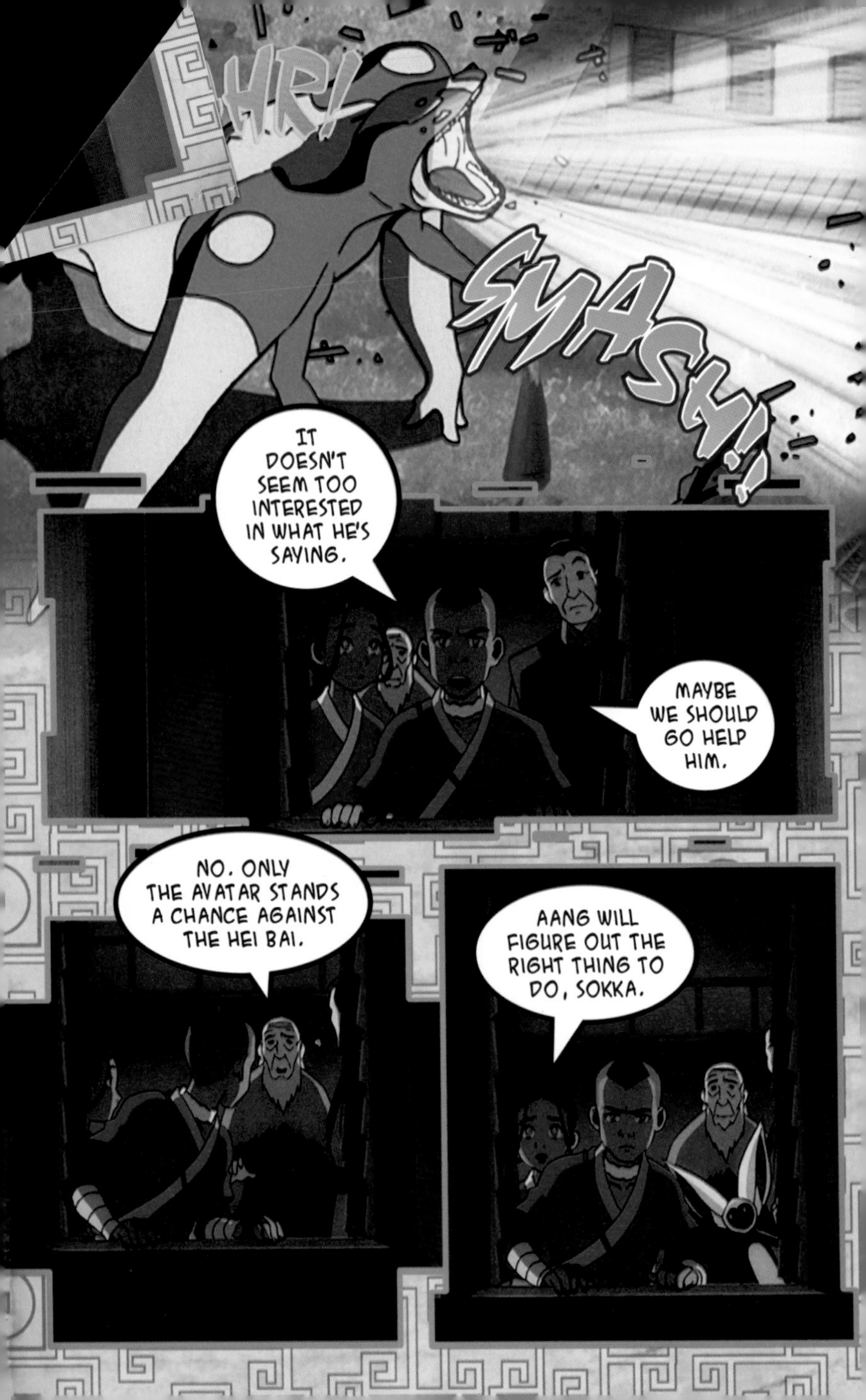
HR!
SMASH!!
IT DOESN'T SEEM TOO INTERESTED IN WHAT HE'S SAYING.
MAYBE WE SHOULD GO HELP HIM.
NO. ONLY THE AVATAR STANDS A CHANCE AGAINST THE HEI BAI.
AANG WILL FIGURE OUT THE RIGHT THING TO DO, SOKKA.

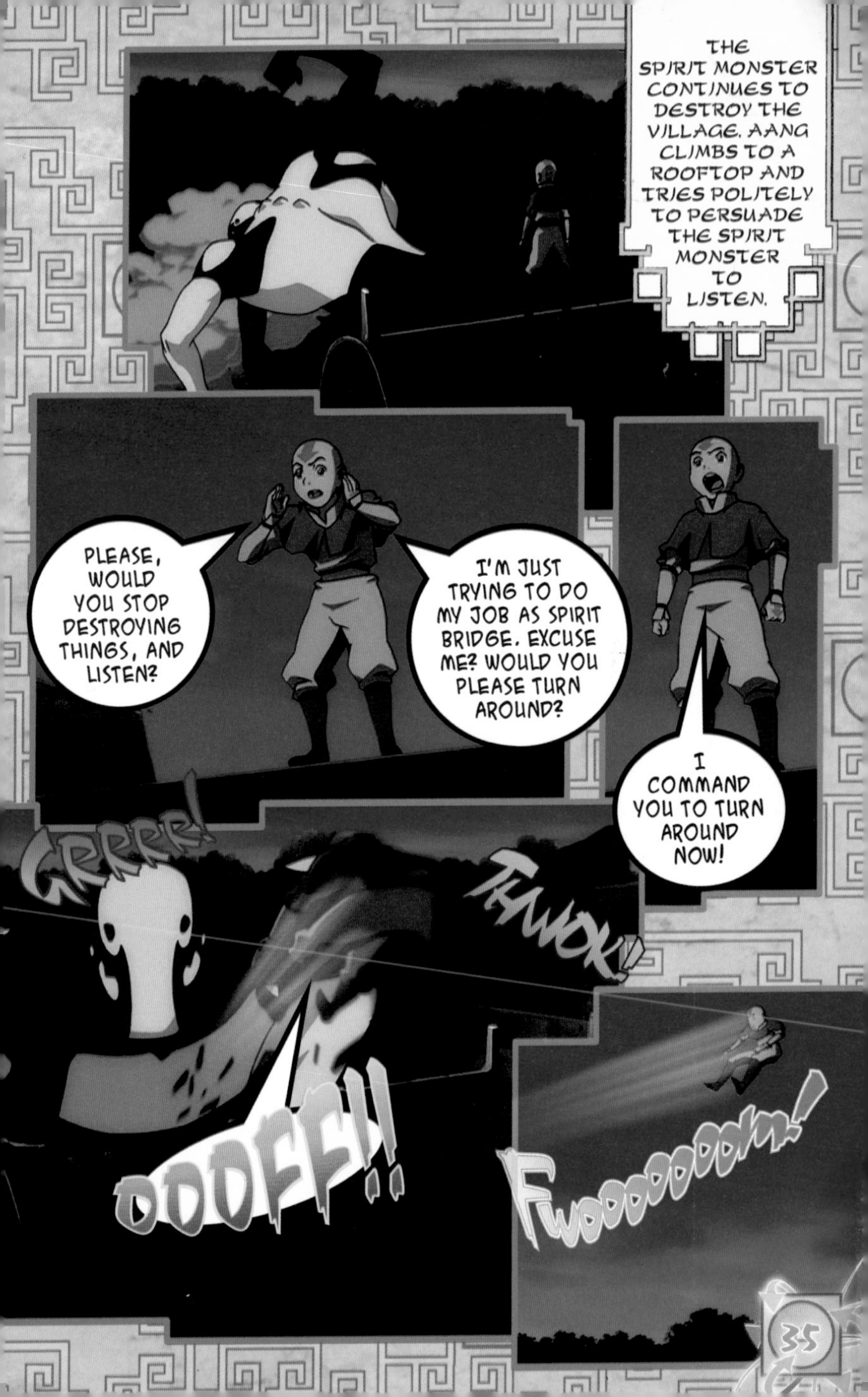
THE SPIRIT MONSTER CONTINUES TO DESTROY THE VILLAGE. AANG CLIMBS TO A ROOFTOP AND TRIES POLITELY TO PERSUADE THE SPIRIT MONSTER TO LISTEN.
PLEASE, WOULD YOU STOP DESTROYING THINGS, AND LISTEN?
I'M JUST TRYING TO DO MY JOB AS SPIRIT BRIDGE. EXCUSE ME? WOULD YOU PLEASE TURN AROUND?
I COMMAND YOU TO TURN AROUND NOW!
GRRRR!
THWOK!
OOOFF!!
FWOOOOOOOM!

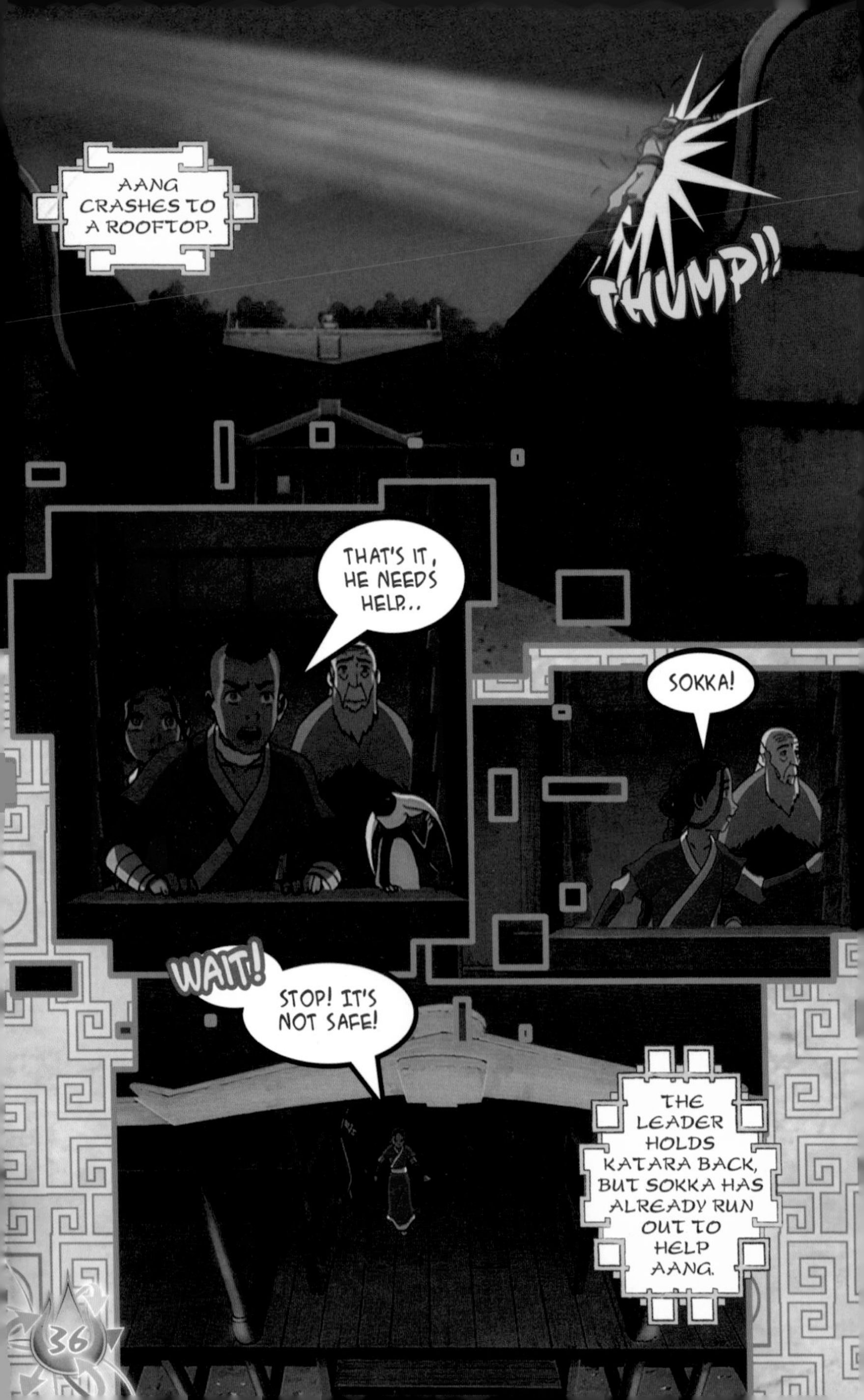
AANG CRASHES TO A ROOFTOP.
THUMP!!
THAT'S IT, HE NEEDS HELP...
SOKKA!
WAIT!
STOP! IT'S NOT SAFE!
THE LEADER HOLDS KATARA BACK, BUT SOKKA HAS ALREADY RUN OUT TO HELP AANG.

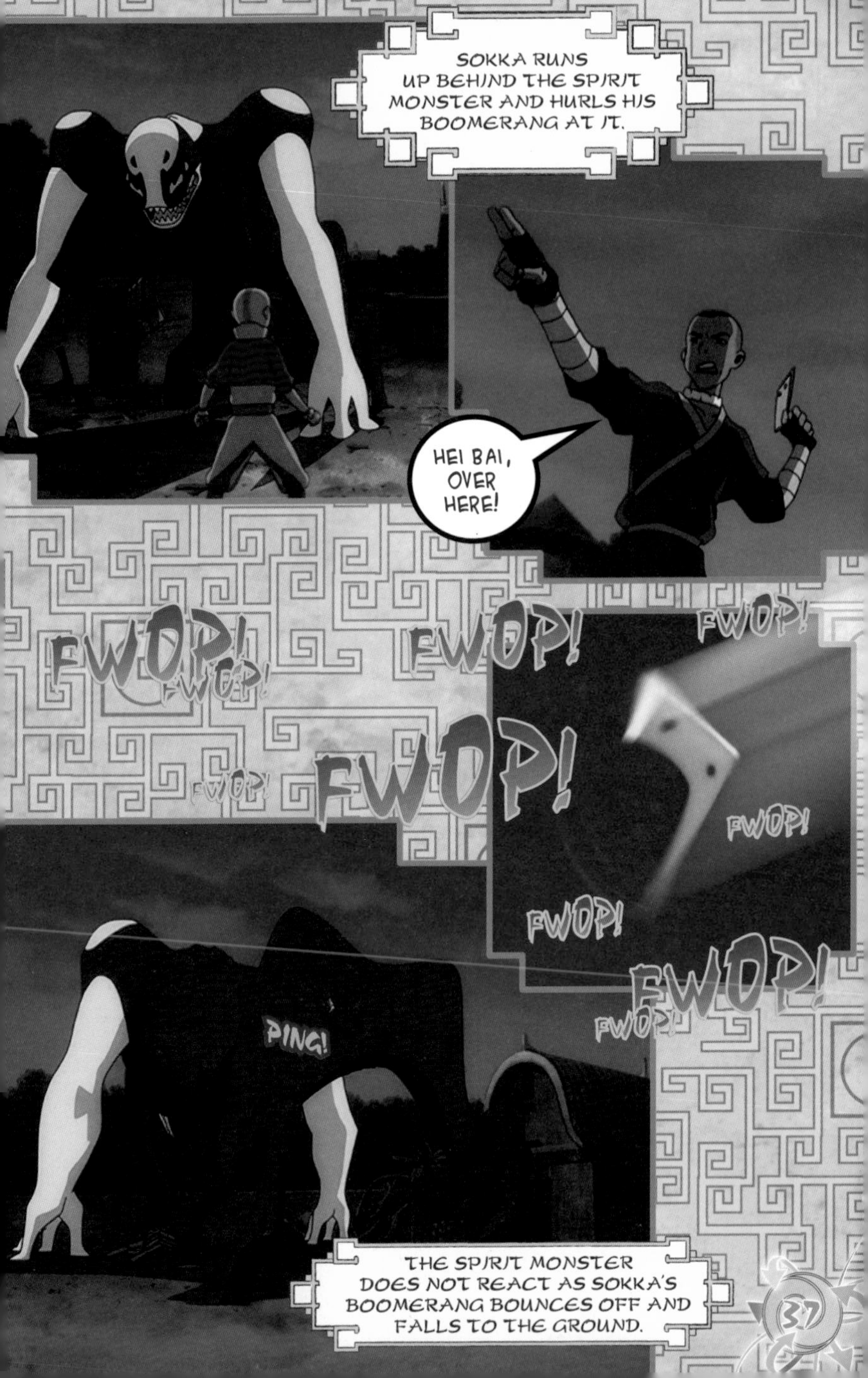
SOKKA RUNS UP BEHIND THE SPIRIT MONSTER AND HURLS HIS BOOMERANG AT IT.
HEI BAI, OVER HERE!
FWOP! FWOP!
FWOP!
FWOP!
FWOP!
FWOP!
FWOP!
FWOP!
FWOP!
FWOP! FWOP!
PING!
THE SPIRIT MONSTER DOES NOT REACT AS SOKKA'S BOOMERANG BOUNCES OFF AND FALLS TO THE GROUND.

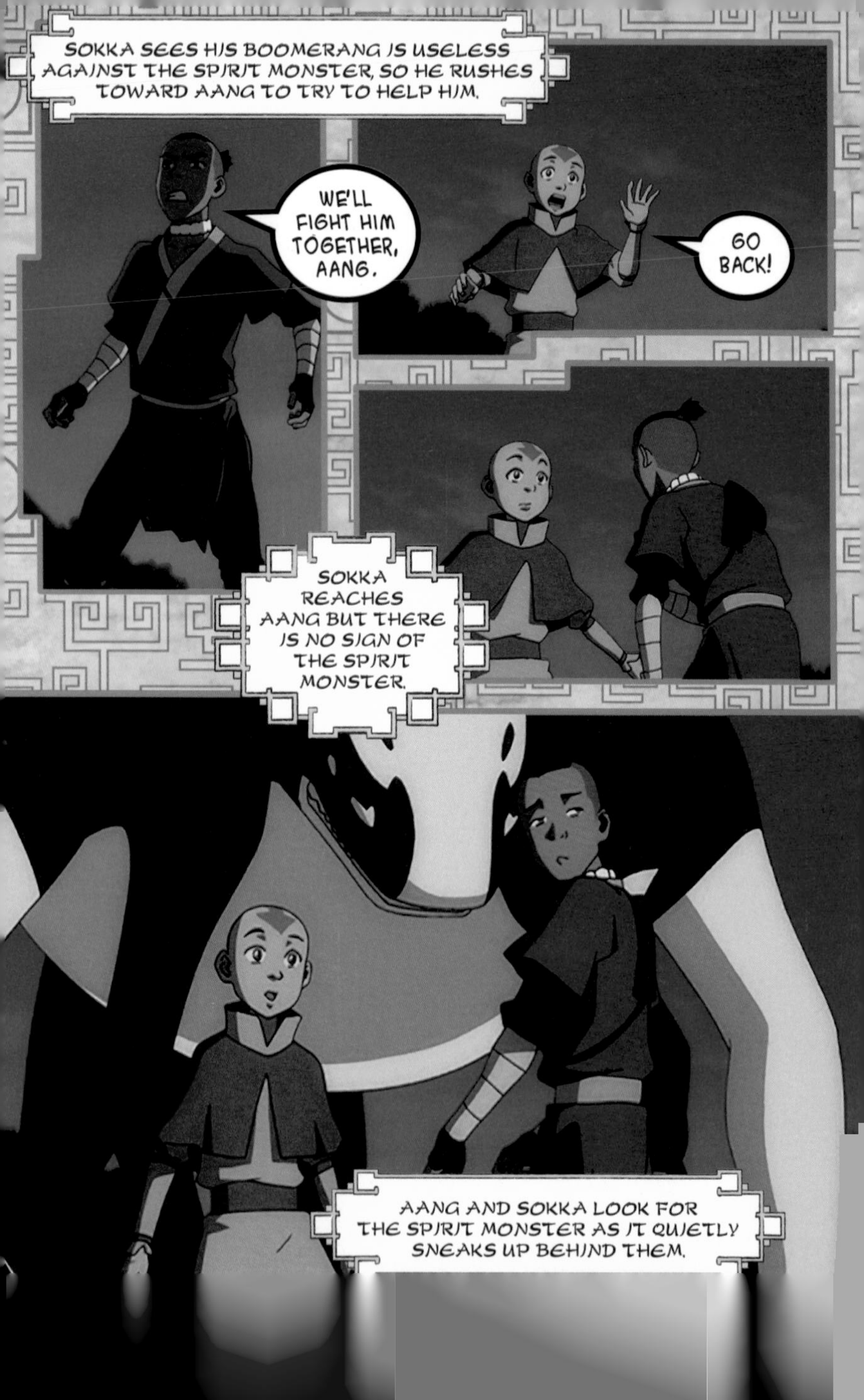
SOKKA SEES HIS BOOMERANG IS USELESS AGAINST THE SPIRIT MONSTER, SO HE RUSHES TOWARD AANG TO TRY TO HELP HIM.
WE'LL FIGHT HIM TOGETHER, AANG.
GO BACK!
SOKKA REACHES AANG BUT THERE IS NO SIGN OF THE SPIRIT MONSTER.
AANG AND SOKKA LOOK FOR THE SPIRIT MONSTER AS IT QUIETLY SNEAKS UP BEHIND THEM.

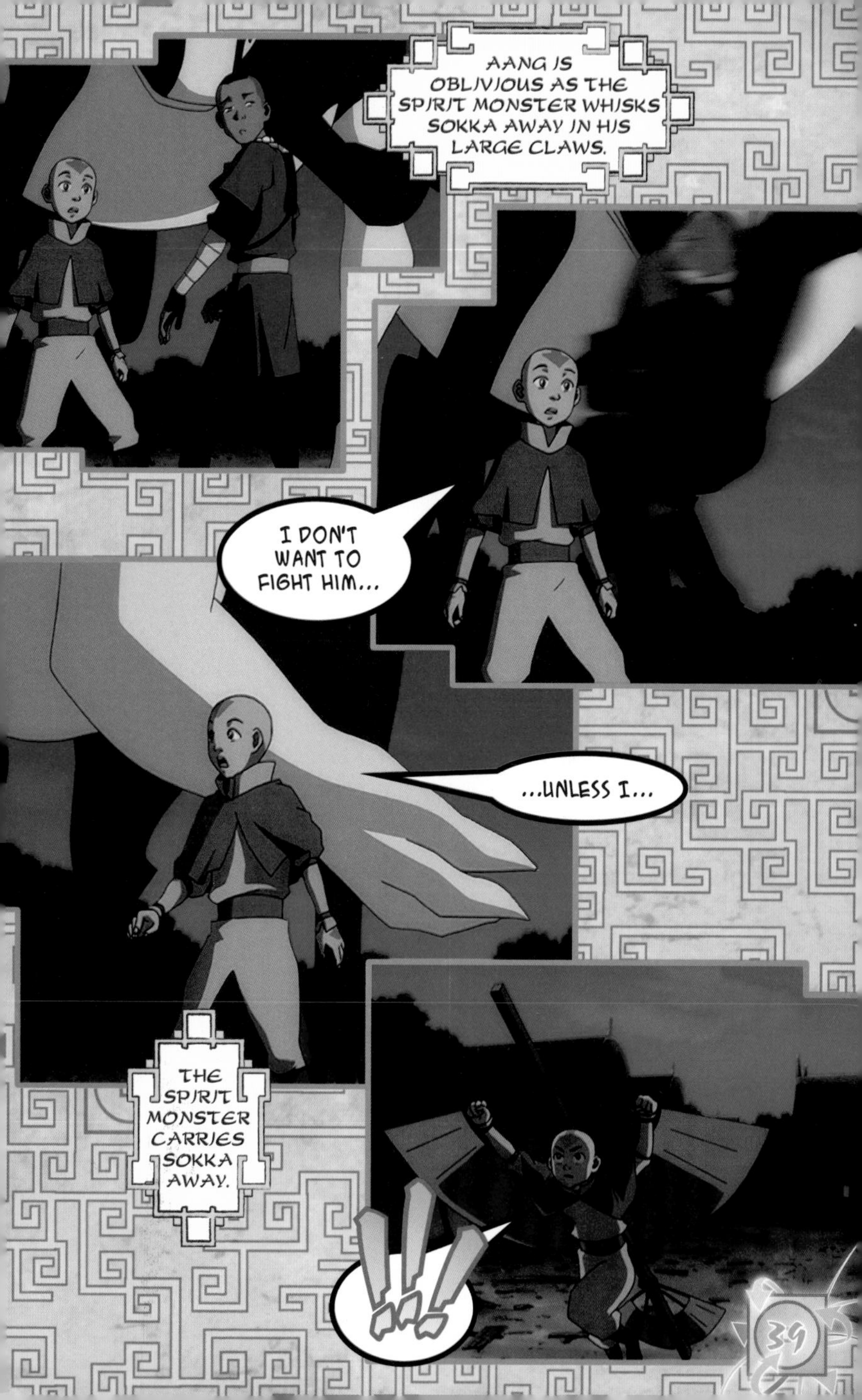
AANG IS OBLIVIOUS AS THE SPIRIT MONSTER WHISKS SOKKA AWAY IN HIS LARGE CLAWS.
I DON'T WANT TO FIGHT HIM...
...UNLESS I...
THE SPIRIT MONSTER CARRIES SOKKA AWAY.
!!!

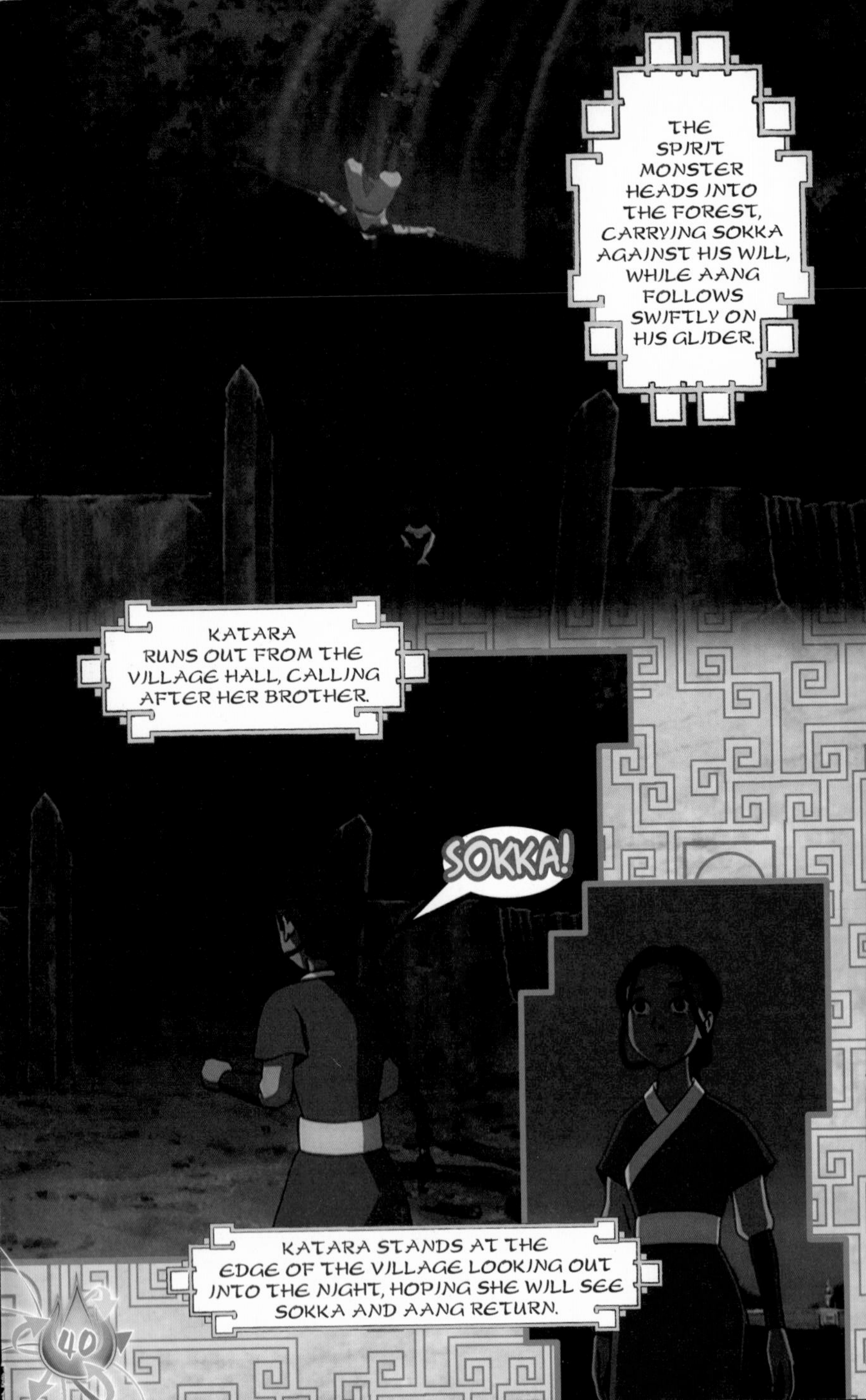
THE SPIRIT MONSTER HEADS INTO THE FOREST, CARRYING SOKKA AGAINST HIS WILL, WHILE AANG FOLLOWS SWIFTLY ON HIS GLIDER.
KATARA RUNS OUT FROM THE VILLAGE HALL, CALLING AFTER HER BROTHER.
SOKKA!
KATARA STANDS AT THE EDGE OF THE VILLAGE LOOKING OUT INTO THE NIGHT, HOPING SHE WILL SEE SOKKA AND AANG RETURN.

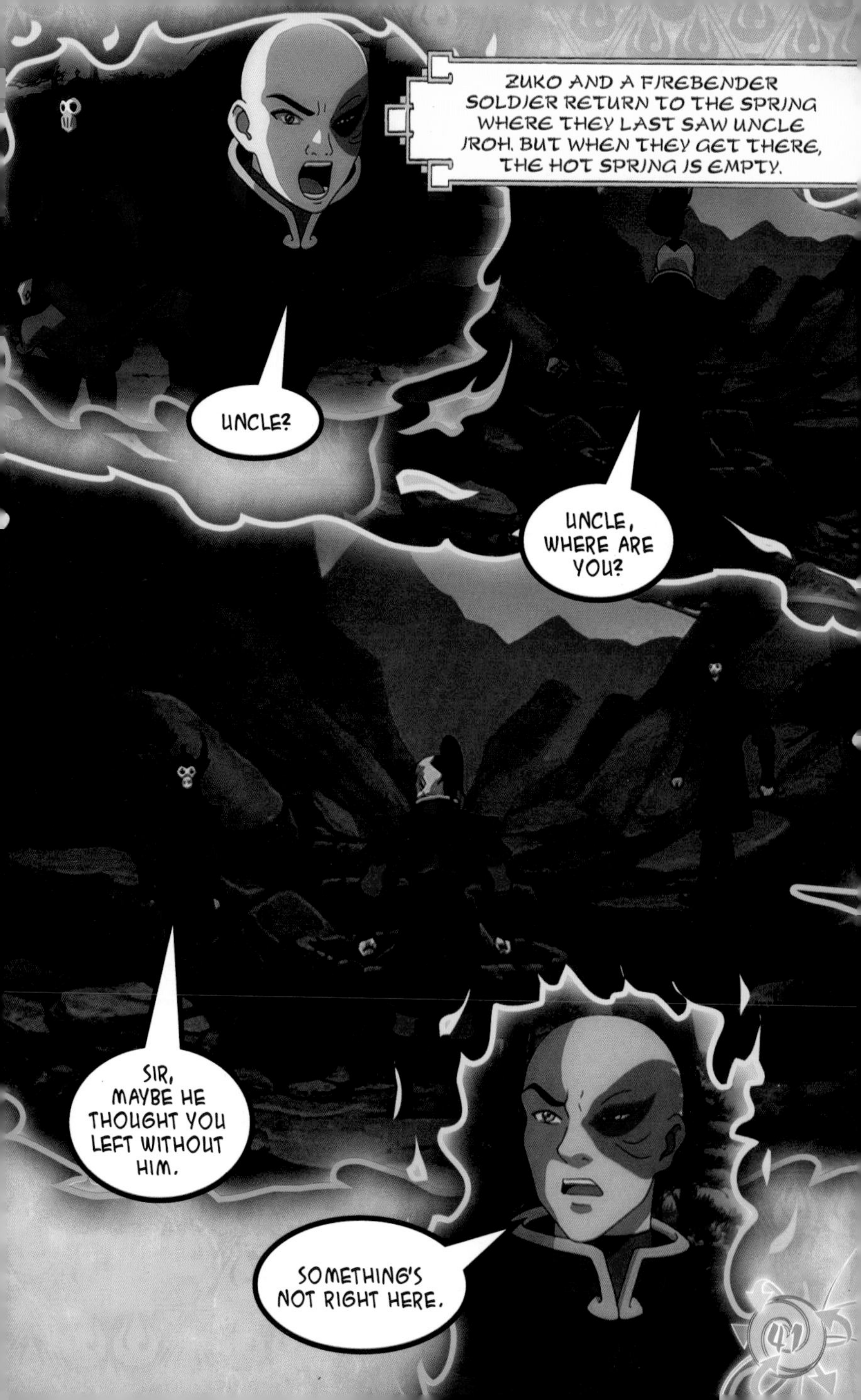
ZUKO AND A FIREBENDER SOLDIER RETURN TO THE SPRING WHERE THEY LAST SAW UNCLE IROH. BUT WHEN THEY GET THERE, THE HOT SPRING IS EMPTY.
UNCLE?
UNCLE, WHERE ARE YOU?
SIR, MAYBE HE THOUGHT YOU LEFT WITHOUT HIM.
SOMETHING'S NOT RIGHT HERE.

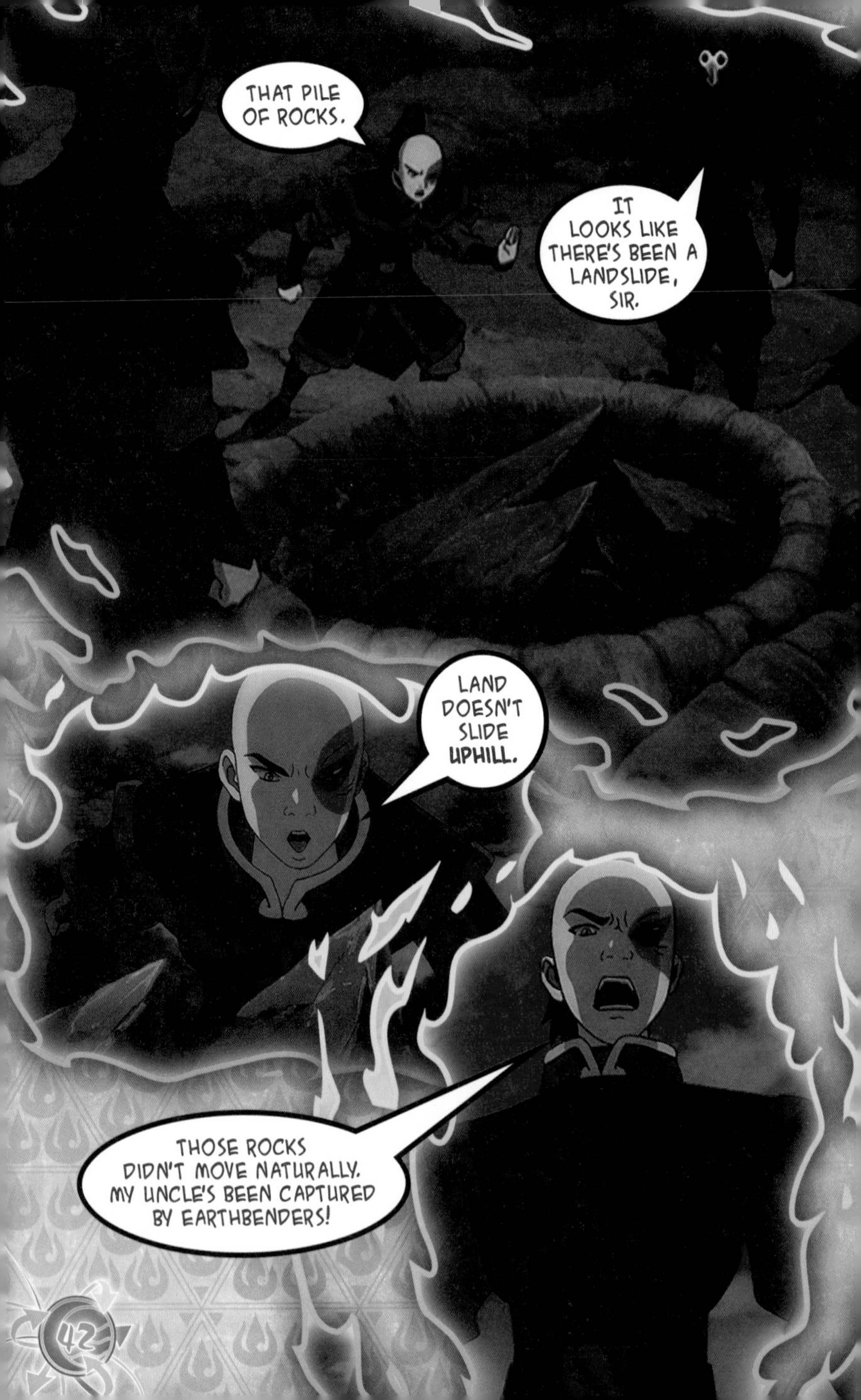
THAT PILE OF ROCKS.
IT LOOKS LIKE THERE'S BEEN A LANDSLIDE, SIR.
LAND DOESN'T SLIDE **UPHILL.**
THOSE ROCKS DIDN'T MOVE NATURALLY. MY UNCLE'S BEEN CAPTURED BY EARTHBENDERS!

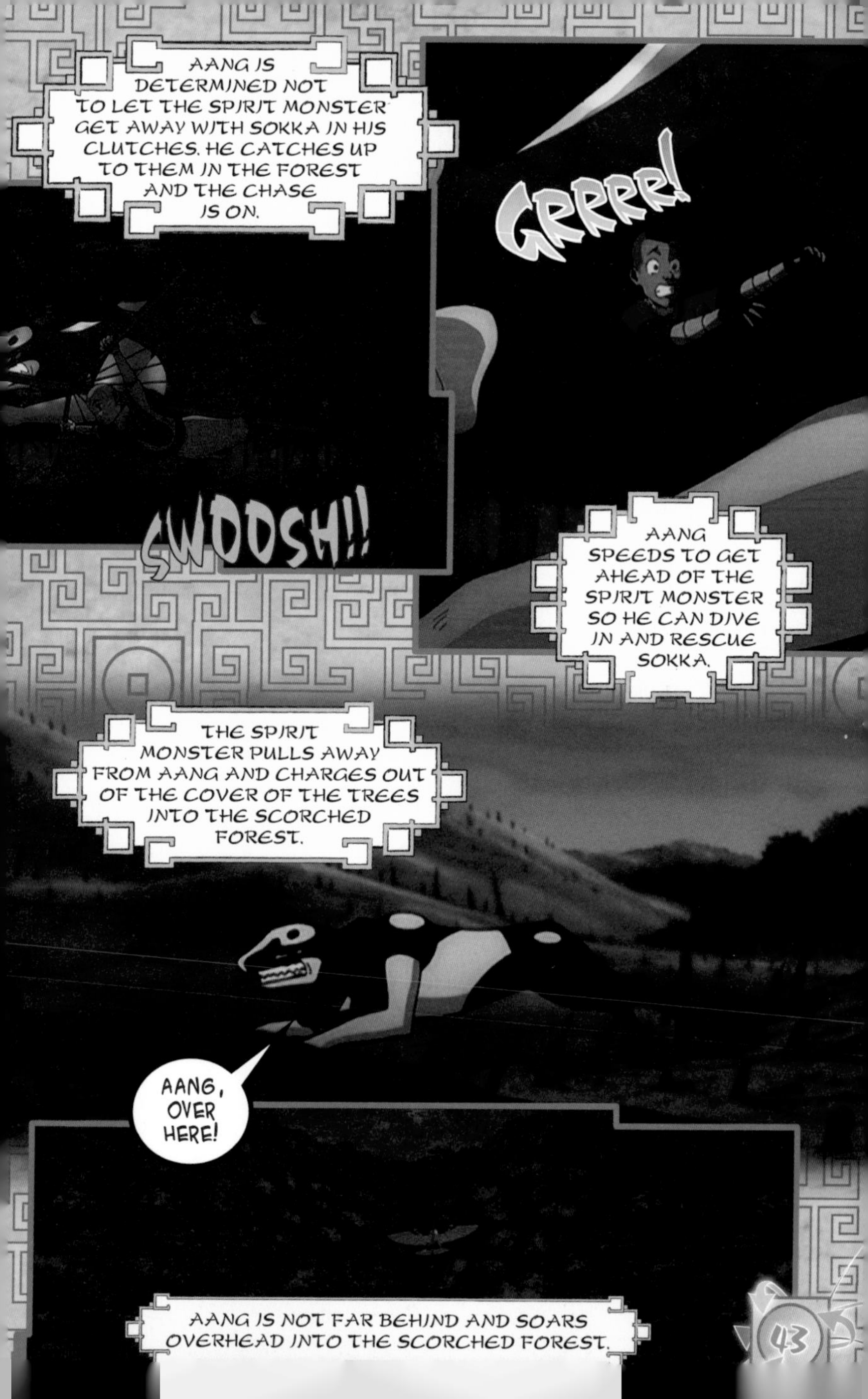
AANG IS DETERMINED NOT TO LET THE SPIRIT MONSTER GET AWAY WITH SOKKA IN HIS CLUTCHES. HE CATCHES UP TO THEM IN THE FOREST AND THE CHASE IS ON.
SWOOSH!!
GRRRR!
AANG SPEEDS TO GET AHEAD OF THE SPIRIT MONSTER SO HE CAN DIVE IN AND RESCUE SOKKA.
THE SPIRIT MONSTER PULLS AWAY FROM AANG AND CHARGES OUT OF THE COVER OF THE TREES INTO THE SCORCHED FOREST.
AANG, OVER HERE!
AANG IS NOT FAR BEHIND AND SOARS OVERHEAD INTO THE SCORCHED FOREST.

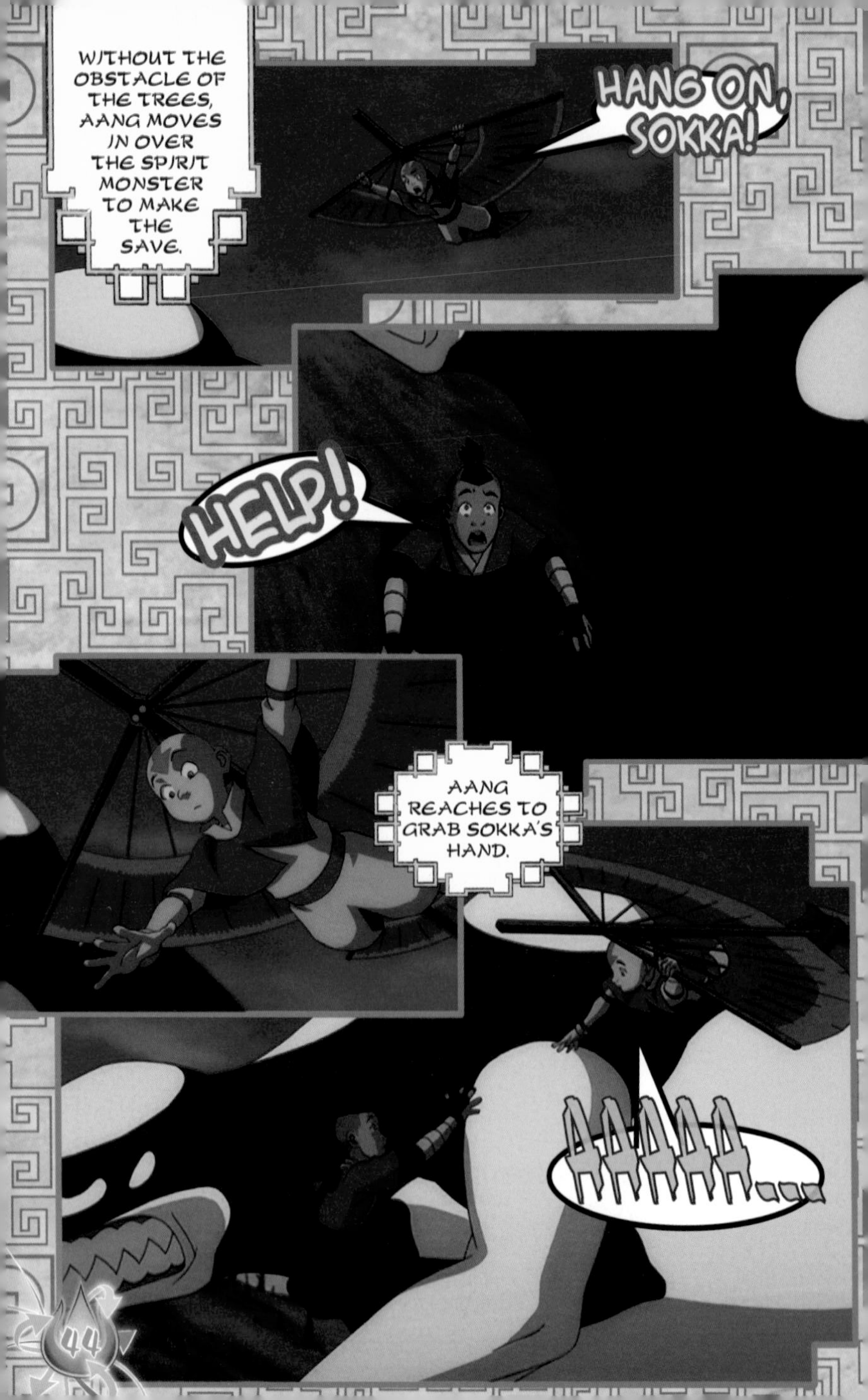
WITHOUT THE OBSTACLE OF THE TREES, AANG MOVES IN OVER THE SPIRIT MONSTER TO MAKE THE SAVE.
HANG ON, SOKKA!
HELP!
AANG REACHES TO GRAB SOKKA'S HAND.
AAAAA...

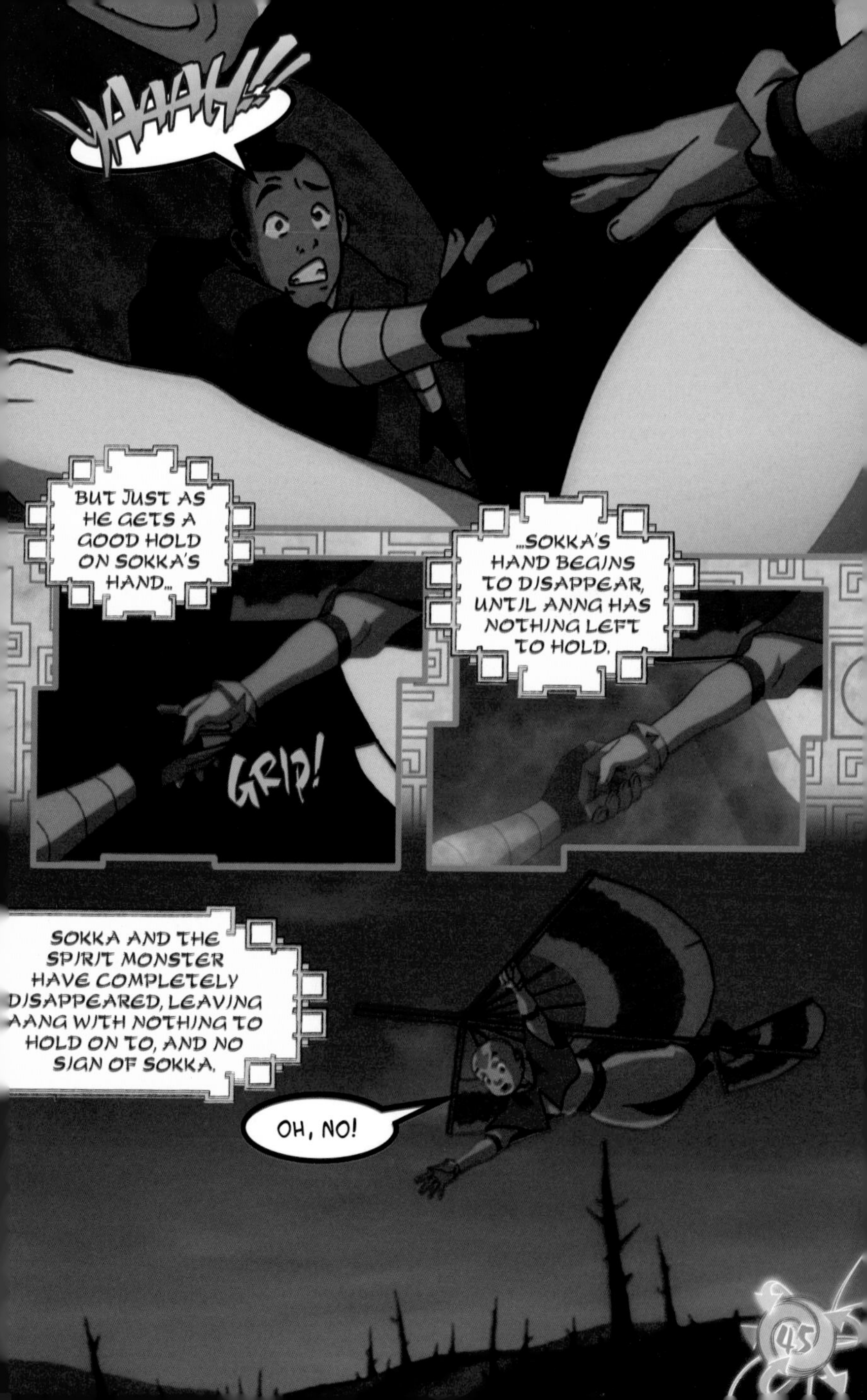

YAAAH!!
BUT JUST AS HE GETS A GOOD HOLD ON SOKKA'S HAND...
GRIP!
...SOKKA'S HAND BEGINS TO DISAPPEAR, UNTIL ANNG HAS NOTHING LEFT TO HOLD.
SOKKA AND THE SPIRIT MONSTER HAVE COMPLETELY DISAPPEARED, LEAVING AANG WITH NOTHING TO HOLD ON TO, AND NO SIGN OF SOKKA.
OH, NO!

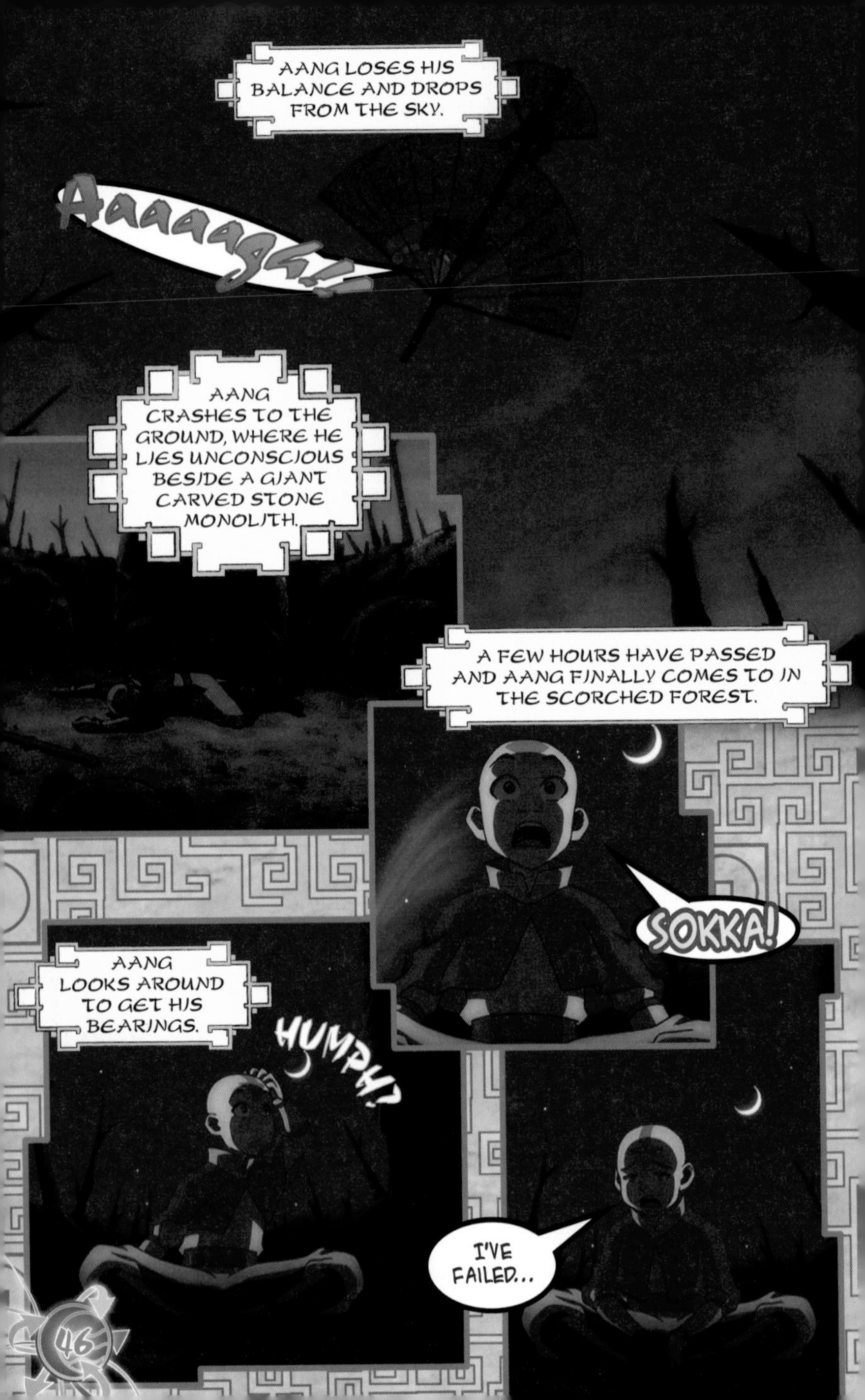

AANG LOSES HIS BALANCE AND DROPS FROM THE SKY.
Aaaaagh!!!
AANG CRASHES TO THE GROUND, WHERE HE LIES UNCONSCIOUS BESIDE A GIANT CARVED STONE MONOLITH.
A FEW HOURS HAVE PASSED AND AANG FINALLY COMES TO IN THE SCORCHED FOREST.
SOKKA!
AANG LOOKS AROUND TO GET HIS BEARINGS.
HUMPH?
I'VE FAILED...

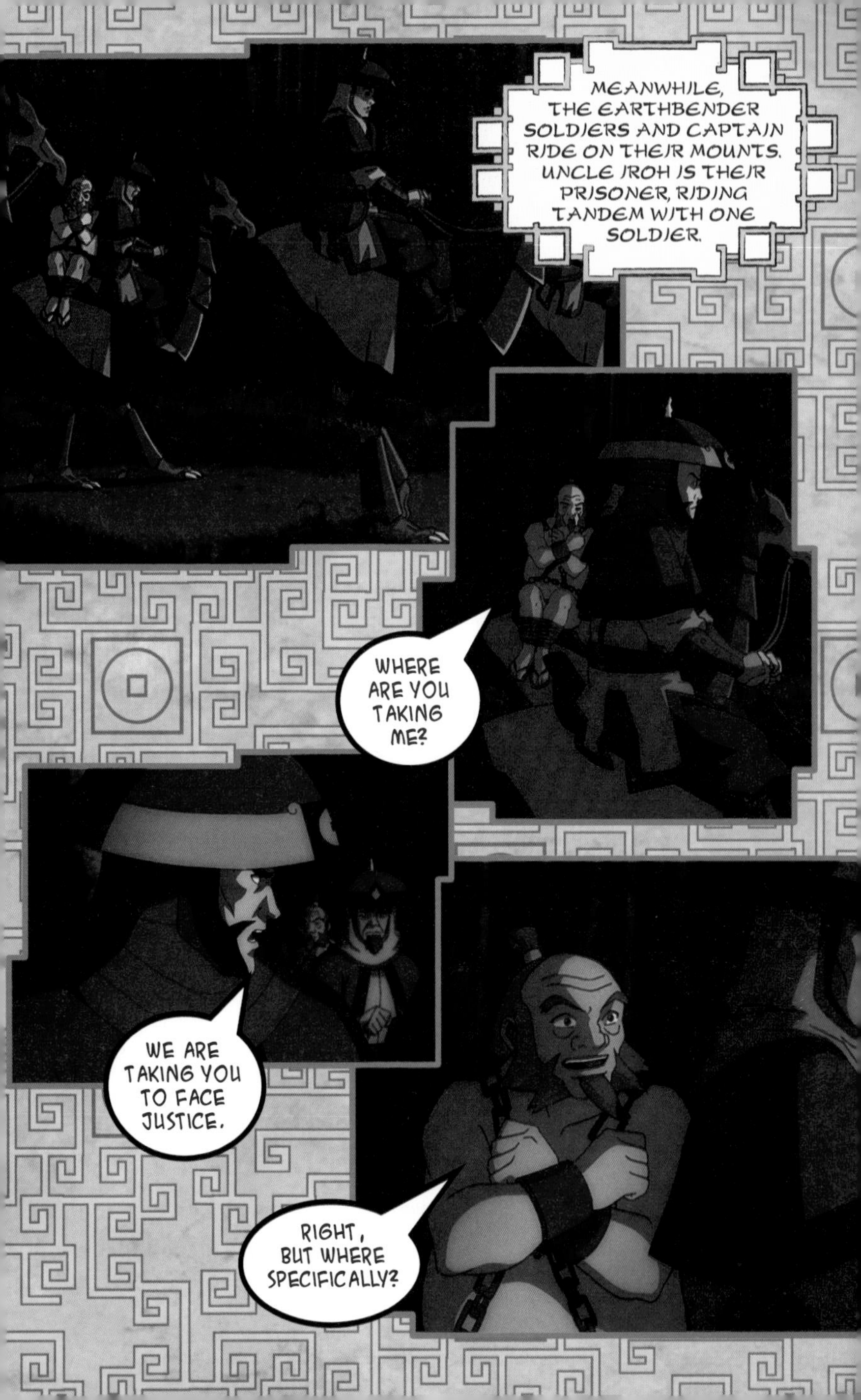
MEANWHILE, THE EARTHBENDER SOLDIERS AND CAPTAIN RIDE ON THEIR MOUNTS. UNCLE IROH IS THEIR PRISONER, RIDING TANDEM WITH ONE SOLDIER.
WHERE ARE YOU TAKING ME?
WE ARE TAKING YOU TO FACE JUSTICE.
RIGHT, BUT WHERE SPECIFICALLY?

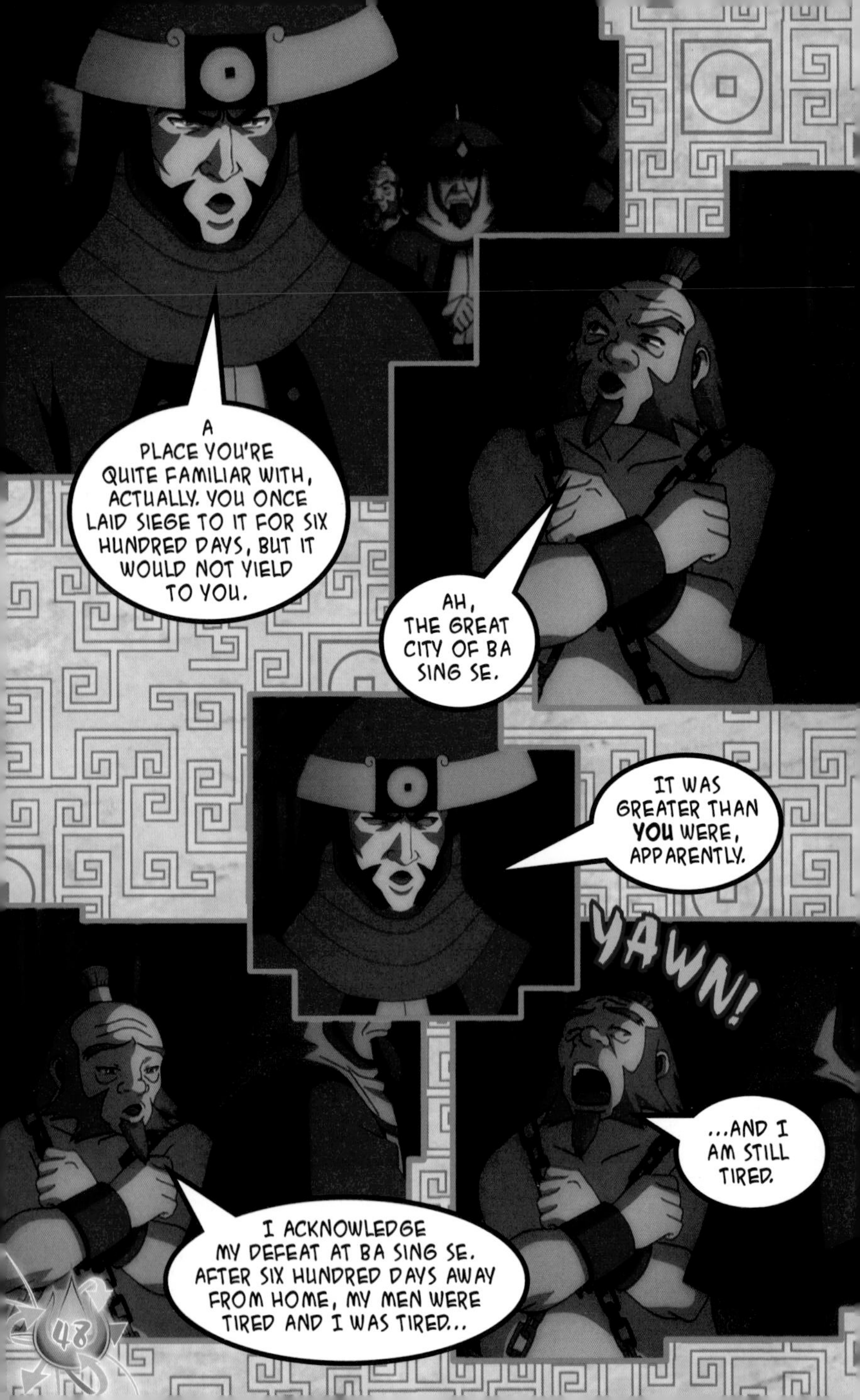
A PLACE YOU'RE QUITE FAMILIAR WITH, ACTUALLY. YOU ONCE LAID SIEGE TO IT FOR SIX HUNDRED DAYS, BUT IT WOULD NOT YIELD TO YOU.
AH, THE GREAT CITY OF BA SING SE.
IT WAS GREATER THAN **YOU** WERE, APPARENTLY.
I ACKNOWLEDGE MY DEFEAT AT BA SING SE. AFTER SIX HUNDRED DAYS AWAY FROM HOME, MY MEN WERE TIRED AND I WAS TIRED...
YAWN!
...AND I AM STILL TIRED.
48

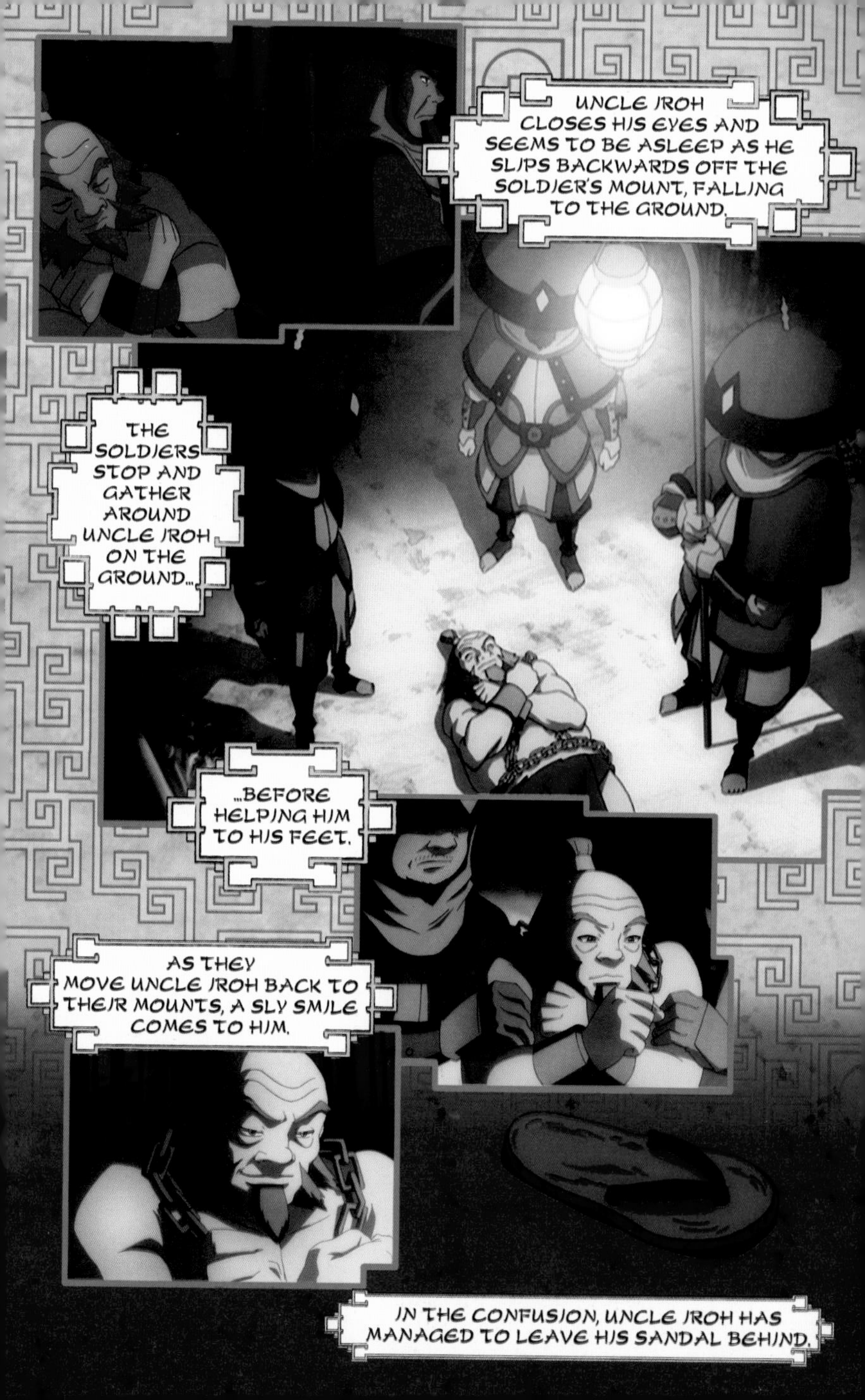
UNCLE IROH CLOSES HIS EYES AND SEEMS TO BE ASLEEP AS HE SLIPS BACKWARDS OFF THE SOLDIER'S MOUNT, FALLING TO THE GROUND.
THE SOLDIERS STOP AND GATHER AROUND UNCLE IROH ON THE GROUND...
...BEFORE HELPING HIM TO HIS FEET.
AS THEY MOVE UNCLE IROH BACK TO THEIR MOUNTS, A SLY SMILE COMES TO HIM.
IN THE CONFUSION, UNCLE IROH HAS MANAGED TO LEAVE HIS SANDAL BEHIND.

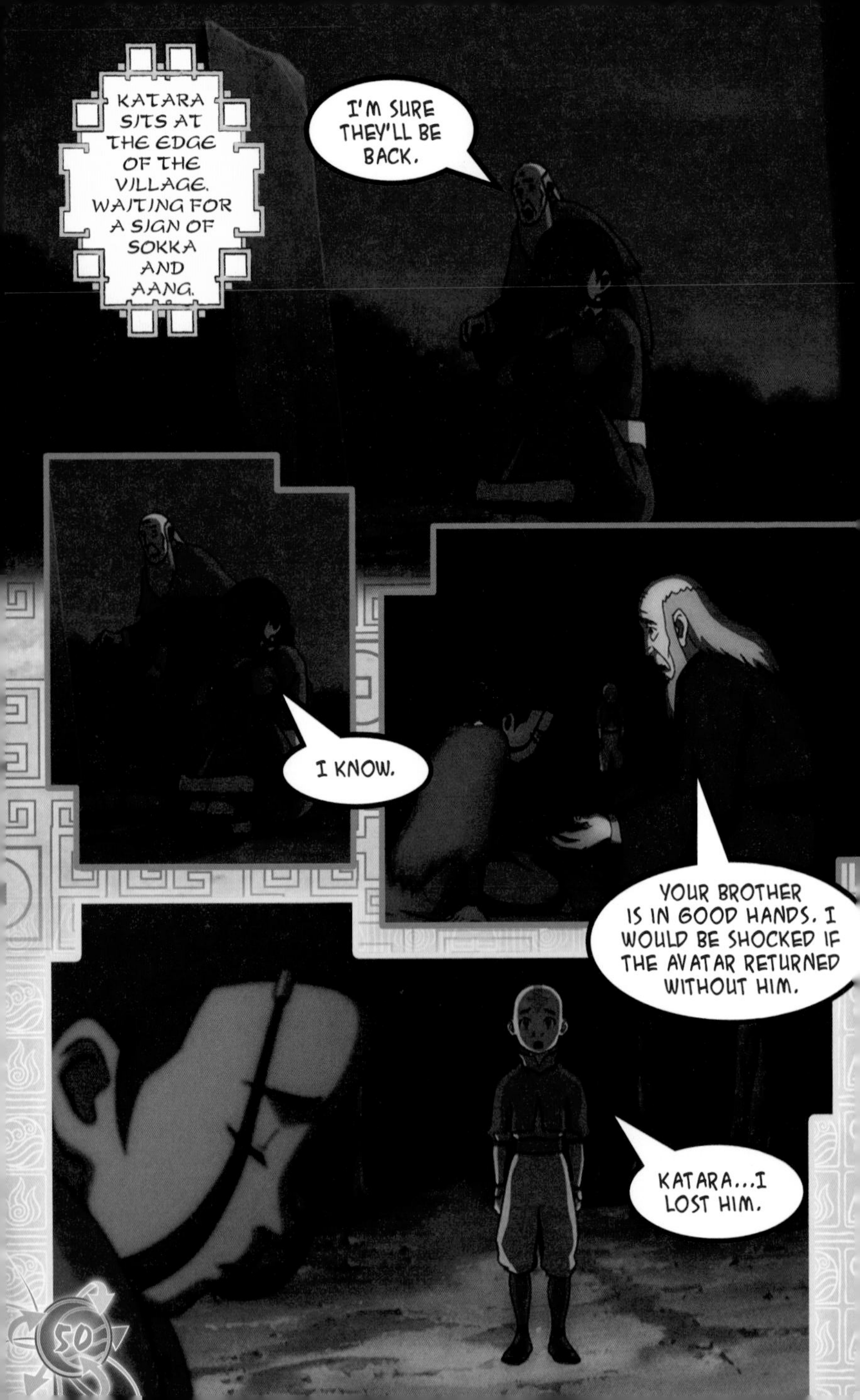
KATARA SITS AT THE EDGE OF THE VILLAGE. WAITING FOR A SIGN OF SOKKA AND AANG.
I'M SURE THEY'LL BE BACK.
I KNOW.
YOUR BROTHER IS IN GOOD HANDS. I WOULD BE SHOCKED IF THE AVATAR RETURNED WITHOUT HIM.
KATARA...I LOST HIM.

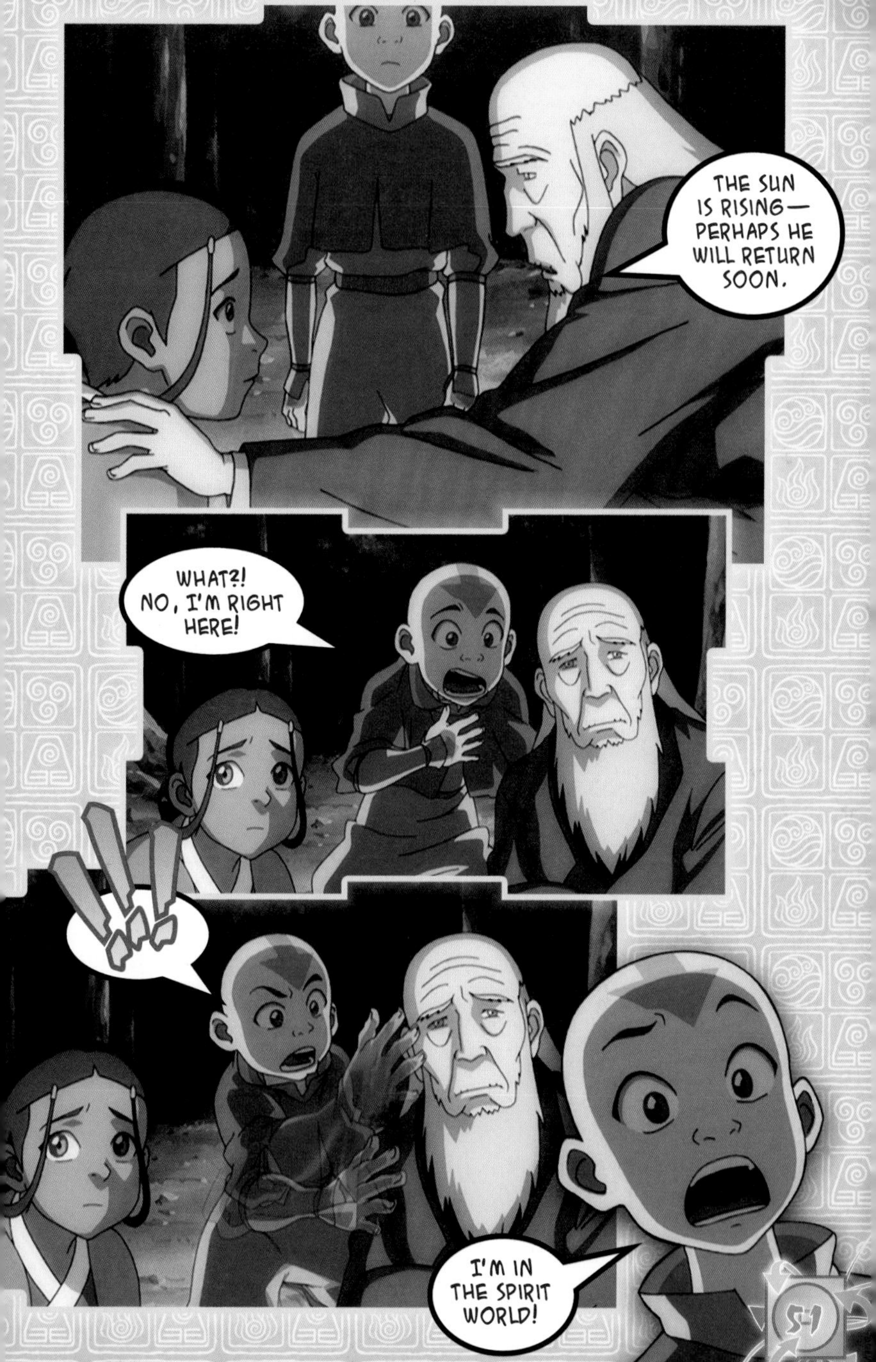
THE SUN IS RISING— PERHAPS HE WILL RETURN SOON.
WHAT?! NO, I'M RIGHT HERE!
!!!
I'M IN THE SPIRIT WORLD!

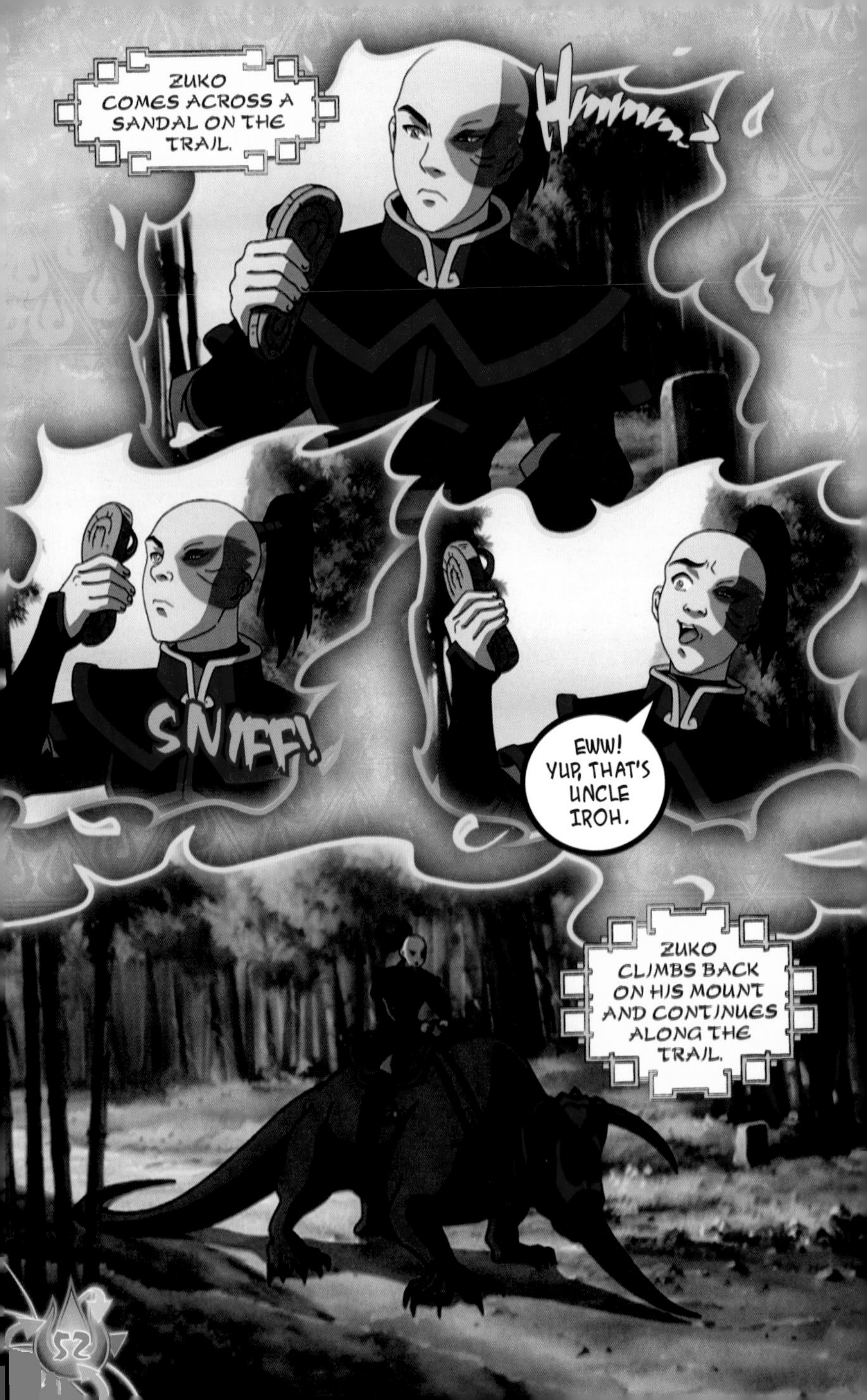
ZUKO COMES ACROSS A SANDAL ON THE TRAIL.
Hmmm?
SNIFF!
EWW! YUP, THAT'S UNCLE IROH.
ZUKO CLIMBS BACK ON HIS MOUNT AND CONTINUES ALONG THE TRAIL.

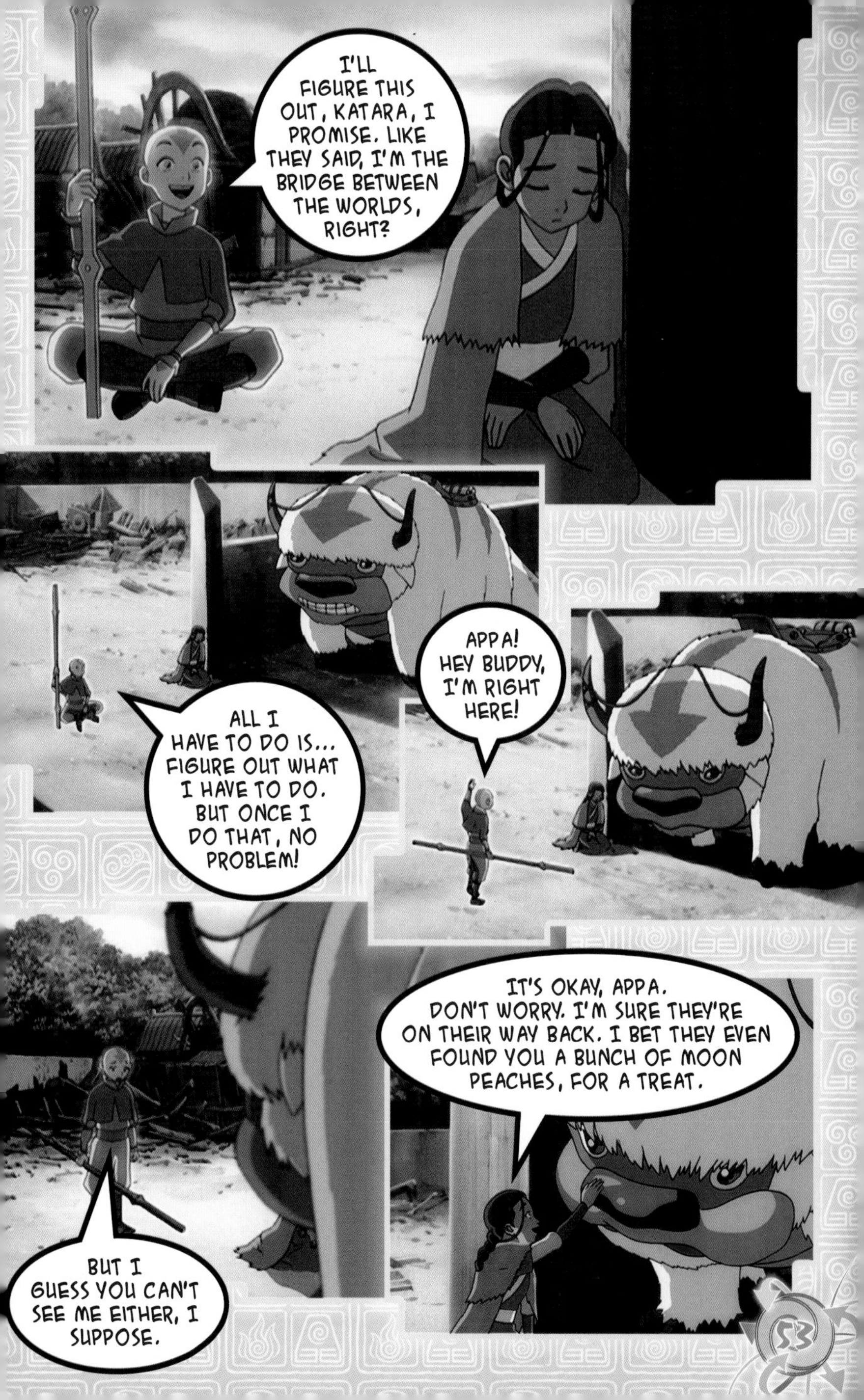
I'LL FIGURE THIS OUT, KATARA, I PROMISE. LIKE THEY SAID, I'M THE BRIDGE BETWEEN THE WORLDS, RIGHT?
ALL I HAVE TO DO IS... FIGURE OUT WHAT I HAVE TO DO. BUT ONCE I DO THAT, NO PROBLEM!
APPA! HEY BUDDY, I'M RIGHT HERE!
BUT I GUESS YOU CAN'T SEE ME EITHER, I SUPPOSE.
IT'S OKAY, APPA. DON'T WORRY. I'M SURE THEY'RE ON THEIR WAY BACK. I BET THEY EVEN FOUND YOU A BUNCH OF MOON PEACHES, FOR A TREAT.
53

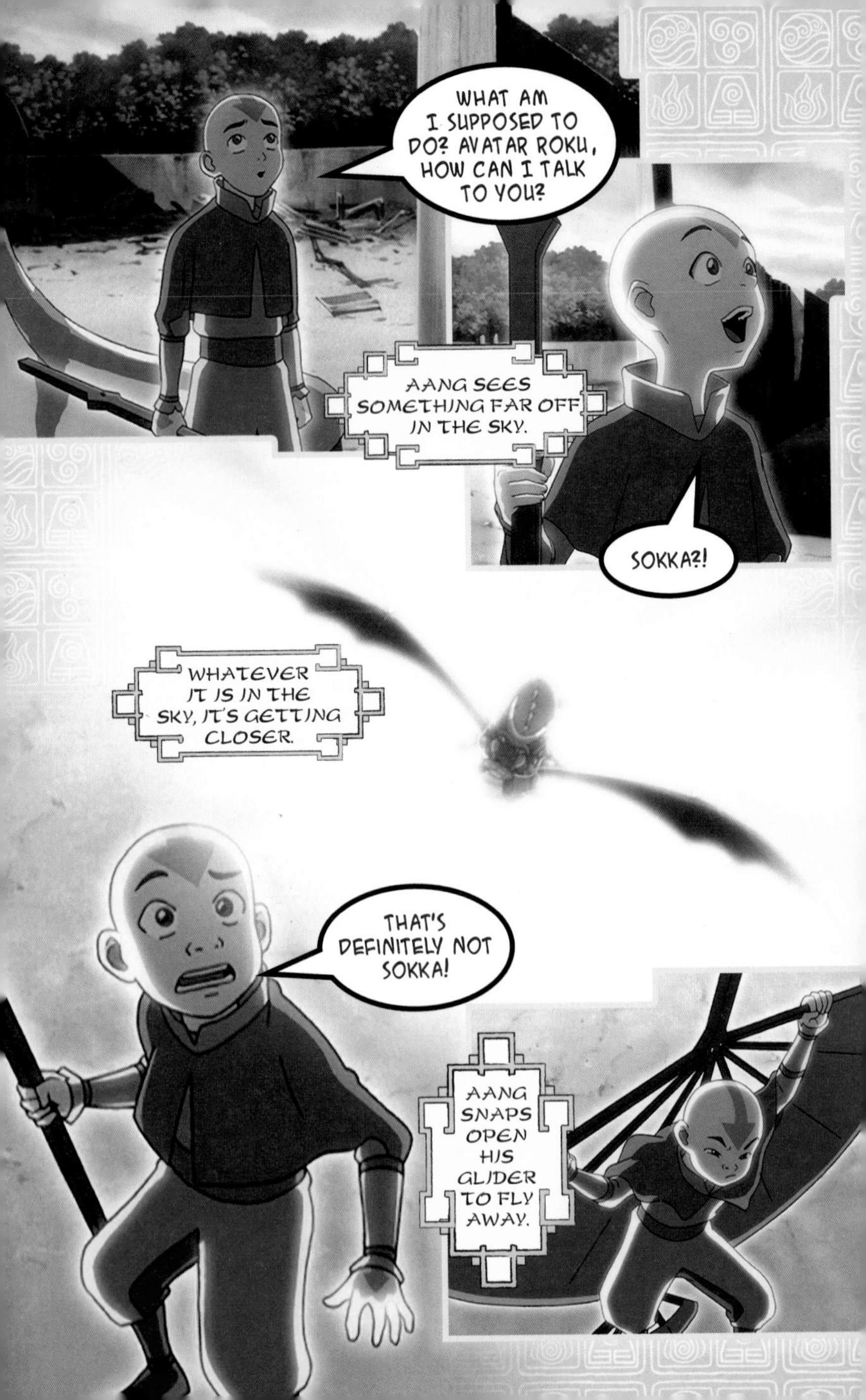
WHAT AM I SUPPOSED TO DO? AVATAR ROKU, HOW CAN I TALK TO YOU?
AANG SEES SOMETHING FAR OFF IN THE SKY.
SOKKA?!
WHATEVER IT IS IN THE SKY, IT'S GETTING CLOSER.
THAT'S DEFINITELY NOT SOKKA!
AANG SNAPS OPEN HIS GLIDER TO FLY AWAY.

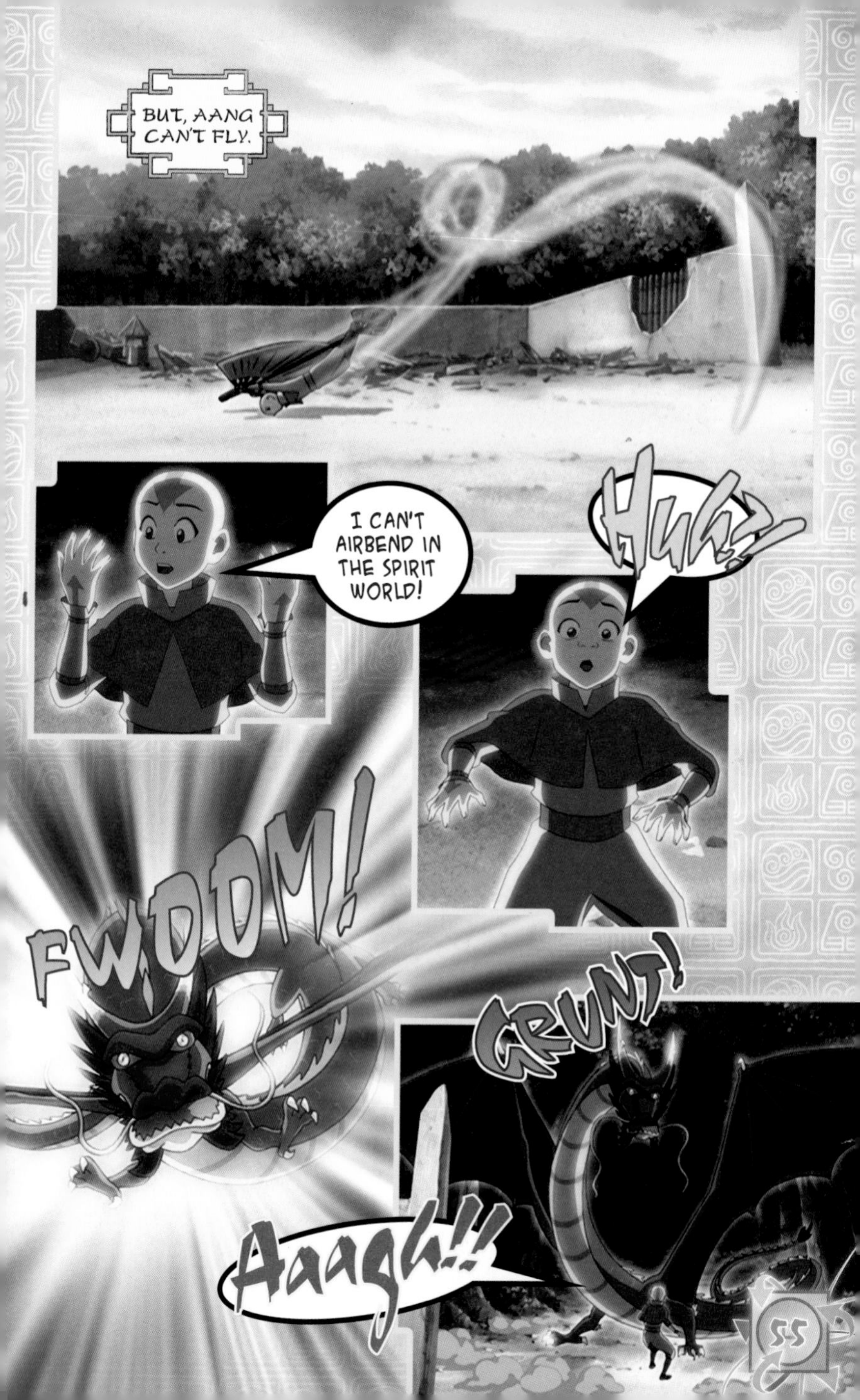

BUT, AANG CAN'T FLY.
I CAN'T AIRBEND IN THE SPIRIT WORLD!
HUH?!
FWOOM!
GRUNT!
Aaagh!!

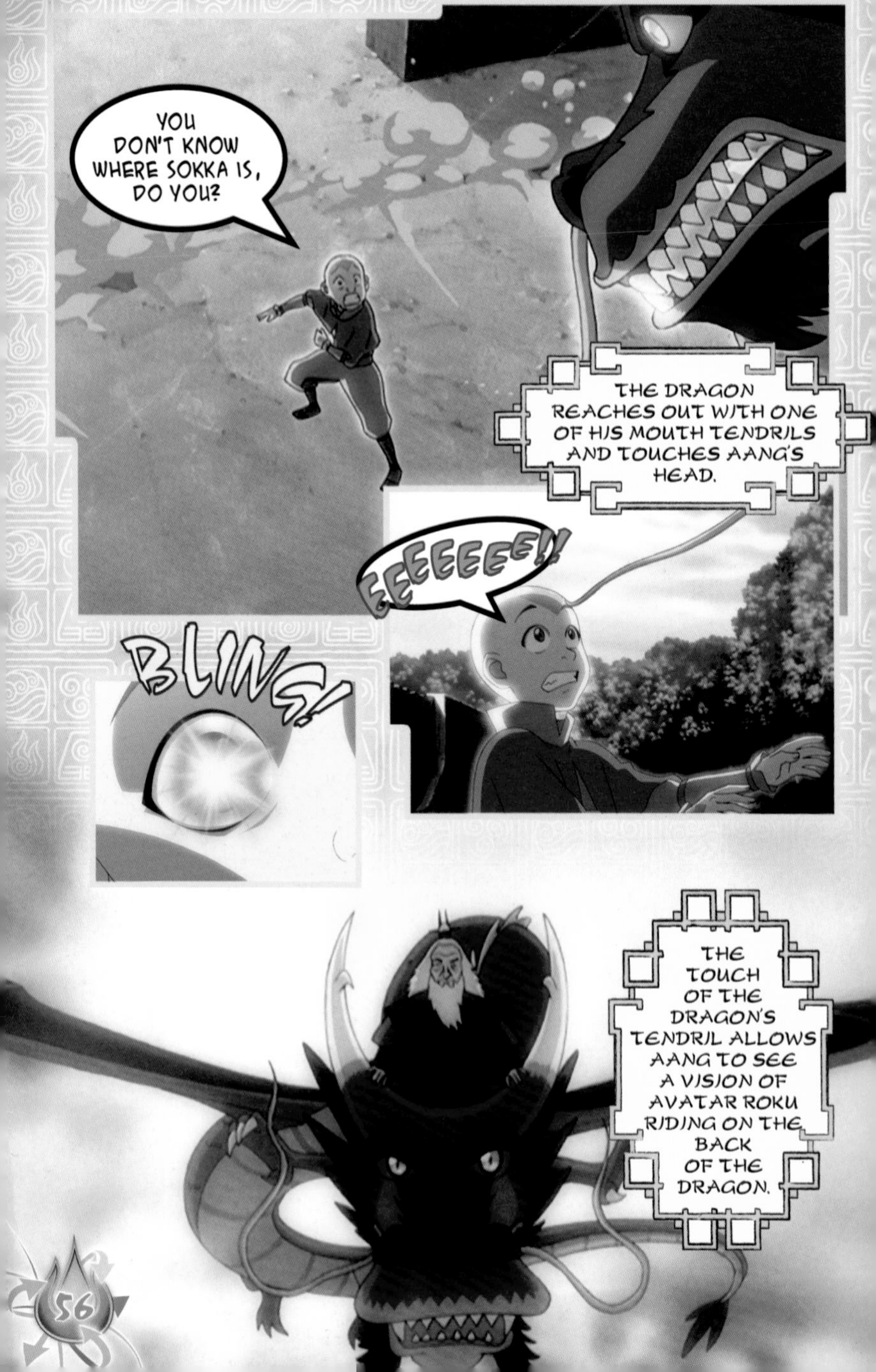
YOU DON'T KNOW WHERE SOKKA IS, DO YOU?
THE DRAGON REACHES OUT WITH ONE OF HIS MOUTH TENDRILS AND TOUCHES AANG'S HEAD.
EEEEEEE!!
BLING!
THE TOUCH OF THE DRAGON'S TENDRIL ALLOWS AANG TO SEE A VISION OF AVATAR ROKU RIDING ON THE BACK OF THE DRAGON.

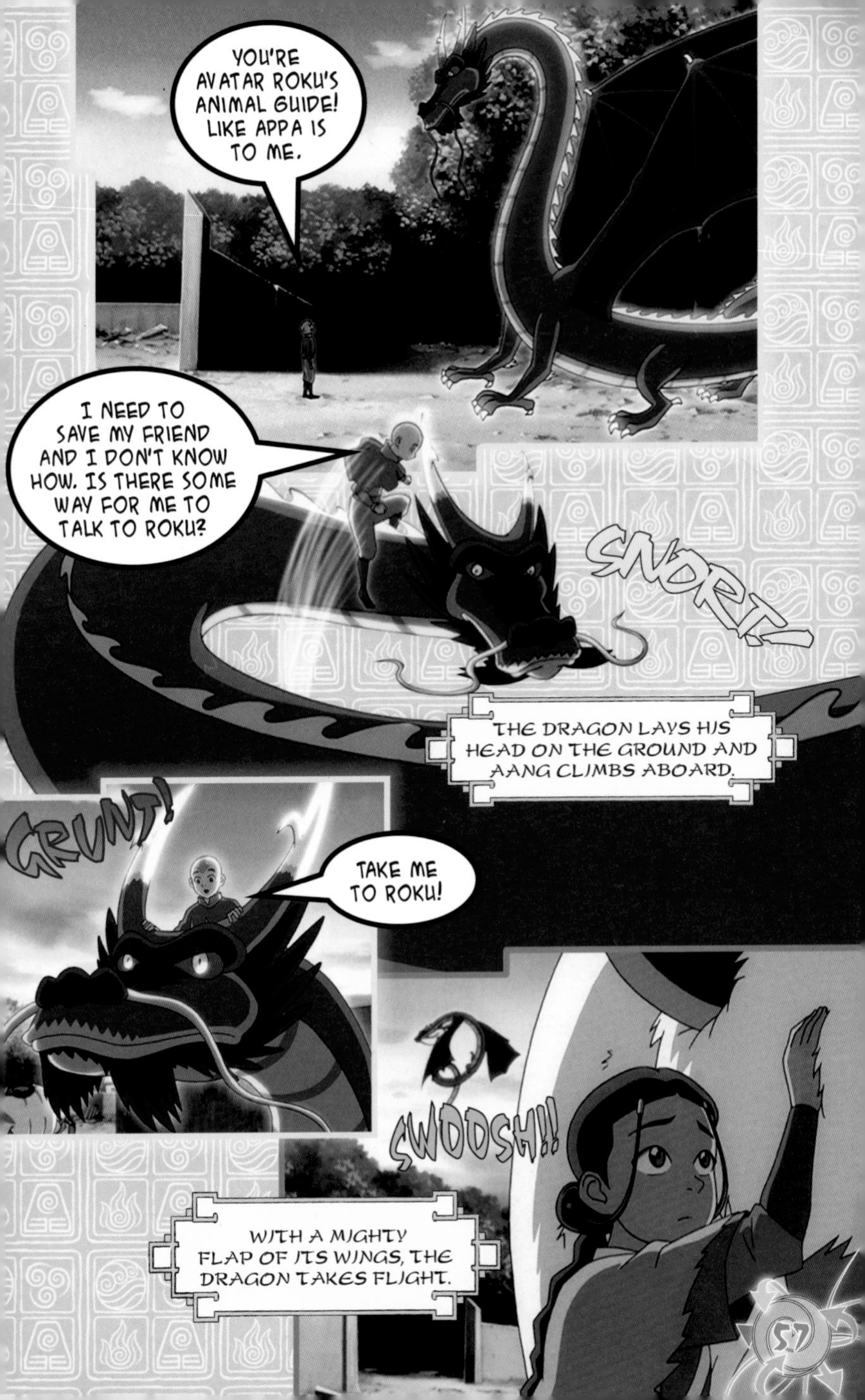

YOU'RE AVATAR ROKU'S ANIMAL GUIDE! LIKE APPA IS TO ME.
I NEED TO SAVE MY FRIEND AND I DON'T KNOW HOW. IS THERE SOME WAY FOR ME TO TALK TO ROKU?
SNORT!
THE DRAGON LAYS HIS HEAD ON THE GROUND AND AANG CLIMBS ABOARD.
GRUNT!
TAKE ME TO ROKU!
SWOOSH!!
WITH A MIGHTY FLAP OF ITS WINGS, THE DRAGON TAKES FLIGHT.

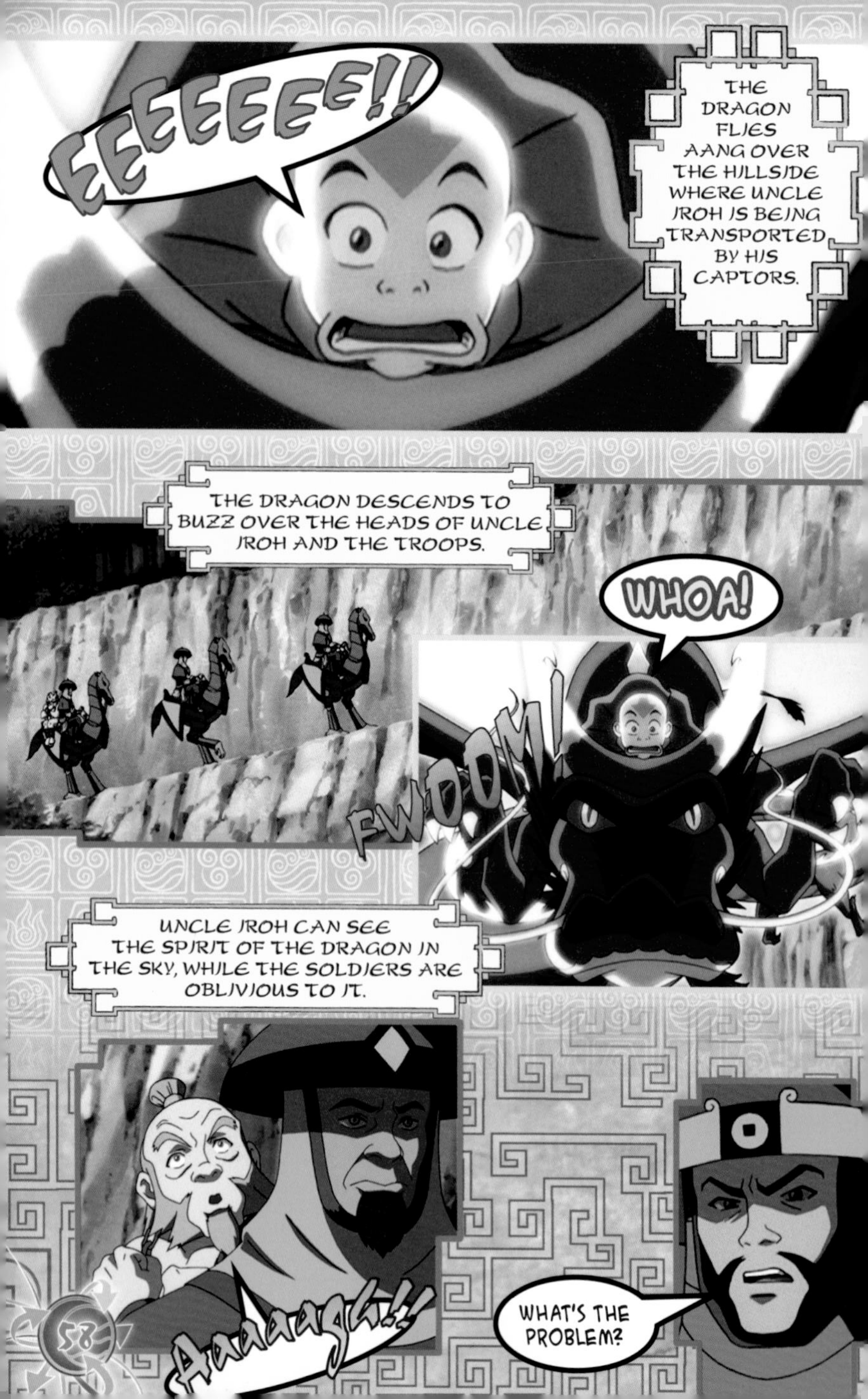
EEEEEEE!!
THE DRAGON FLIES AANG OVER THE HILLSIDE WHERE UNCLE IROH IS BEING TRANSPORTED BY HIS CAPTORS.
THE DRAGON DESCENDS TO BUZZ OVER THE HEADS OF UNCLE IROH AND THE TROOPS.
WHOA!
FWOOM!
UNCLE IROH CAN SEE THE SPIRIT OF THE DRAGON IN THE SKY, WHILE THE SOLDIERS ARE OBLIVIOUS TO IT.
Aaaaagh!!
WHAT'S THE PROBLEM?

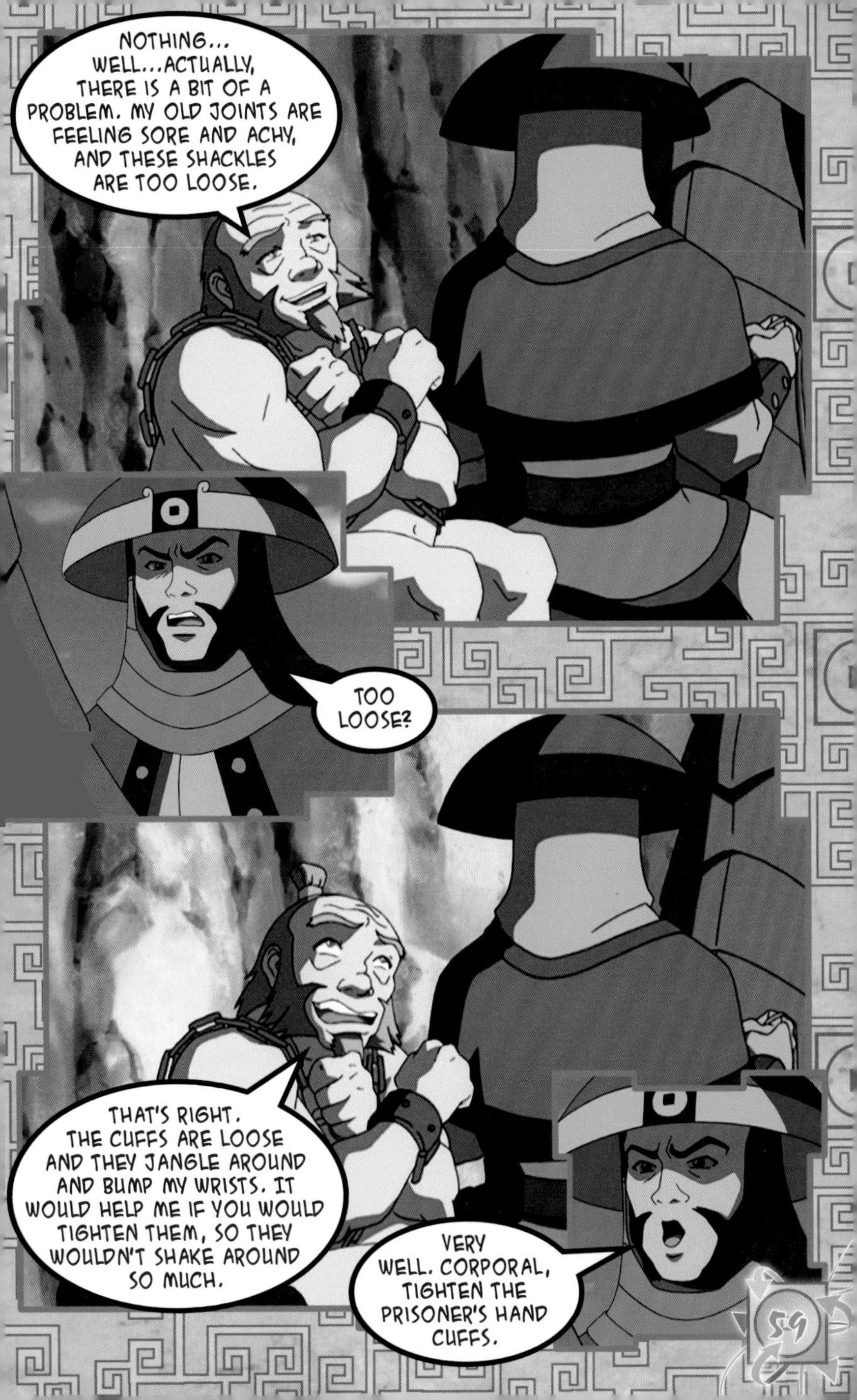

NOTHING... WELL...ACTUALLY, THERE IS A BIT OF A PROBLEM. MY OLD JOINTS ARE FEELING SORE AND ACHY, AND THESE SHACKLES ARE TOO LOOSE.
TOO LOOSE?
THAT'S RIGHT. THE CUFFS ARE LOOSE AND THEY JANGLE AROUND AND BUMP MY WRISTS. IT WOULD HELP ME IF YOU WOULD TIGHTEN THEM, SO THEY WOULDN'T SHAKE AROUND SO MUCH.
VERY WELL. CORPORAL, TIGHTEN THE PRISONER'S HAND CUFFS.

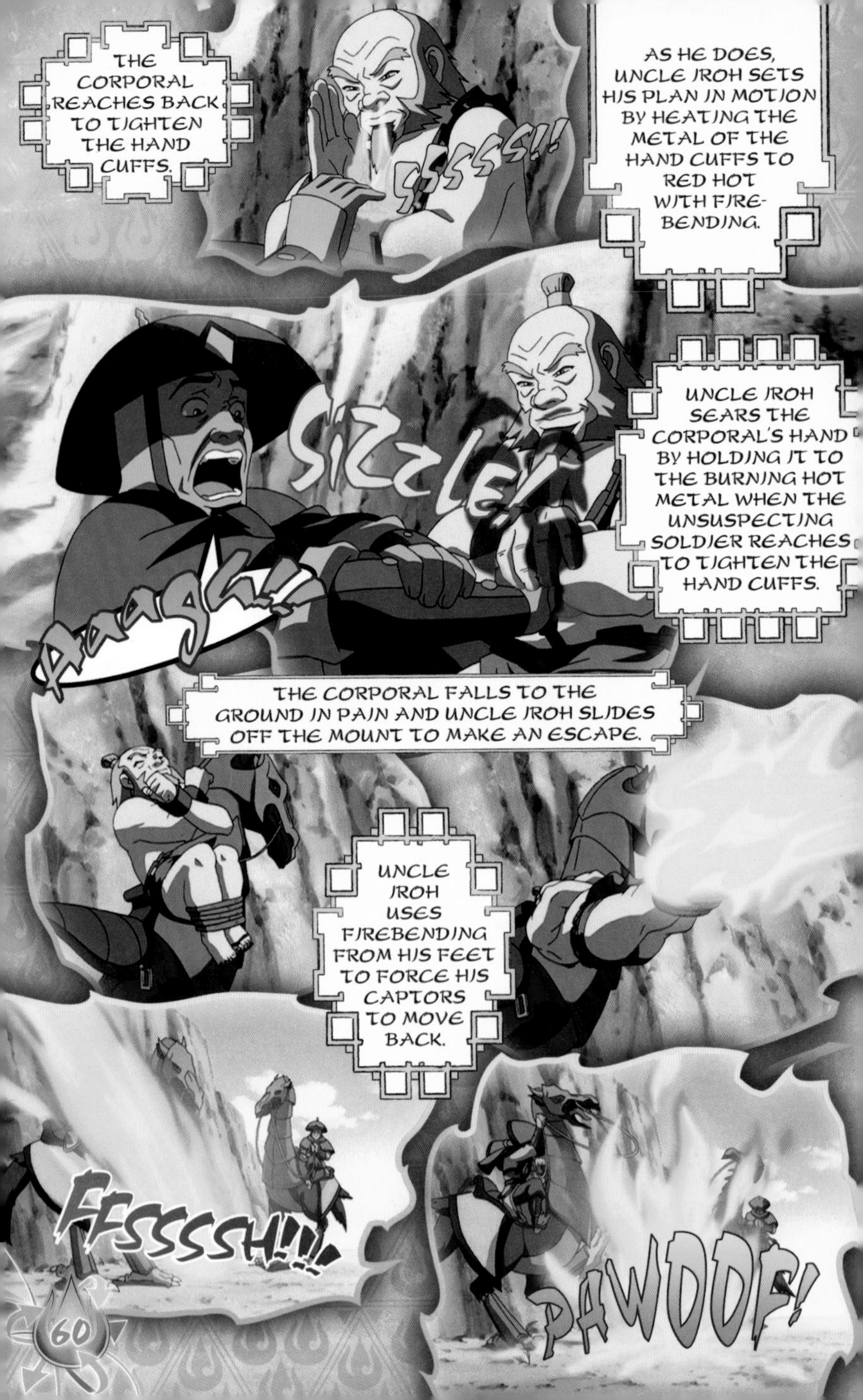

THE CORPORAL REACHES BACK TO TIGHTEN THE HAND CUFFS.
SSSSSS!!
AS HE DOES, UNCLE IROH SETS HIS PLAN IN MOTION BY HEATING THE METAL OF THE HAND CUFFS TO RED HOT WITH FIRE-BENDING.
SIZZLE!
AAAGH!!
UNCLE IROH SEARS THE CORPORAL'S HAND BY HOLDING IT TO THE BURNING HOT METAL WHEN THE UNSUSPECTING SOLDIER REACHES TO TIGHTEN THE HAND CUFFS.
THE CORPORAL FALLS TO THE GROUND IN PAIN AND UNCLE IROH SLIDES OFF THE MOUNT TO MAKE AN ESCAPE.
UNCLE IROH USES FIREBENDING FROM HIS FEET TO FORCE HIS CAPTORS TO MOVE BACK.
FFSSSSH!!!
PAWOOF!

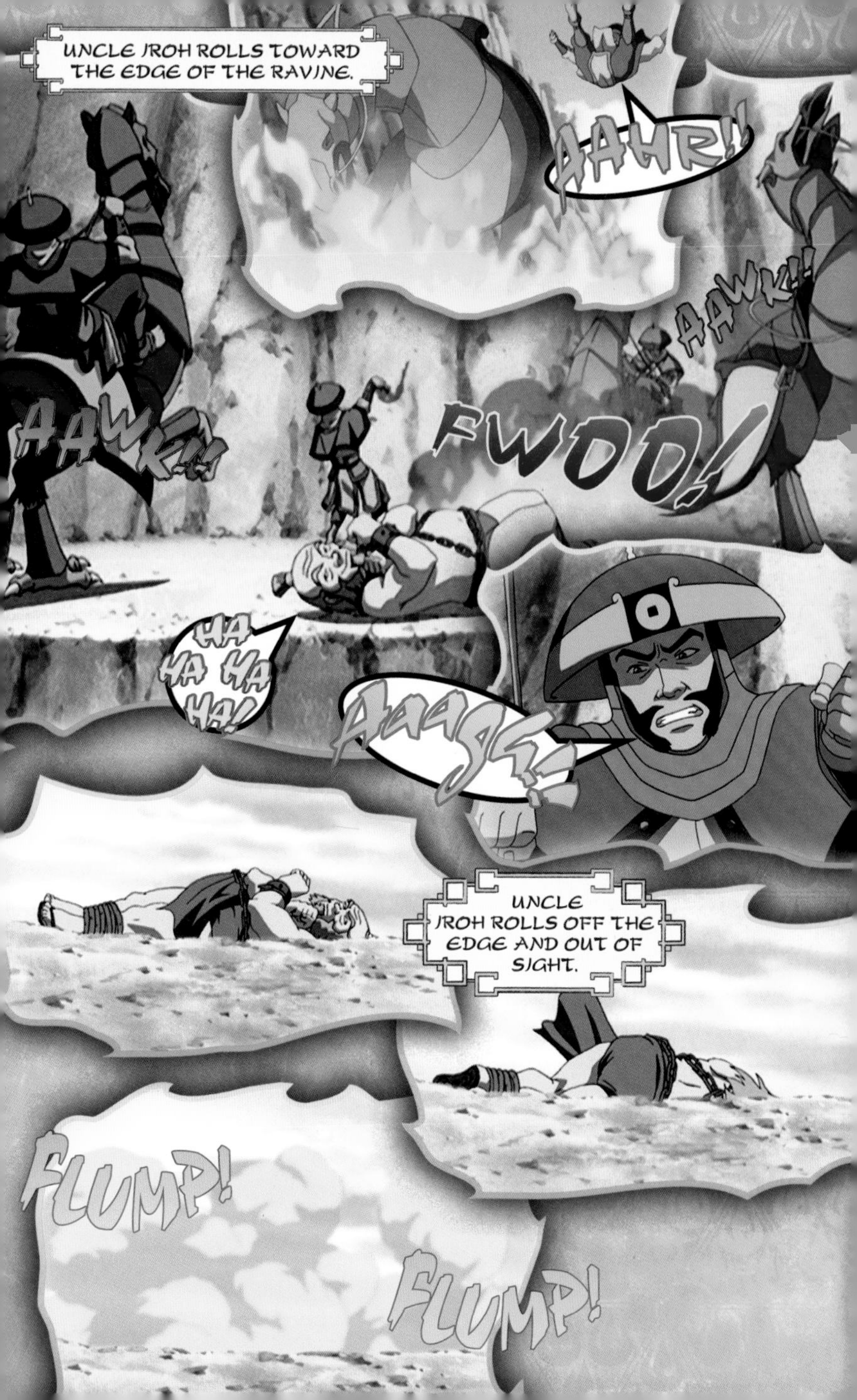
UNCLE IROH ROLLS TOWARD THE EDGE OF THE RAVINE.
AAHR!!
AAWK!!
AAWK!!
FWOO!
HA HA HA HA!
AAAGH!!
UNCLE IROH ROLLS OFF THE EDGE AND OUT OF SIGHT.
FLUMP!
FLUMP!

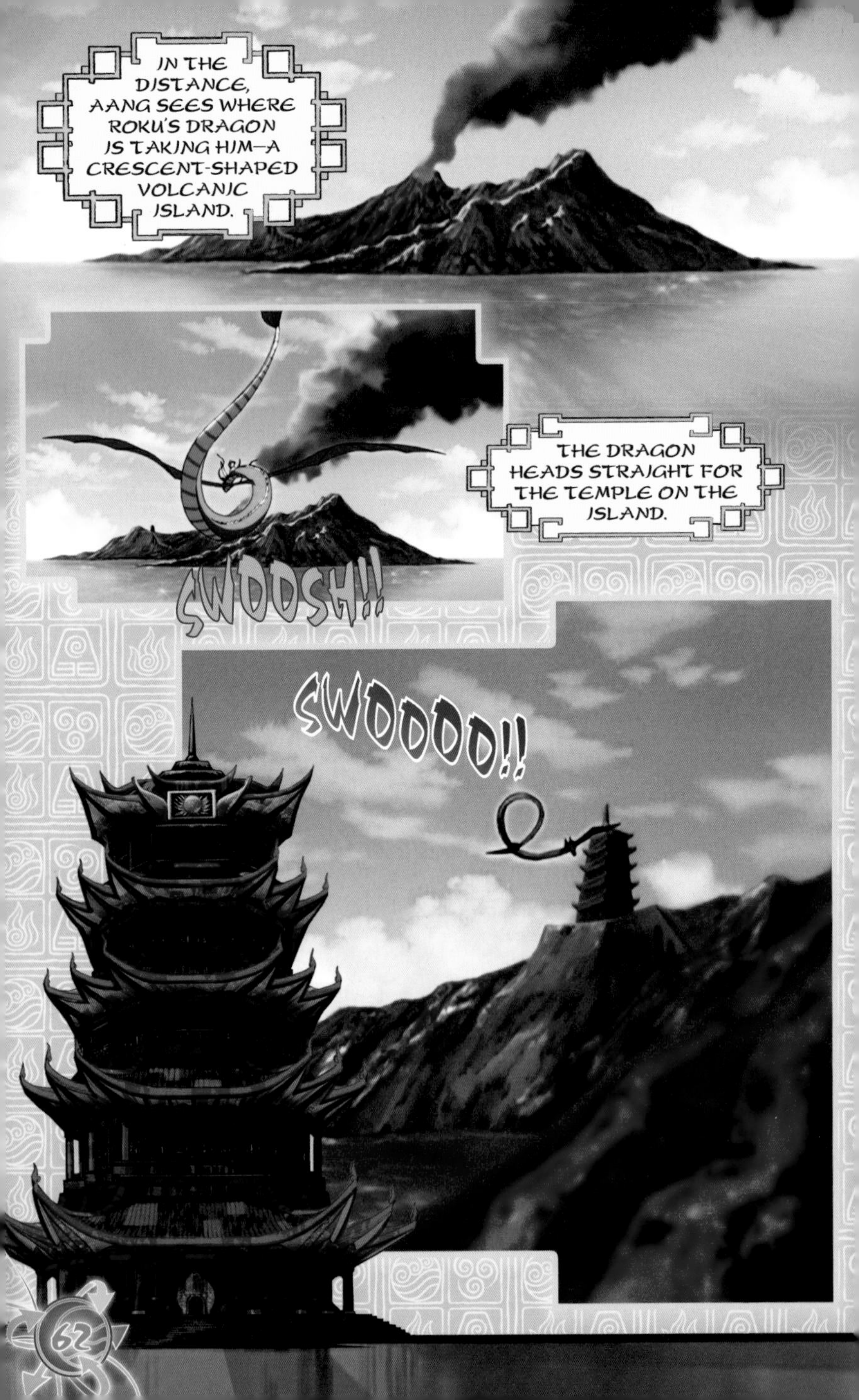
IN THE DISTANCE, AANG SEES WHERE ROKU'S DRAGON IS TAKING HIM—A CRESCENT-SHAPED VOLCANIC ISLAND.
SWOOSH!!
THE DRAGON HEADS STRAIGHT FOR THE TEMPLE ON THE ISLAND.
SWOOOO!!

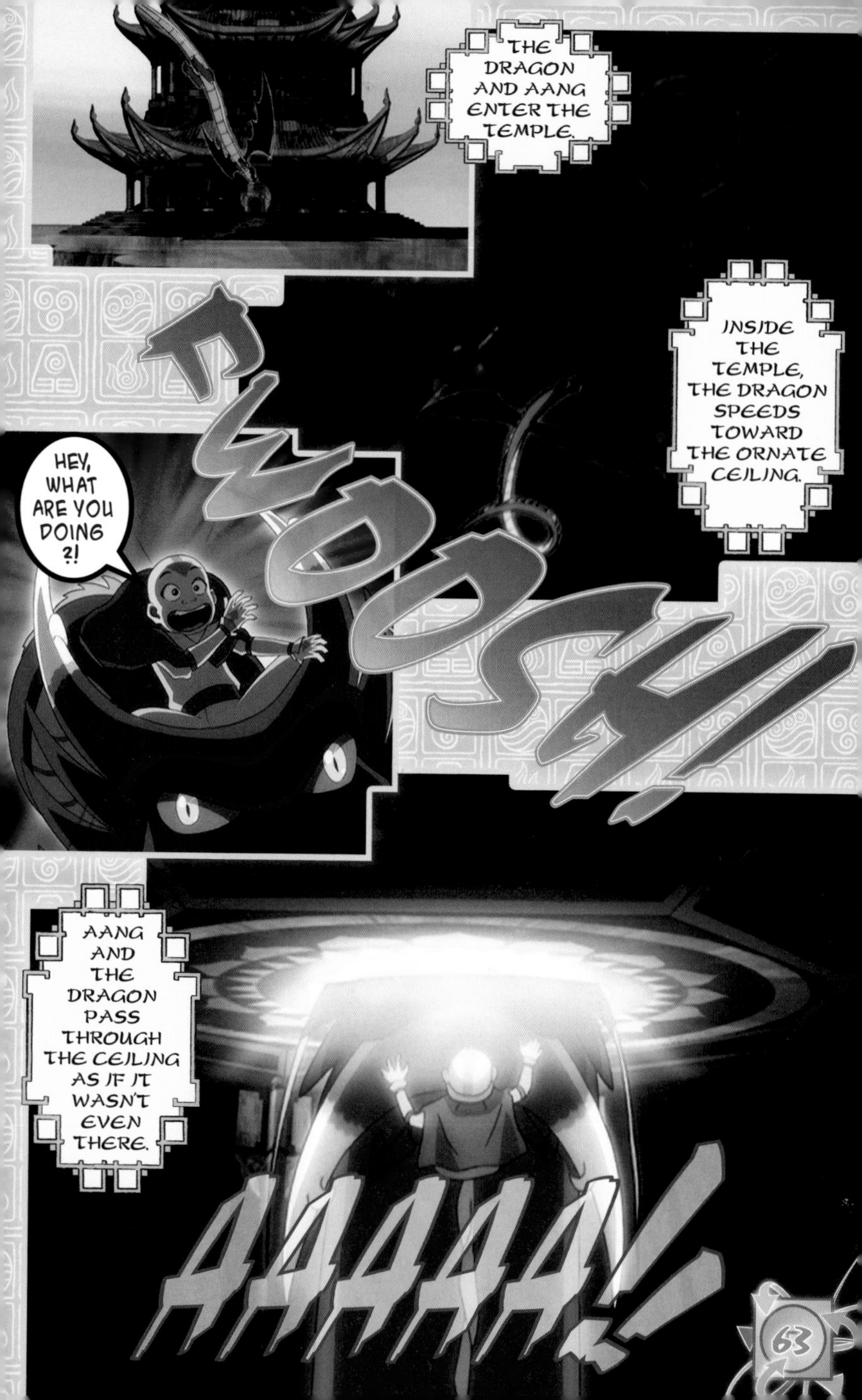

THE DRAGON AND AANG ENTER THE TEMPLE.
INSIDE THE TEMPLE, THE DRAGON SPEEDS TOWARD THE ORNATE CEILING.
HEY, WHAT ARE YOU DOING ?!
FWOOSH!
AANG AND THE DRAGON PASS THROUGH THE CEILING AS IF IT WASN'T EVEN THERE.
AAAAA!

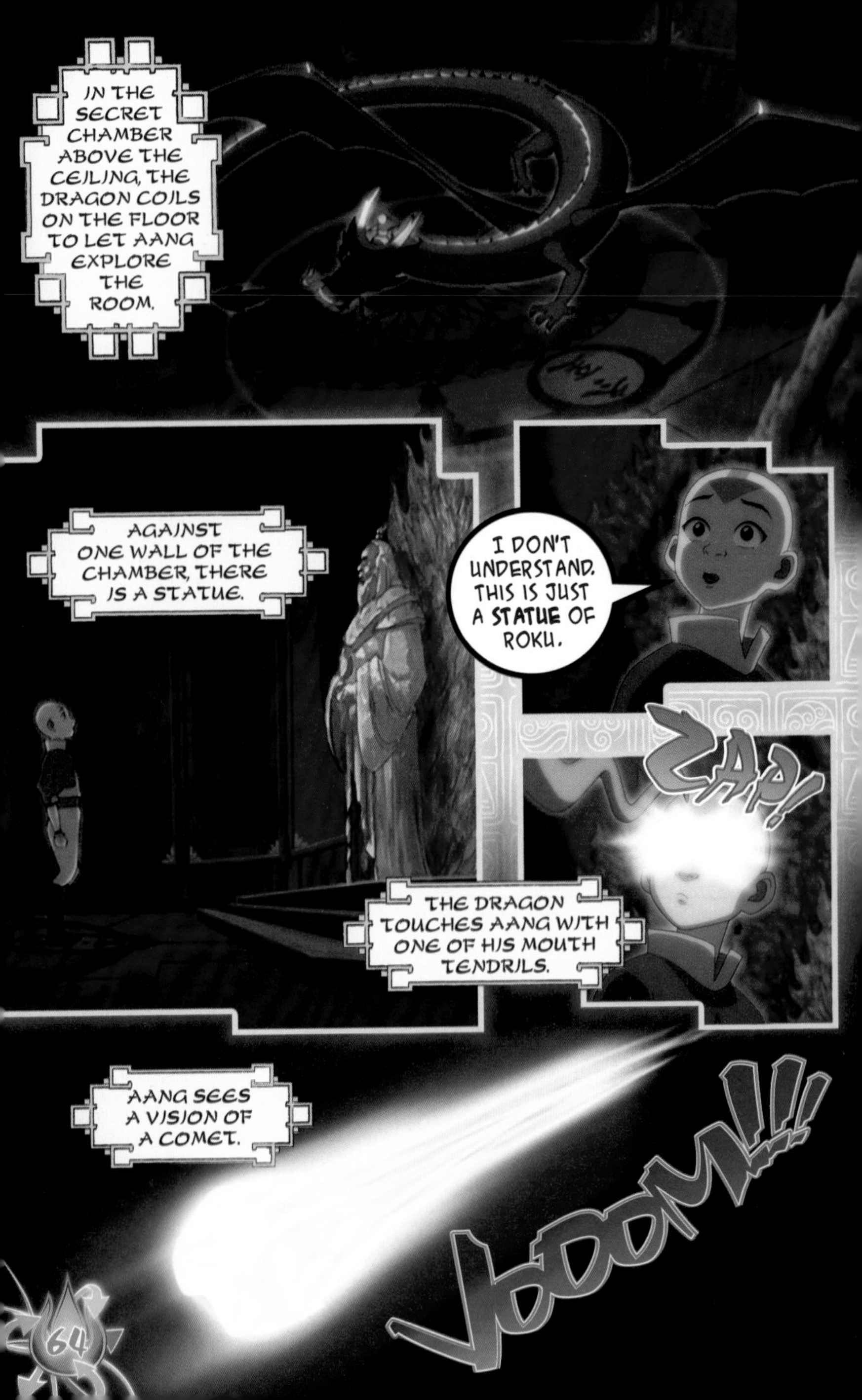
IN THE SECRET CHAMBER ABOVE THE CEILING, THE DRAGON COILS ON THE FLOOR TO LET AANG EXPLORE THE ROOM.
AGAINST ONE WALL OF THE CHAMBER, THERE IS A STATUE.
I DON'T UNDERSTAND. THIS IS JUST A **STATUE** OF ROKU.
ZAP!
THE DRAGON TOUCHES AANG WITH ONE OF HIS MOUTH TENDRILS.
AANG SEES A VISION OF A COMET.
VOOOM!!!

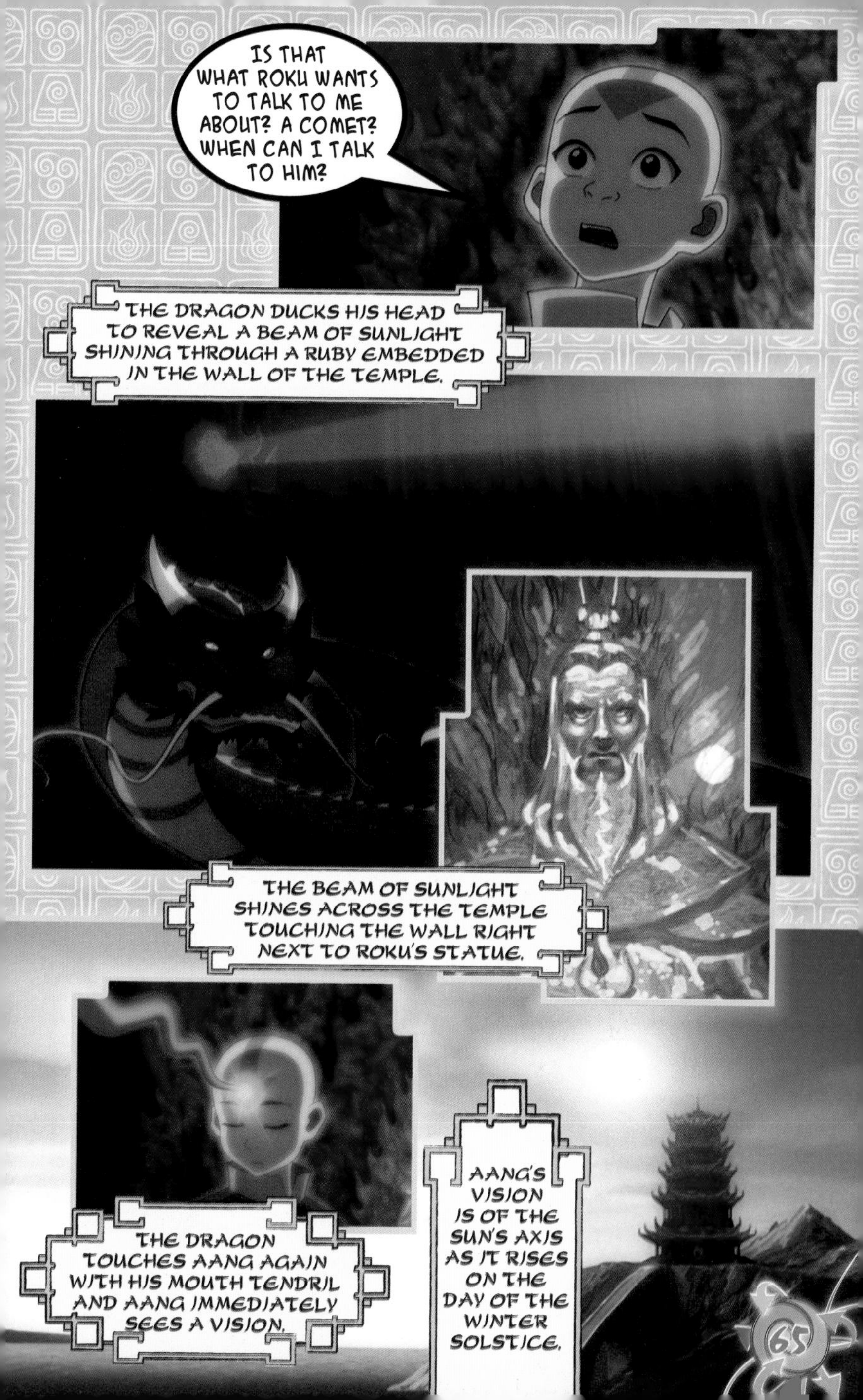

IS THAT WHAT ROKU WANTS TO TALK TO ME ABOUT? A COMET? WHEN CAN I TALK TO HIM?
THE DRAGON DUCKS HIS HEAD TO REVEAL A BEAM OF SUNLIGHT SHINING THROUGH A RUBY EMBEDDED IN THE WALL OF THE TEMPLE.
THE BEAM OF SUNLIGHT SHINES ACROSS THE TEMPLE TOUCHING THE WALL RIGHT NEXT TO ROKU'S STATUE.
THE DRAGON TOUCHES AANG AGAIN WITH HIS MOUTH TENDRIL AND AANG IMMEDIATELY SEES A VISION.
AANG'S VISION IS OF THE SUN'S AXIS AS IT RISES ON THE DAY OF THE WINTER SOLSTICE.

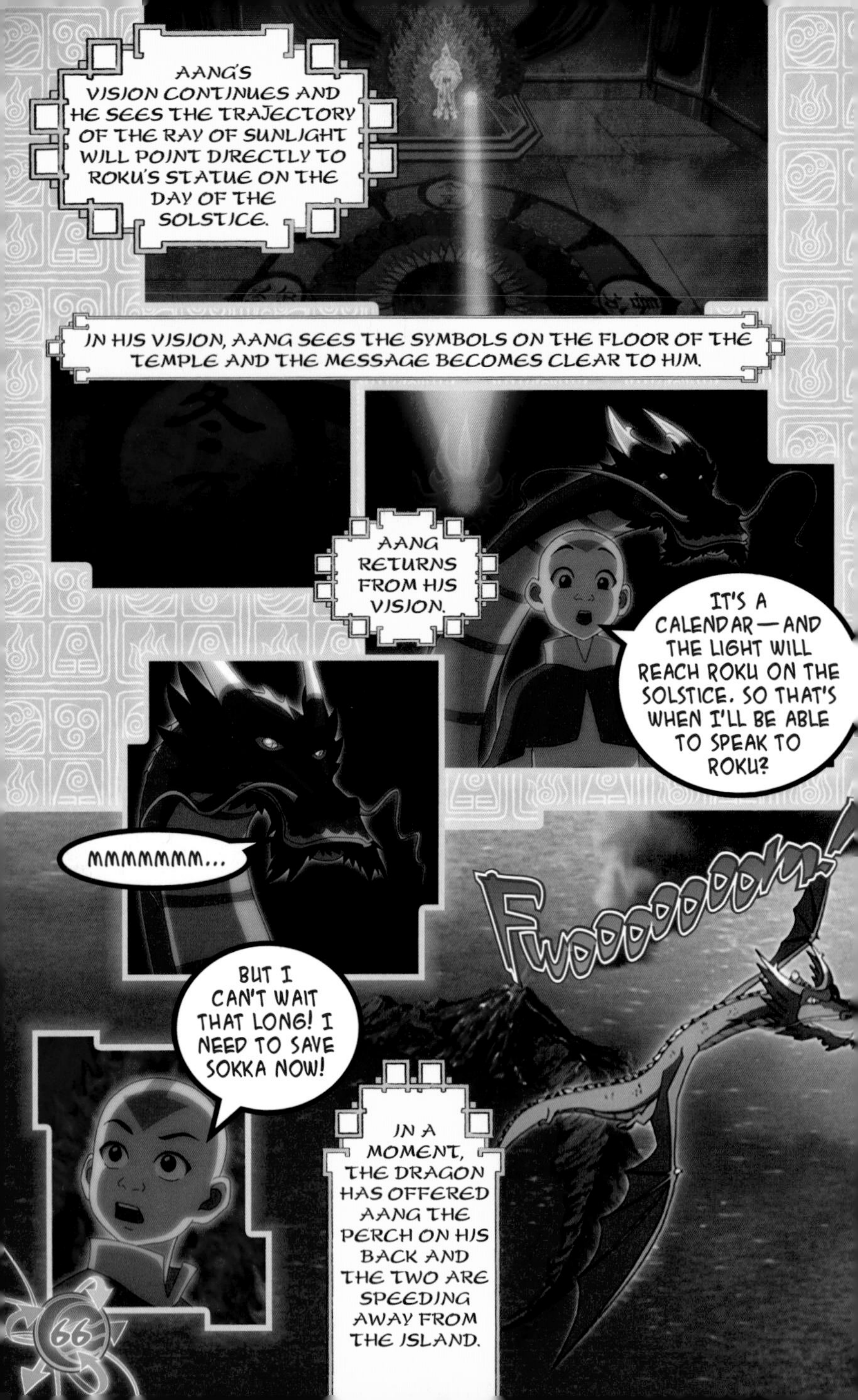
AANG'S VISION CONTINUES AND HE SEES THE TRAJECTORY OF THE RAY OF SUNLIGHT WILL POINT DIRECTLY TO ROKU'S STATUE ON THE DAY OF THE SOLSTICE.
IN HIS VISION, AANG SEES THE SYMBOLS ON THE FLOOR OF THE TEMPLE AND THE MESSAGE BECOMES CLEAR TO HIM.
AANG RETURNS FROM HIS VISION.
IT'S A CALENDAR—AND THE LIGHT WILL REACH ROKU ON THE SOLSTICE. SO THAT'S WHEN I'LL BE ABLE TO SPEAK TO ROKU?
MMMMMMM...
BUT I CAN'T WAIT THAT LONG! I NEED TO SAVE SOKKA NOW!
FWOOOOOOOM!
IN A MOMENT, THE DRAGON HAS OFFERED AANG THE PERCH ON HIS BACK AND THE TWO ARE SPEEDING AWAY FROM THE ISLAND.

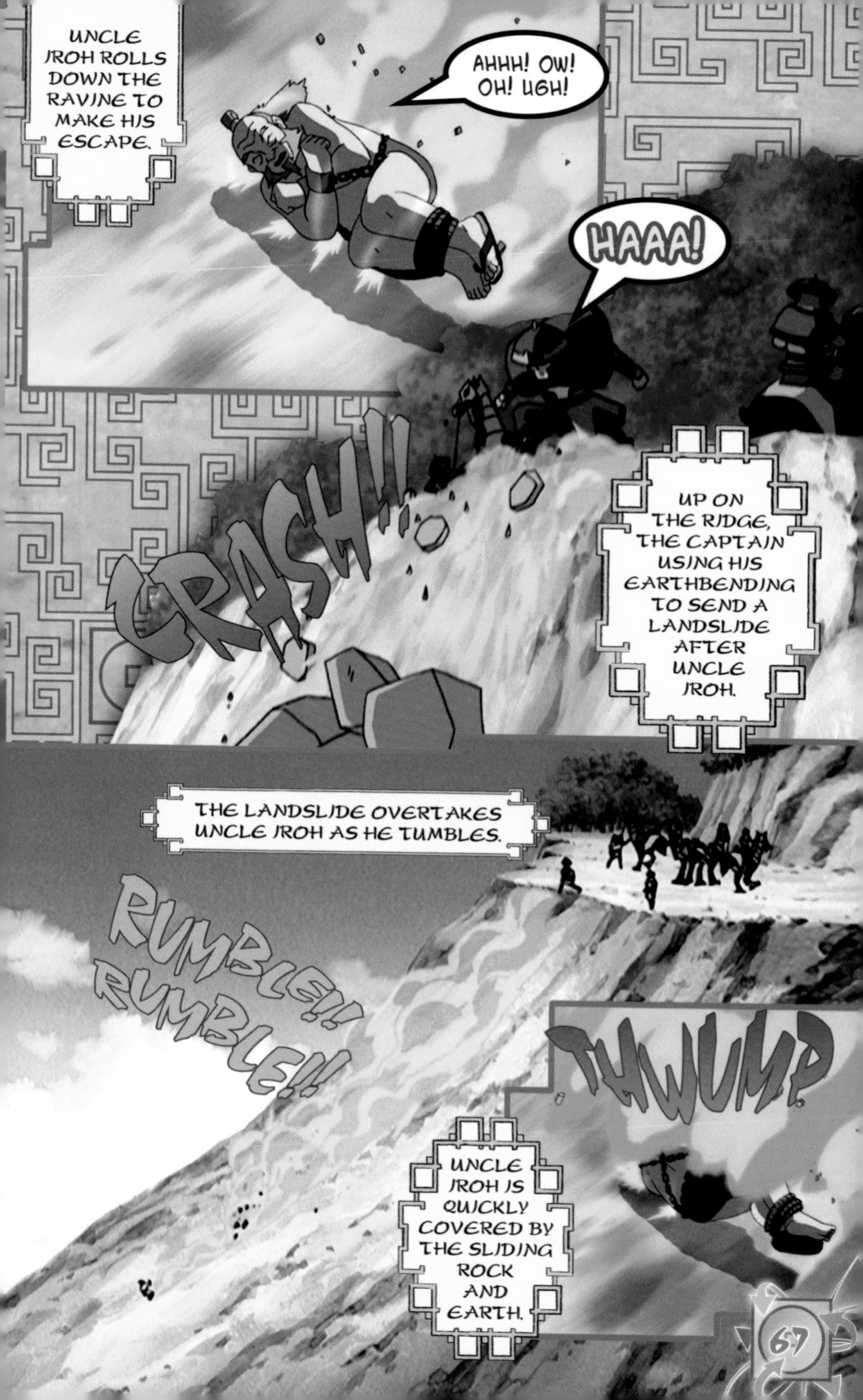
UNCLE IROH ROLLS DOWN THE RAVINE TO MAKE HIS ESCAPE.
AHHH! OW! OH! UGH!
HAAA!
CRASH!!
UP ON THE RIDGE, THE CAPTAIN USING HIS EARTHBENDING TO SEND A LANDSLIDE AFTER UNCLE IROH.
THE LANDSLIDE OVERTAKES UNCLE IROH AS HE TUMBLES.
RUMBLE!! RUMBLE!!
THWUMP
UNCLE IROH IS QUICKLY COVERED BY THE SLIDING ROCK AND EARTH.

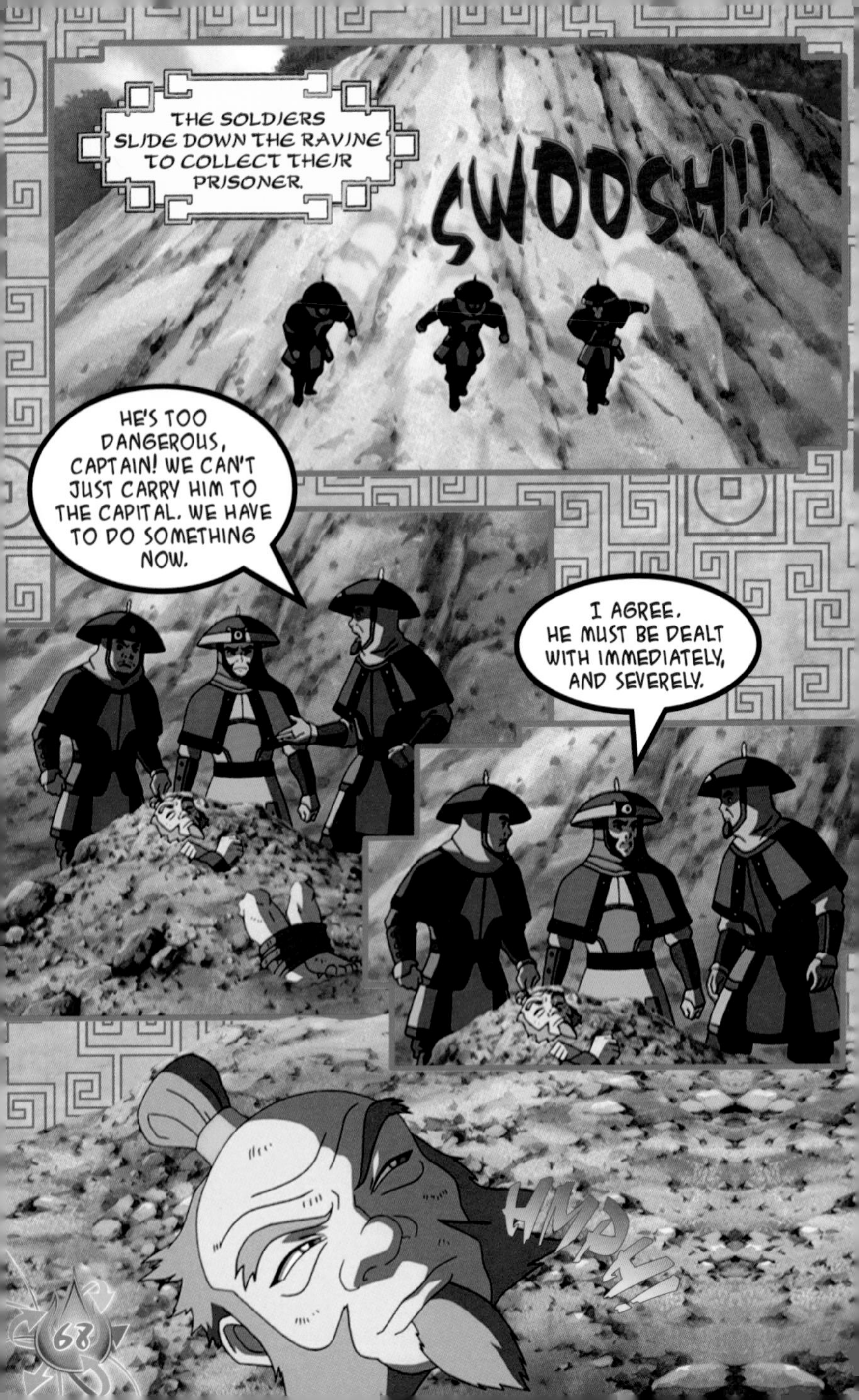
THE SOLDIERS SLIDE DOWN THE RAVINE TO COLLECT THEIR PRISONER.
SWOOSH!!
HE'S TOO DANGEROUS, CAPTAIN! WE CAN'T JUST CARRY HIM TO THE CAPITAL. WE HAVE TO DO SOMETHING NOW.
I AGREE. HE MUST BE DEALT WITH IMMEDIATELY, AND SEVERELY.
HMPH!!

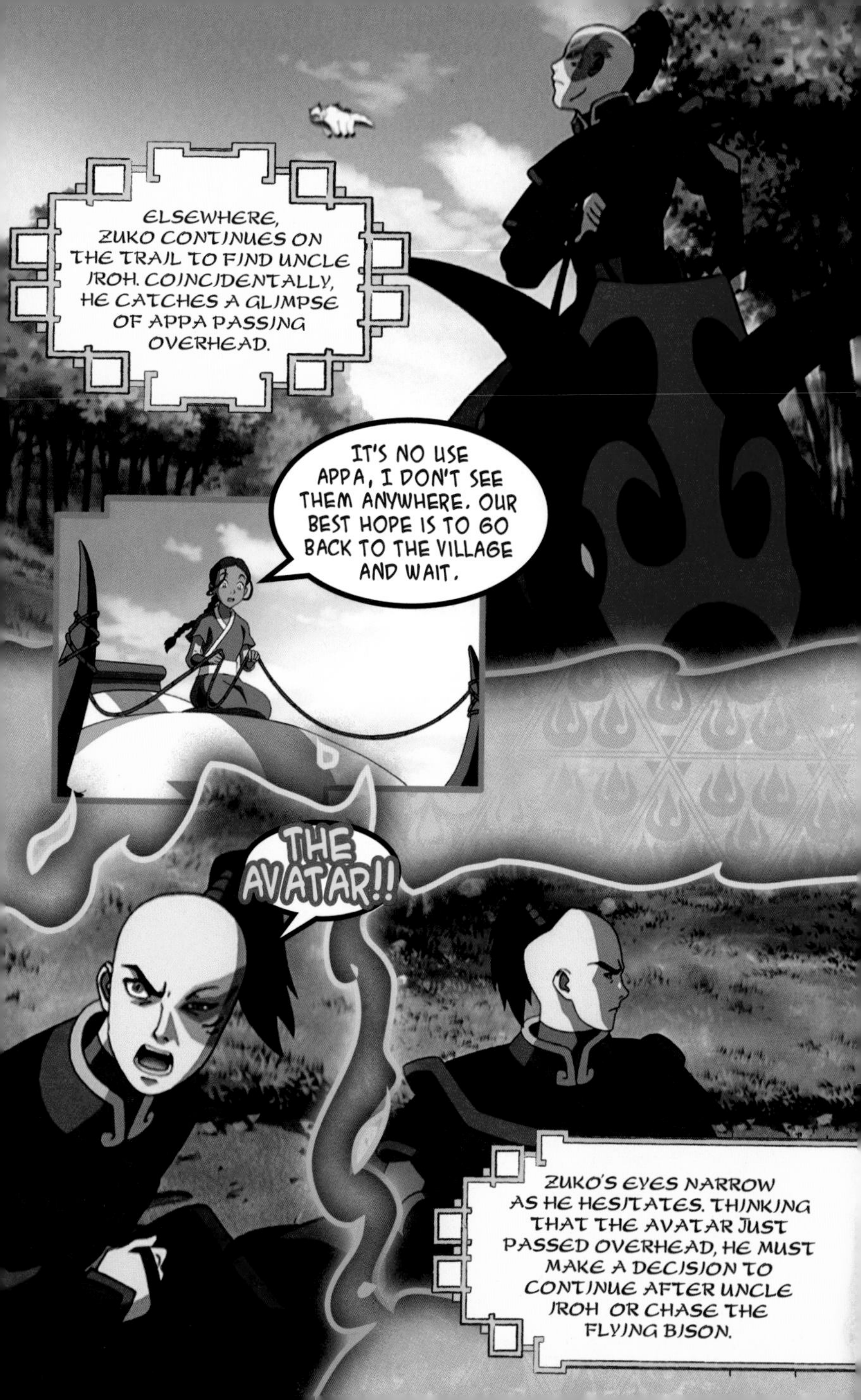
ELSEWHERE, ZUKO CONTINUES ON THE TRAIL TO FIND UNCLE IROH. COINCIDENTALLY, HE CATCHES A GLIMPSE OF APPA PASSING OVERHEAD.
IT'S NO USE APPA, I DON'T SEE THEM ANYWHERE. OUR BEST HOPE IS TO GO BACK TO THE VILLAGE AND WAIT.
THE AVATAR!!
ZUKO'S EYES NARROW AS HE HESITATES. THINKING THAT THE AVATAR JUST PASSED OVERHEAD, HE MUST MAKE A DECISION TO CONTINUE AFTER UNCLE IROH OR CHASE THE FLYING BISON.

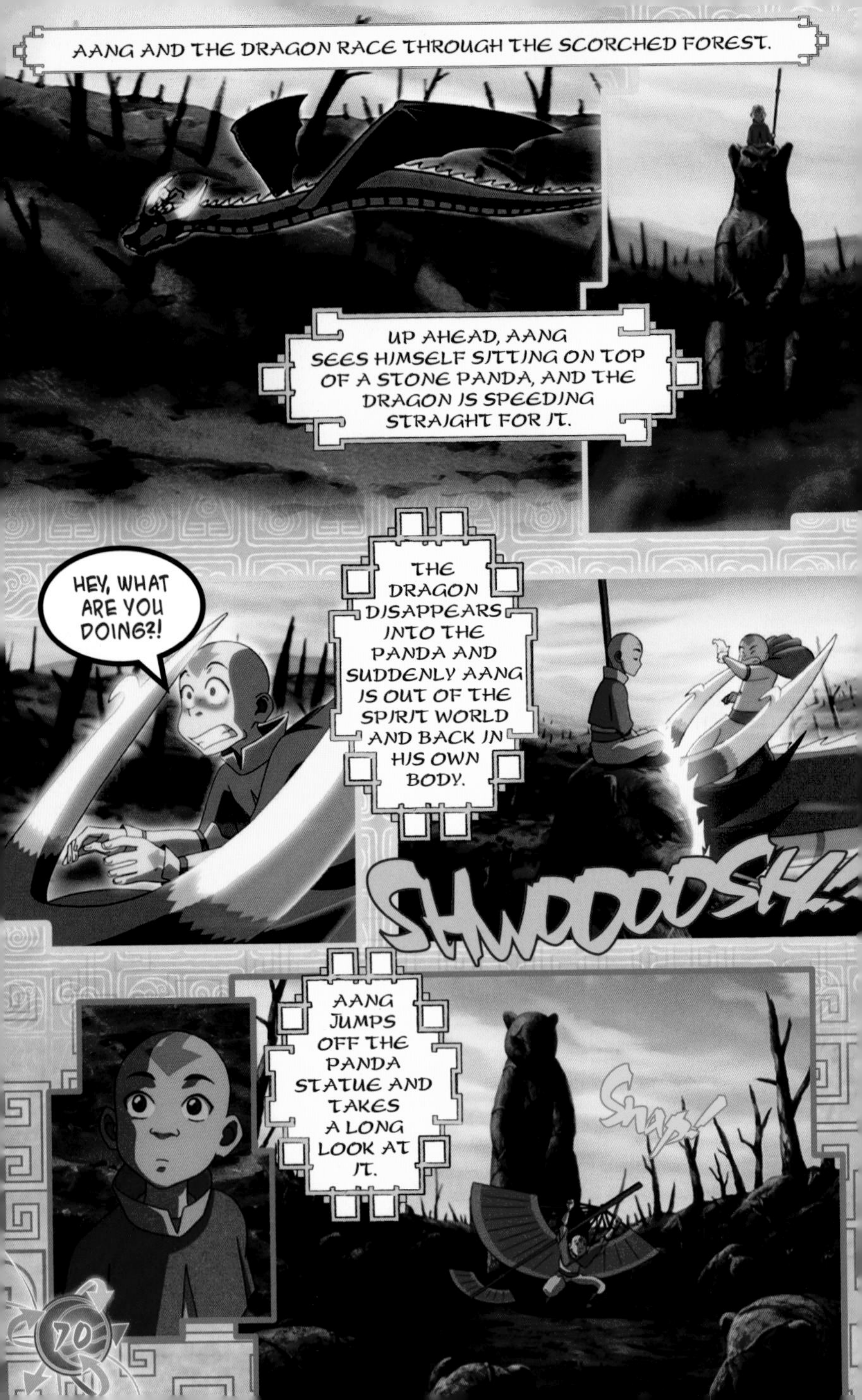
AANG AND THE DRAGON RACE THROUGH THE SCORCHED FOREST.
UP AHEAD, AANG SEES HIMSELF SITTING ON TOP OF A STONE PANDA, AND THE DRAGON IS SPEEDING STRAIGHT FOR IT.
HEY, WHAT ARE YOU DOING?!
THE DRAGON DISAPPEARS INTO THE PANDA AND SUDDENLY AANG IS OUT OF THE SPIRIT WORLD AND BACK IN HIS OWN BODY.
SHWOOOOSH!
AANG JUMPS OFF THE PANDA STATUE AND TAKES A LONG LOOK AT IT.
Snap!

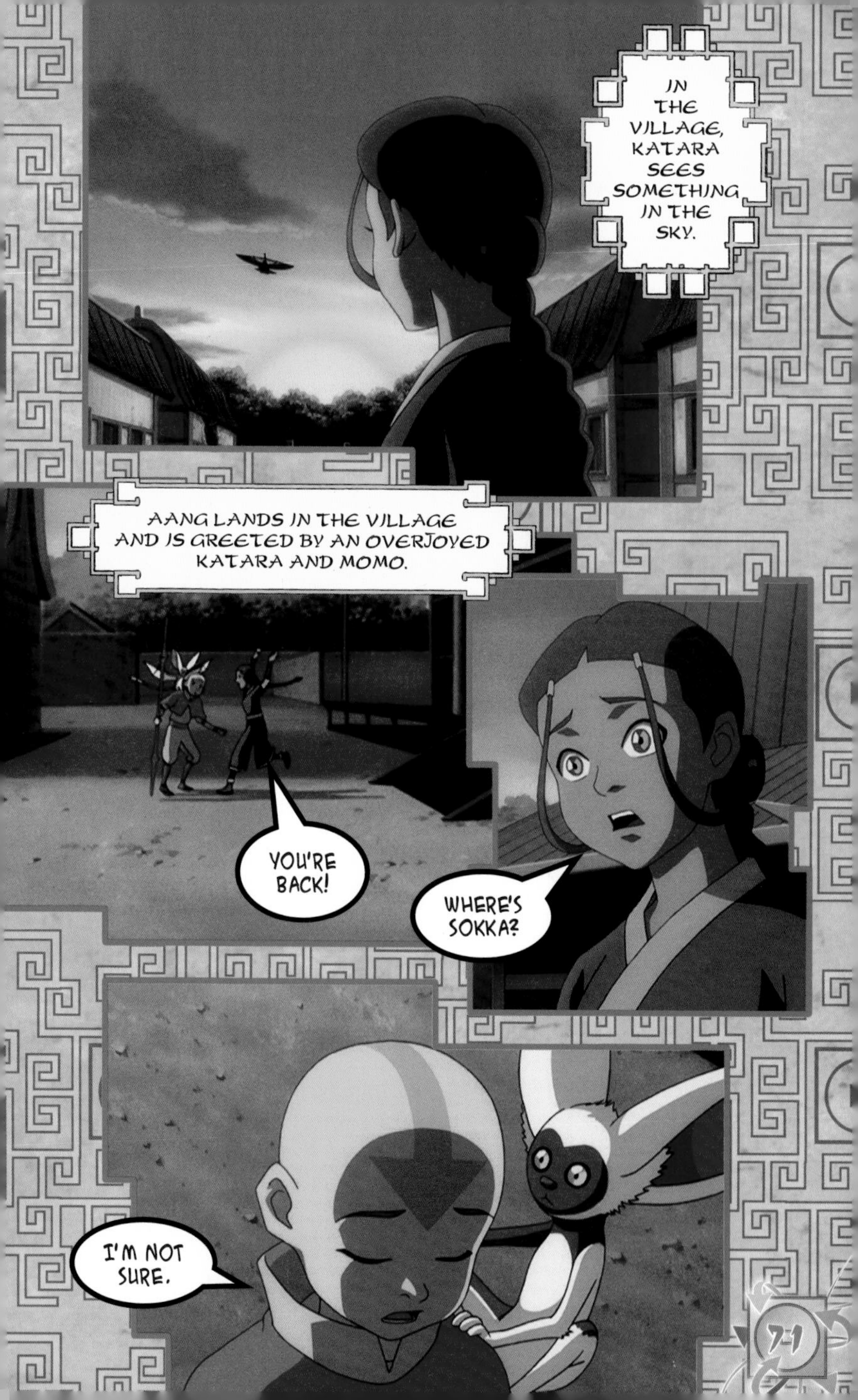
IN THE VILLAGE, KATARA SEES SOMETHING IN THE SKY.
AANG LANDS IN THE VILLAGE AND IS GREETED BY AN OVERJOYED KATARA AND MOMO.
YOU'RE BACK!
WHERE'S SOKKA?
I'M NOT SURE.
71

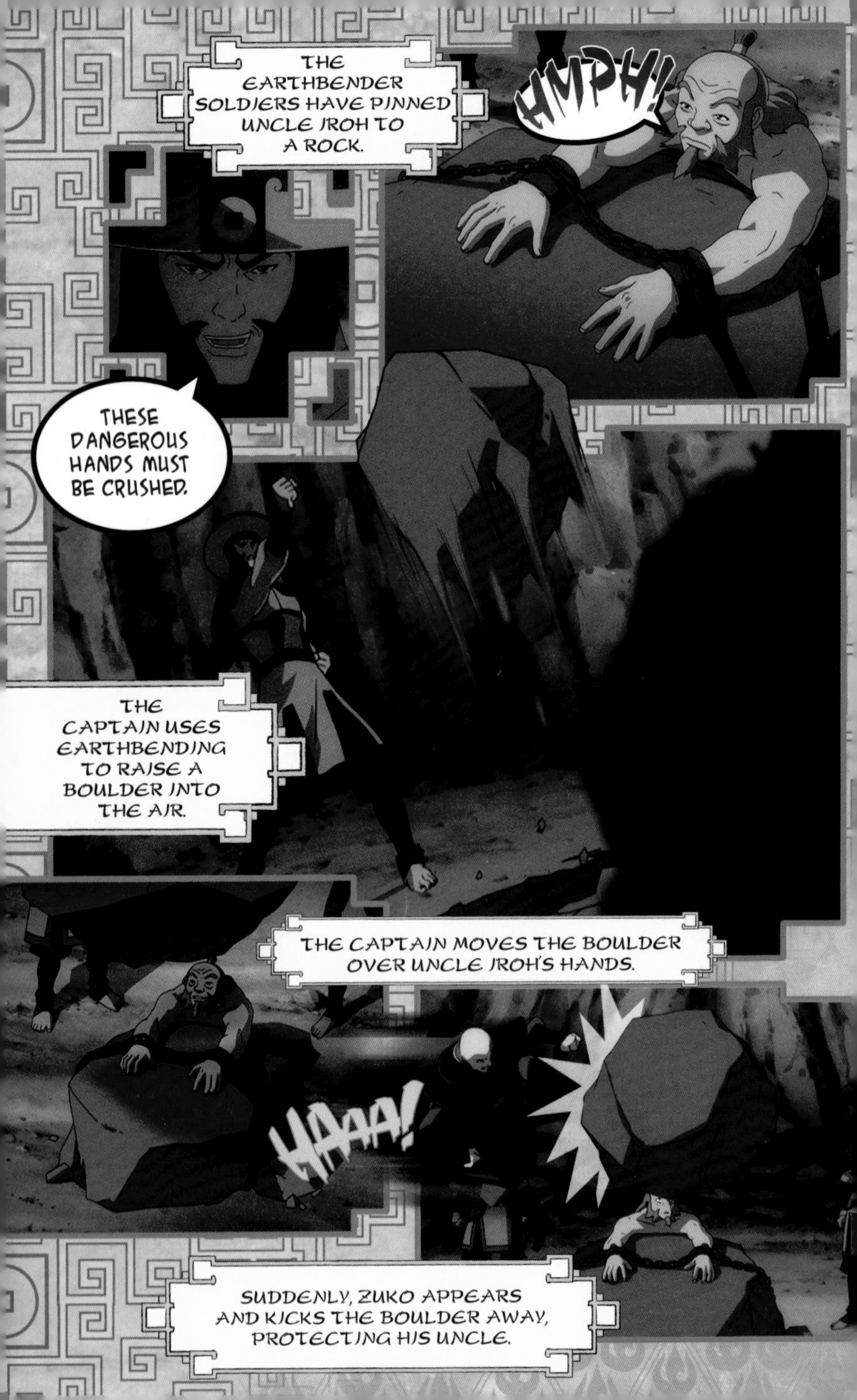
THE EARTHBENDER SOLDIERS HAVE PINNED UNCLE IROH TO A ROCK.
HMPH!
THESE DANGEROUS HANDS MUST BE CRUSHED.
THE CAPTAIN USES EARTHBENDING TO RAISE A BOULDER INTO THE AIR.
THE CAPTAIN MOVES THE BOULDER OVER UNCLE IROH'S HANDS.
HAAA!
SUDDENLY, ZUKO APPEARS AND KICKS THE BOULDER AWAY, PROTECTING HIS UNCLE.

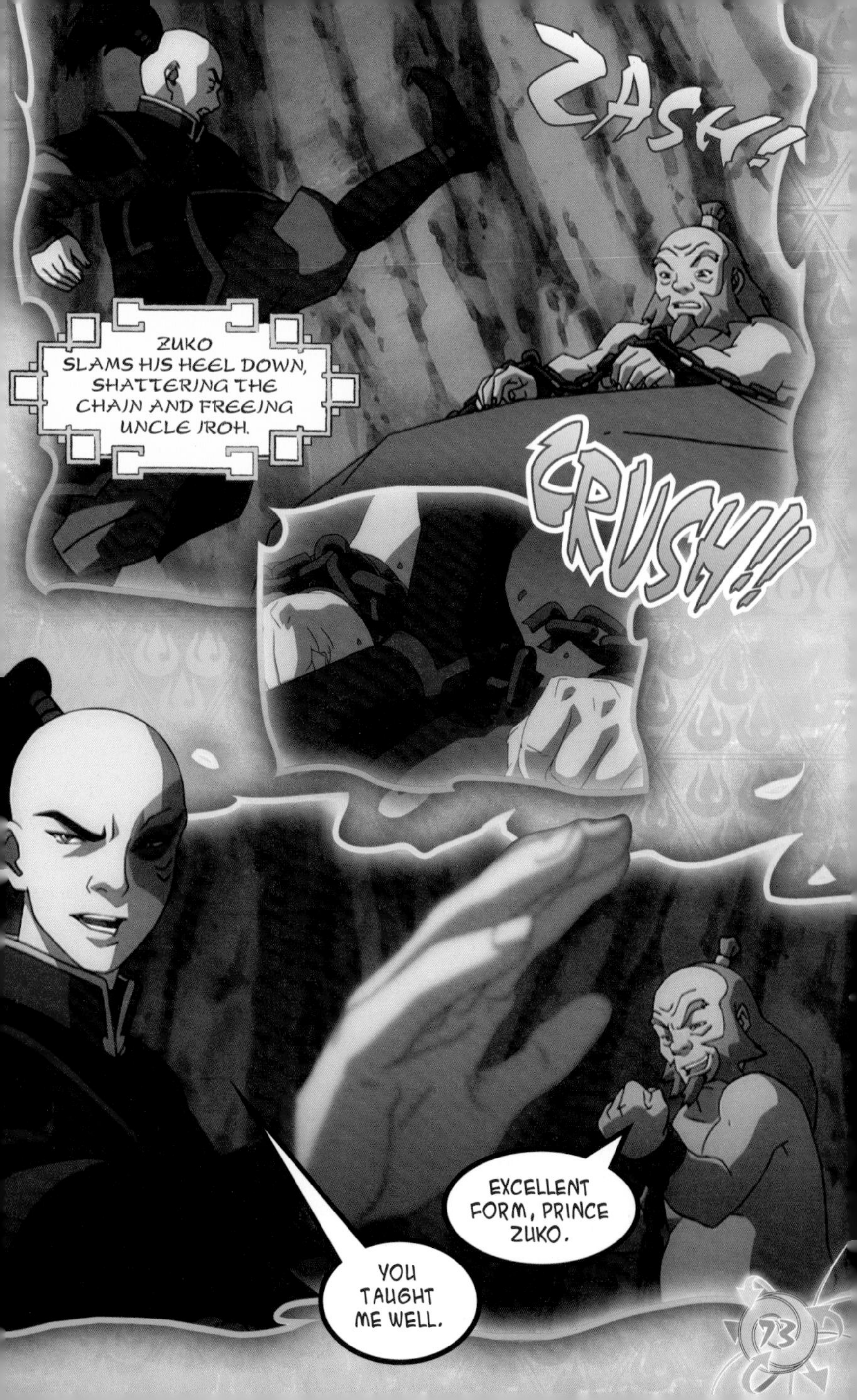
ZASH!
ZUKO SLAMS HIS HEEL DOWN, SHATTERING THE CHAIN AND FREEING UNCLE IROH.
CRUSH!!
EXCELLENT FORM, PRINCE ZUKO.
YOU TAUGHT ME WELL.

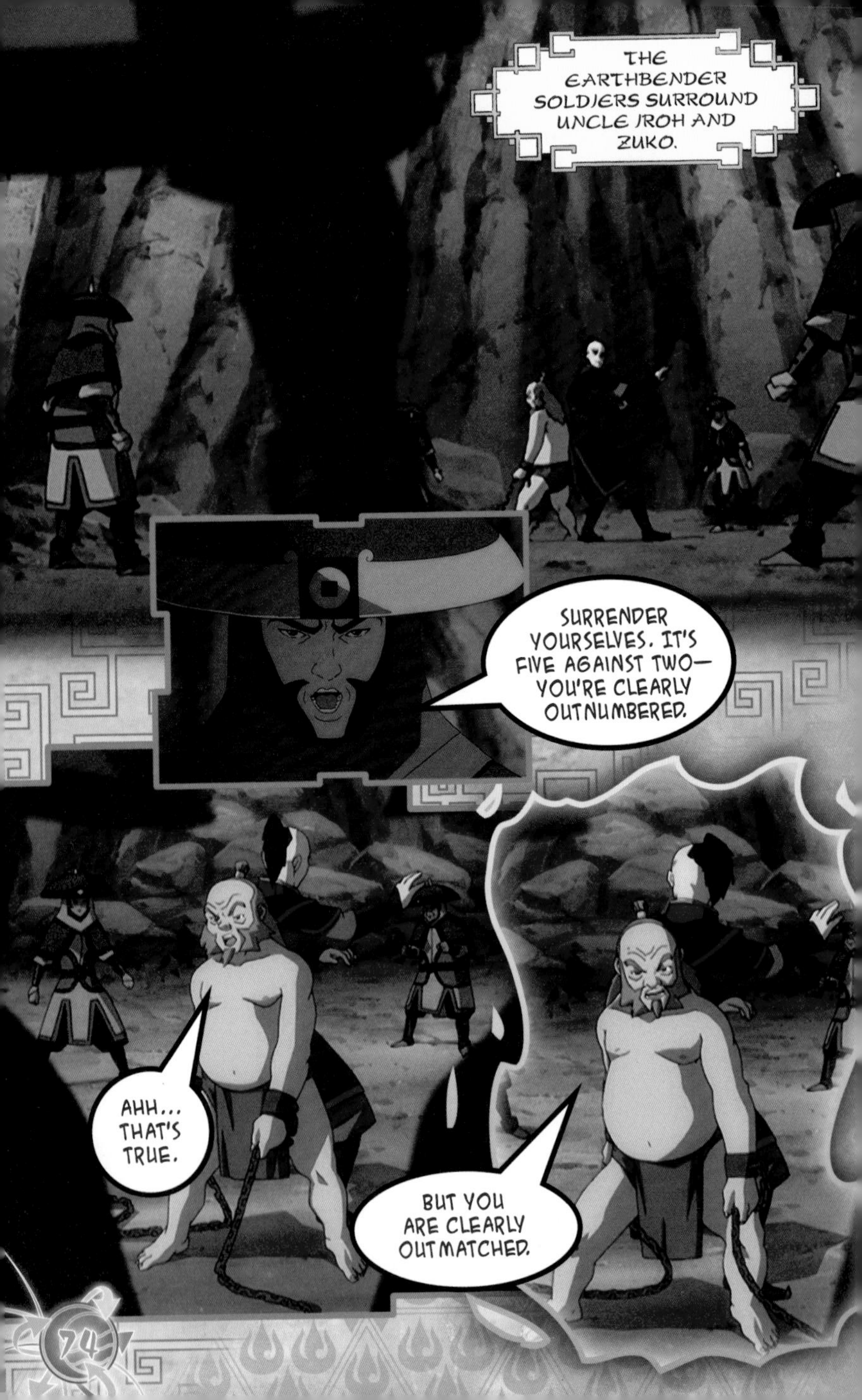
THE EARTHBENDER SOLDIERS SURROUND UNCLE IROH AND ZUKO.
SURRENDER YOURSELVES. IT'S FIVE AGAINST TWO— YOU'RE CLEARLY OUTNUMBERED.
AHH... THAT'S TRUE.
BUT YOU ARE CLEARLY OUTMATCHED.

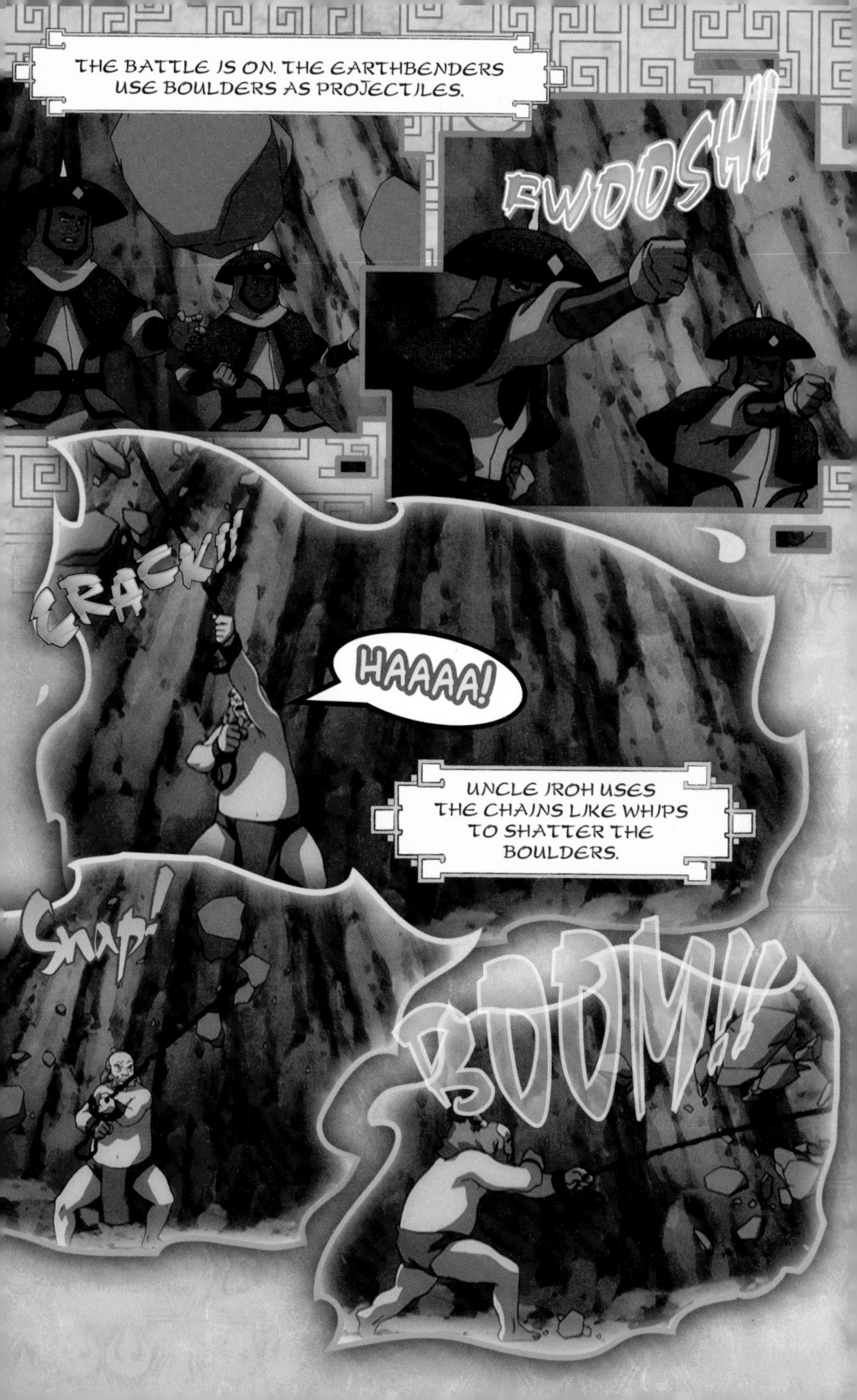
THE BATTLE IS ON. THE EARTHBENDERS USE BOULDERS AS PROJECTILES.
FWOOSH!
CRACK!!
HAAAA!
UNCLE IROH USES THE CHAINS LIKE WHIPS TO SHATTER THE BOULDERS.
Snap!
BOOM!!

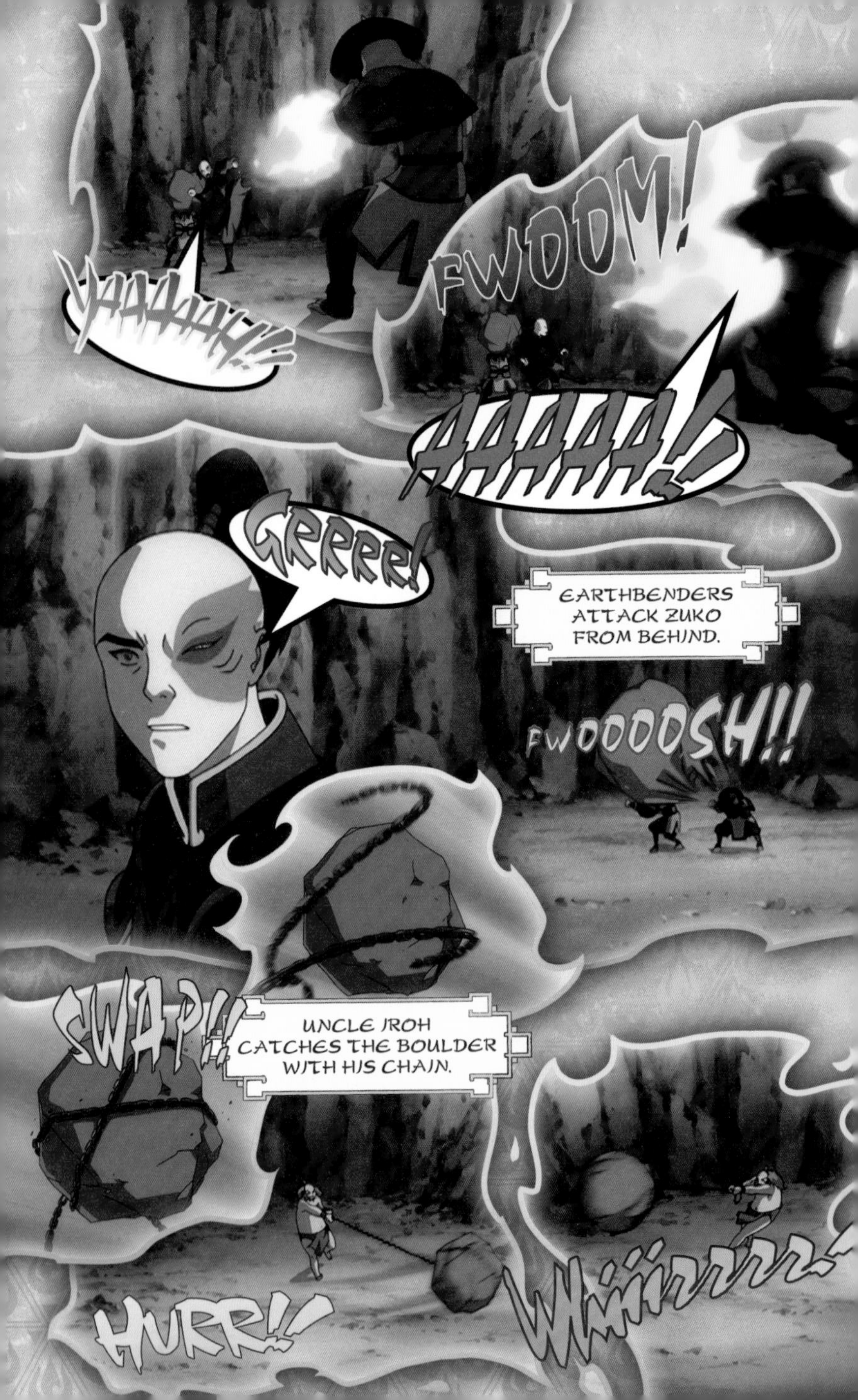
YAAAAH!!
FWOOM!
AAAAA!!
GRRRR!
EARTHBENDERS ATTACK ZUKO FROM BEHIND.
FWOOOOSH!!
SWAP!!
UNCLE IROH CATCHES THE BOULDER WITH HIS CHAIN.
HURR!!
Whiirrrr!

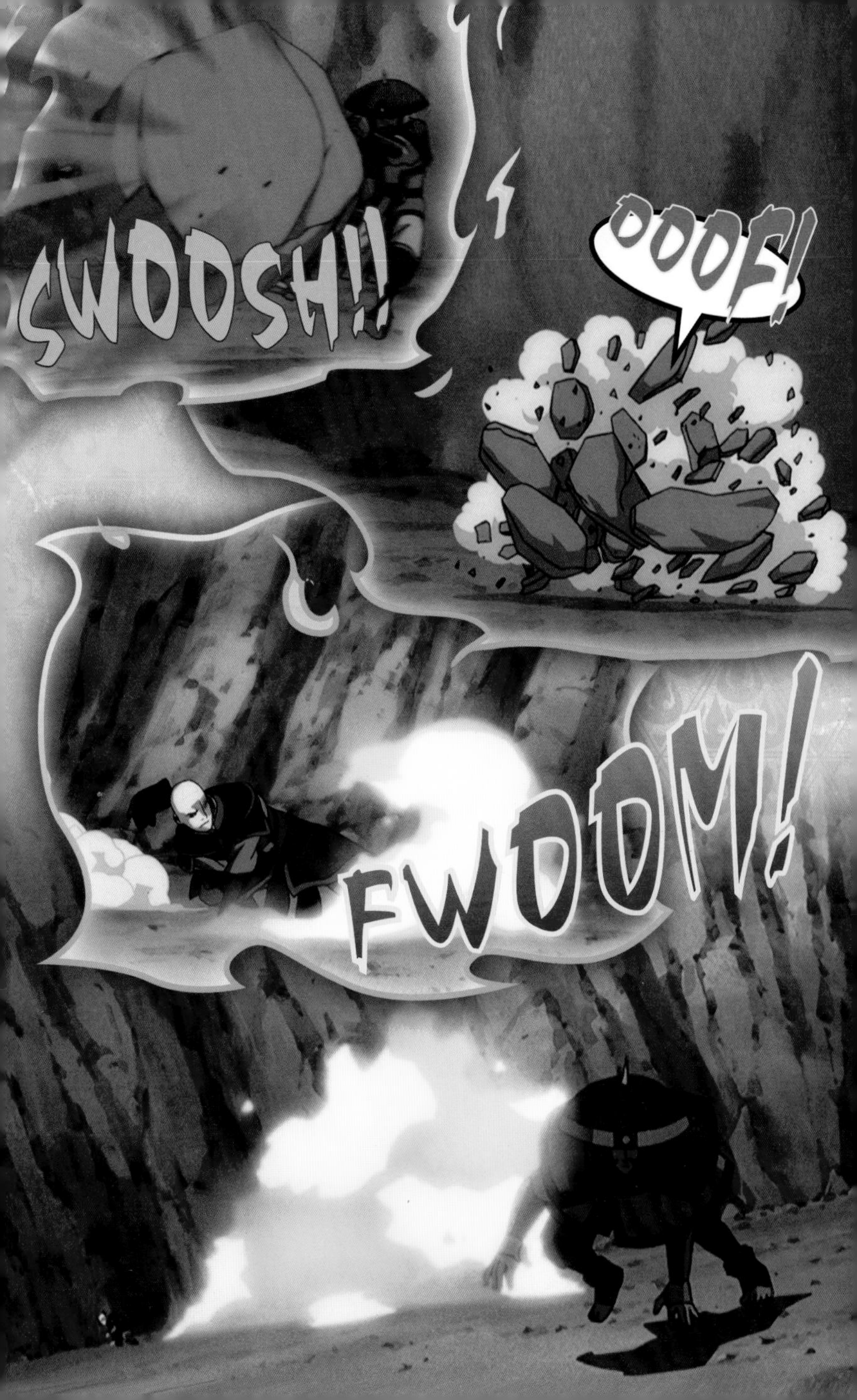
SWOOSH!!
OOOF!
FWOOM!

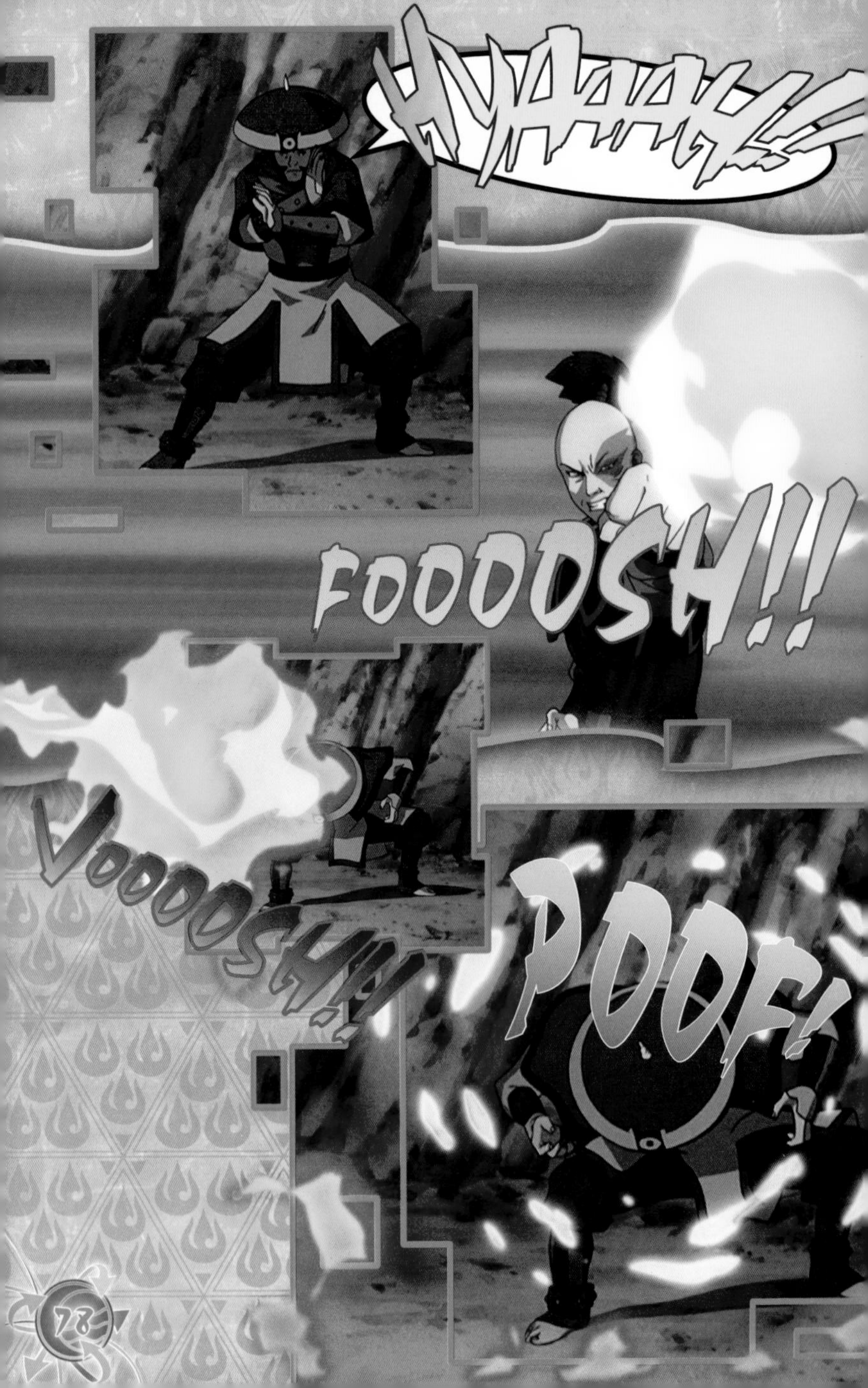
HYAAAH!!
FOOOOSH!!
VOOOOSH!!
POOF!

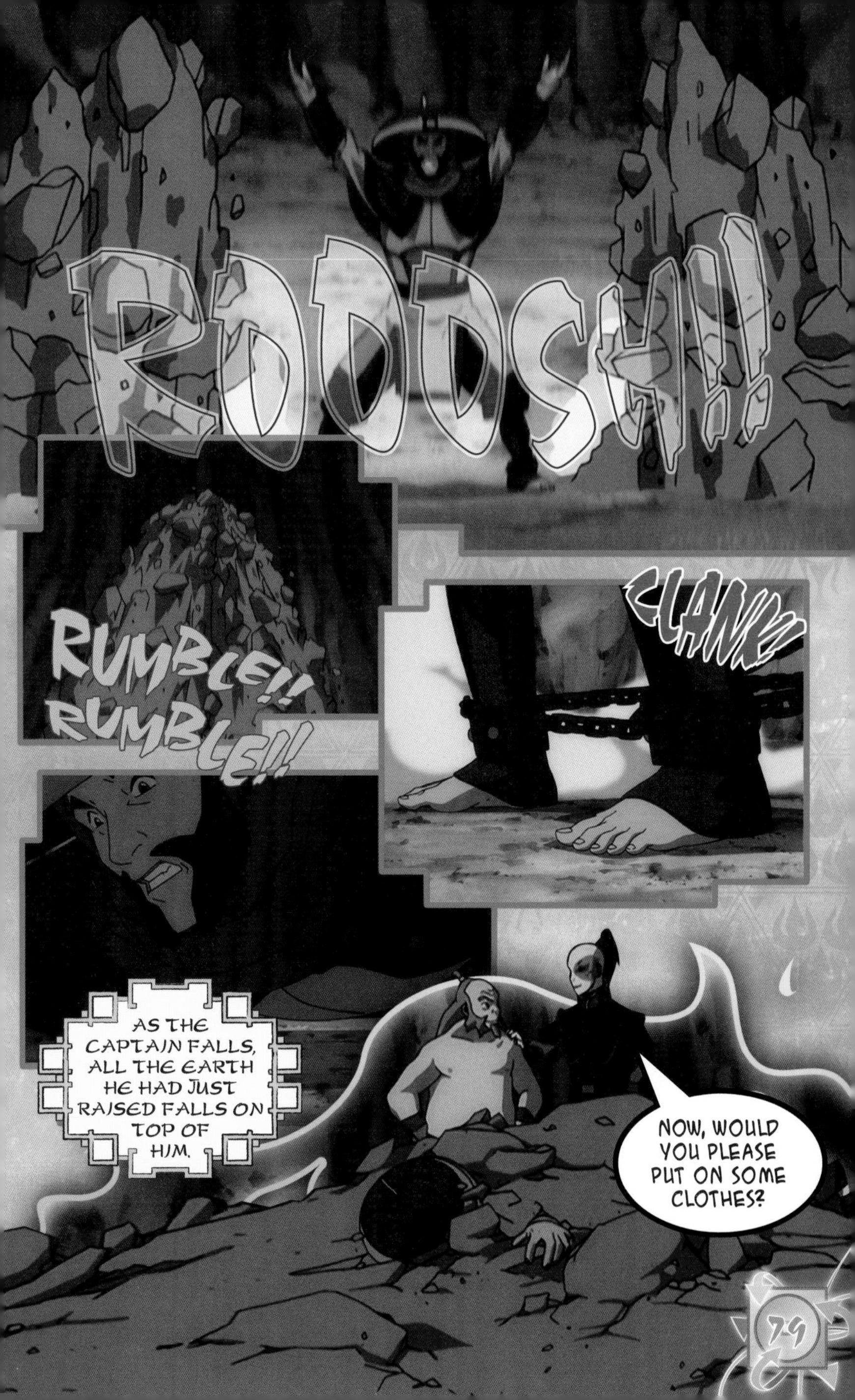
ROOOSH!!
RUMBLE!! RUMBLE!!
CLANK!!
AS THE CAPTAIN FALLS, ALL THE EARTH HE HAD JUST RAISED FALLS ON TOP OF HIM.
NOW, WOULD YOU PLEASE PUT ON SOME CLOTHES?
79

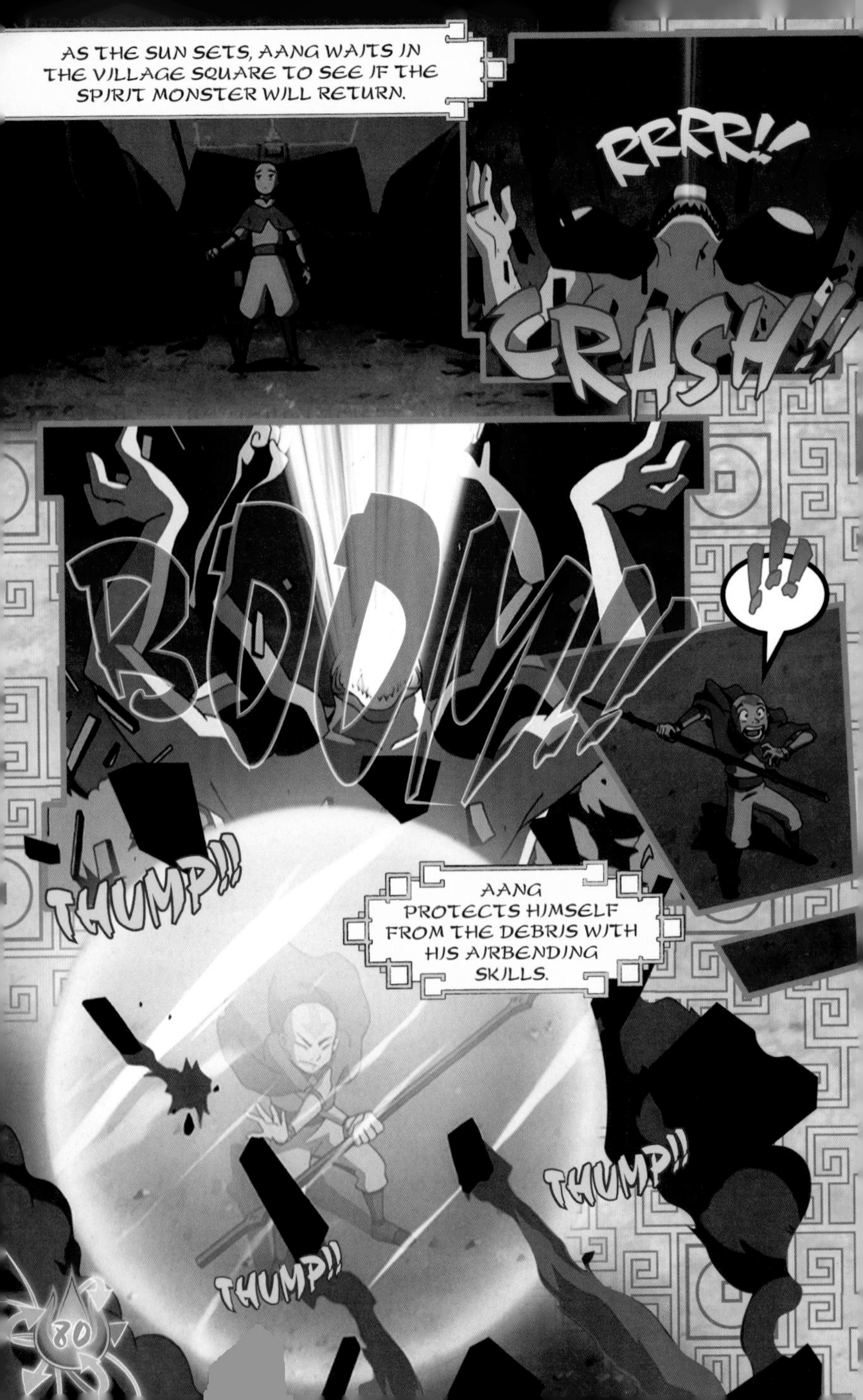
AS THE SUN SETS, AANG WAITS IN THE VILLAGE SQUARE TO SEE IF THE SPIRIT MONSTER WILL RETURN.
RRRR!!
CRASH!!
BOOM!!
!!
THUMP!!
AANG PROTECTS HIMSELF FROM THE DEBRIS WITH HIS AIRBENDING SKILLS.
THUMP!!
THUMP!!

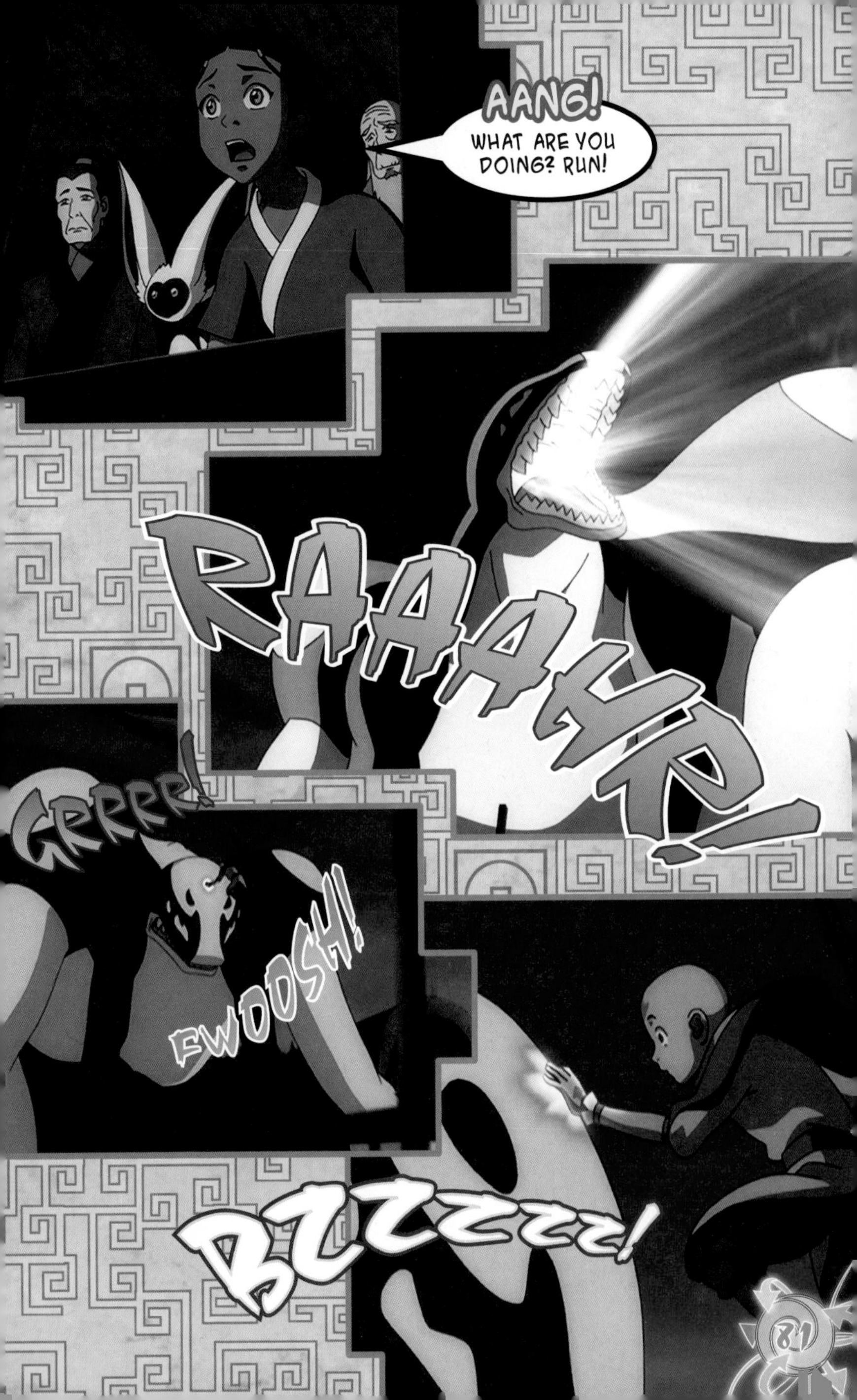
AANG!
WHAT ARE YOU DOING? RUN!
RAAAHR!
GRRRR!
FWOOSH!
BZZZZZZ!

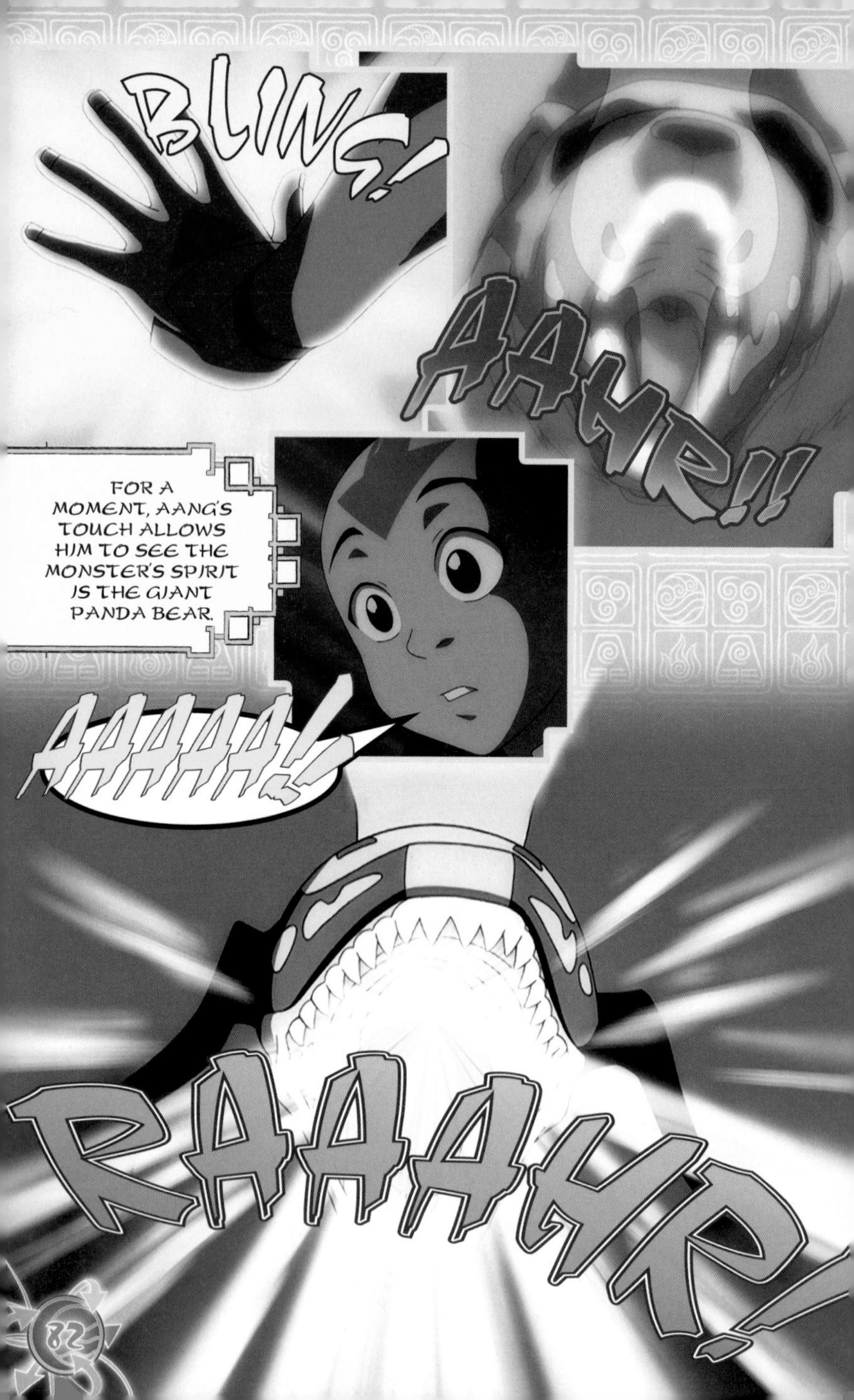
BLING!
AAHR!!
FOR A MOMENT, AANG'S TOUCH ALLOWS HIM TO SEE THE MONSTER'S SPIRIT IS THE GIANT PANDA BEAR.
AAAAA!
RAAAHR!

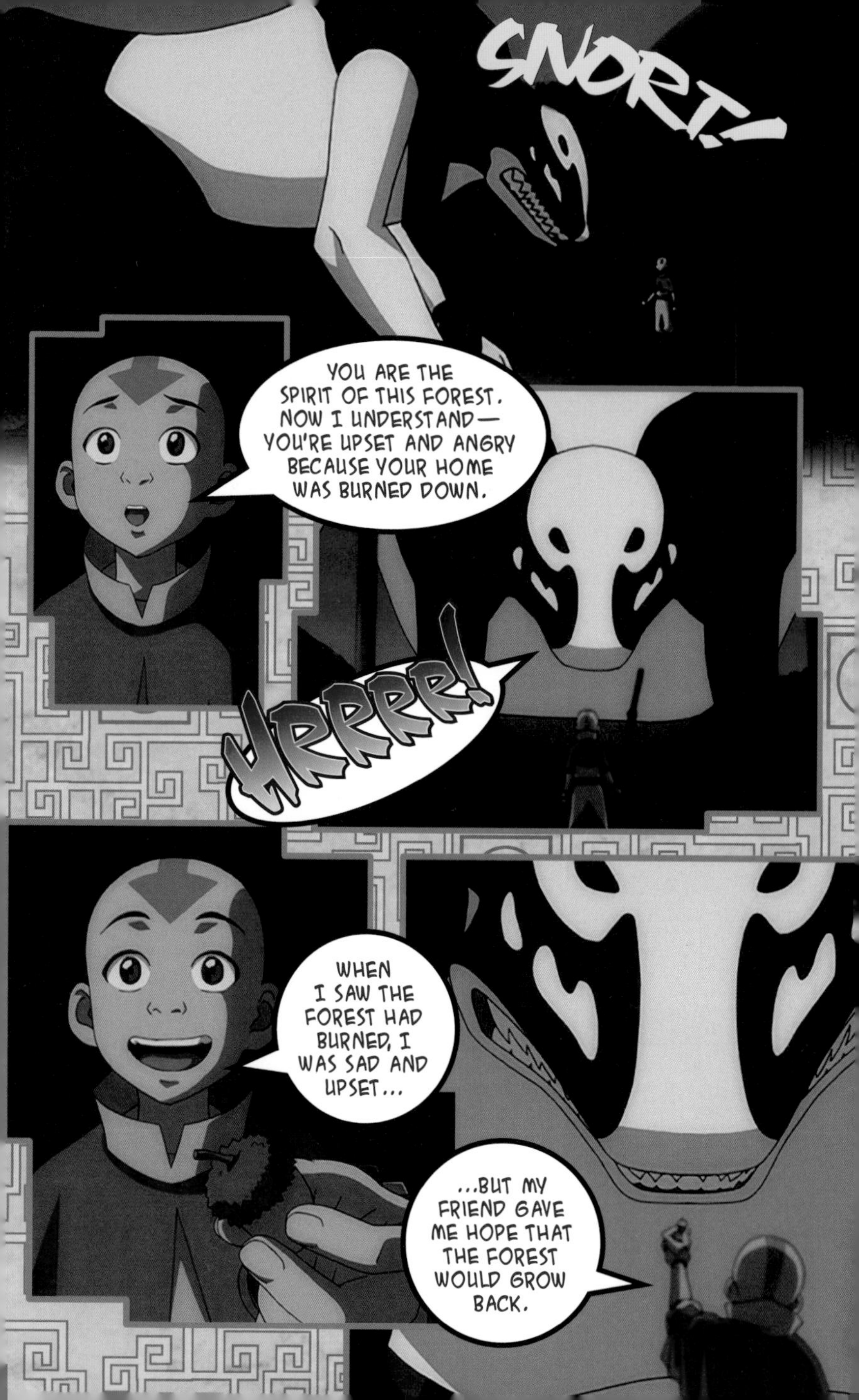
SNORT!
YOU ARE THE SPIRIT OF THIS FOREST. NOW I UNDERSTAND— YOU'RE UPSET AND ANGRY BECAUSE YOUR HOME WAS BURNED DOWN.
HRRRR!
WHEN I SAW THE FOREST HAD BURNED, I WAS SAD AND UPSET...
...BUT MY FRIEND GAVE ME HOPE THAT THE FOREST WOULD GROW BACK.

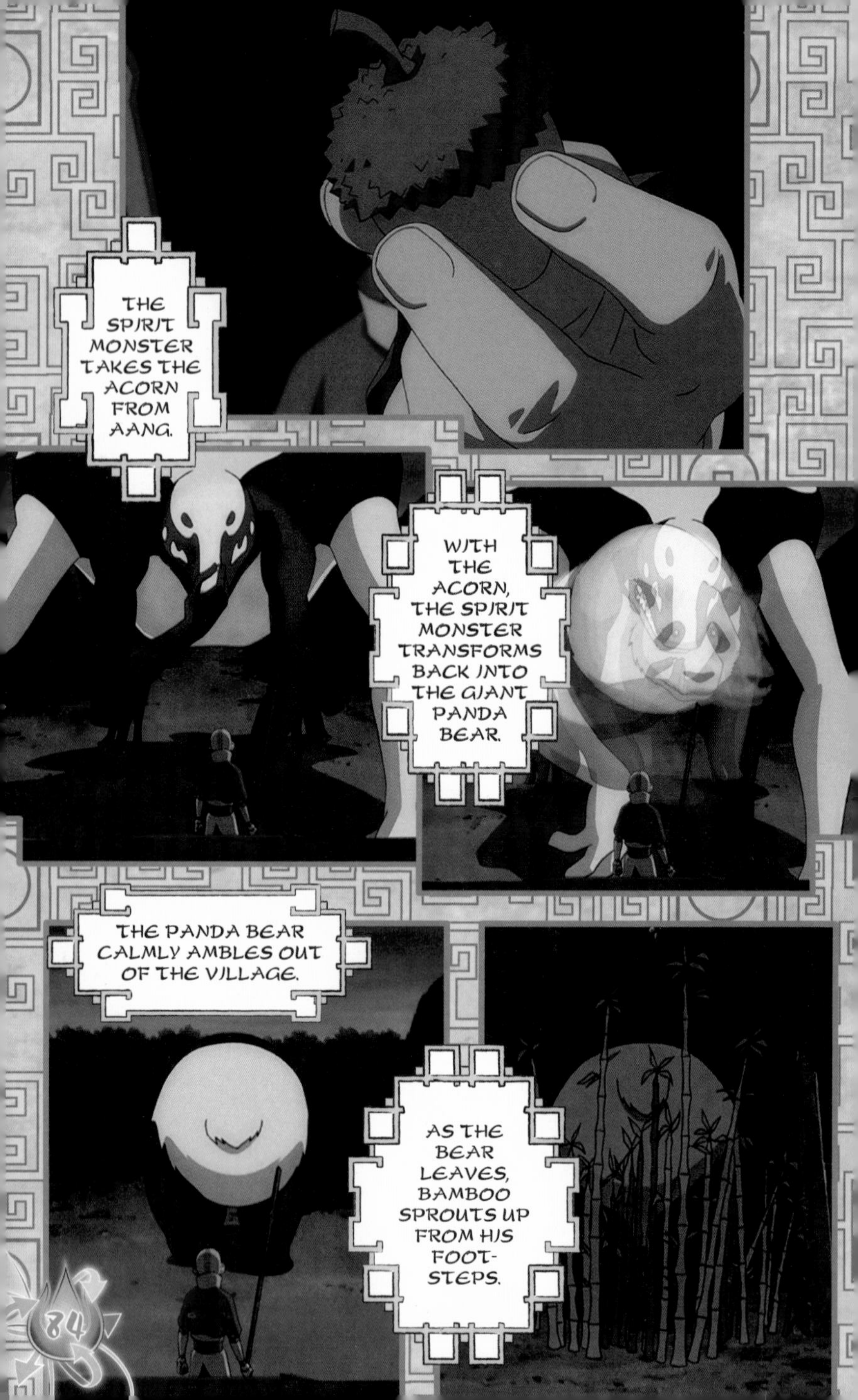
THE SPIRIT MONSTER TAKES THE ACORN FROM AANG.
WITH THE ACORN, THE SPIRIT MONSTER TRANSFORMS BACK INTO THE GIANT PANDA BEAR.
THE PANDA BEAR CALMLY AMBLES OUT OF THE VILLAGE.
AS THE BEAR LEAVES, BAMBOO SPROUTS UP FROM HIS FOOT-STEPS.

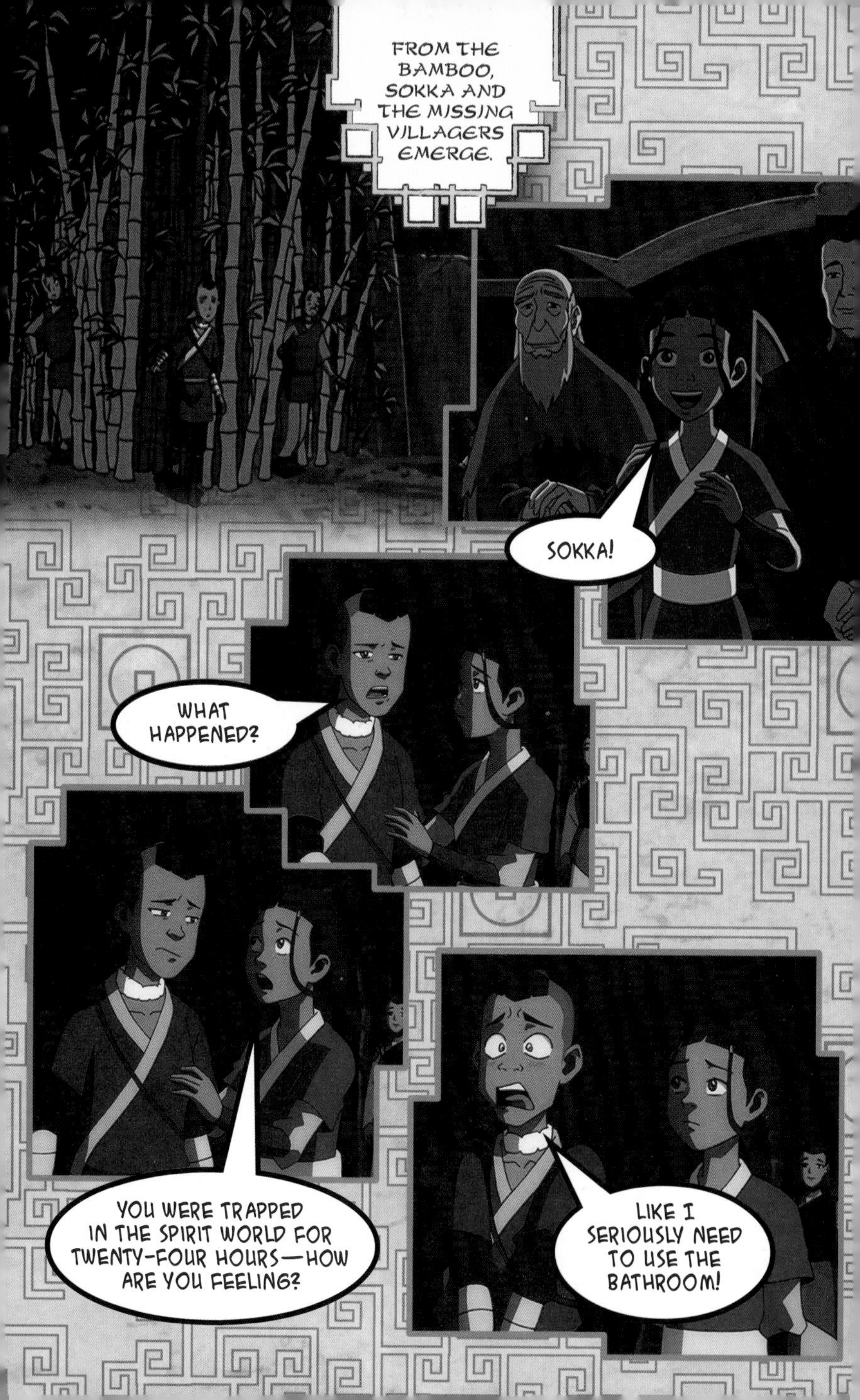
FROM THE BAMBOO, SOKKA AND THE MISSING VILLAGERS EMERGE.
SOKKA!
WHAT HAPPENED?
YOU WERE TRAPPED IN THE SPIRIT WORLD FOR TWENTY-FOUR HOURS—HOW ARE YOU FEELING?
LIKE I SERIOUSLY NEED TO USE THE BATHROOM!

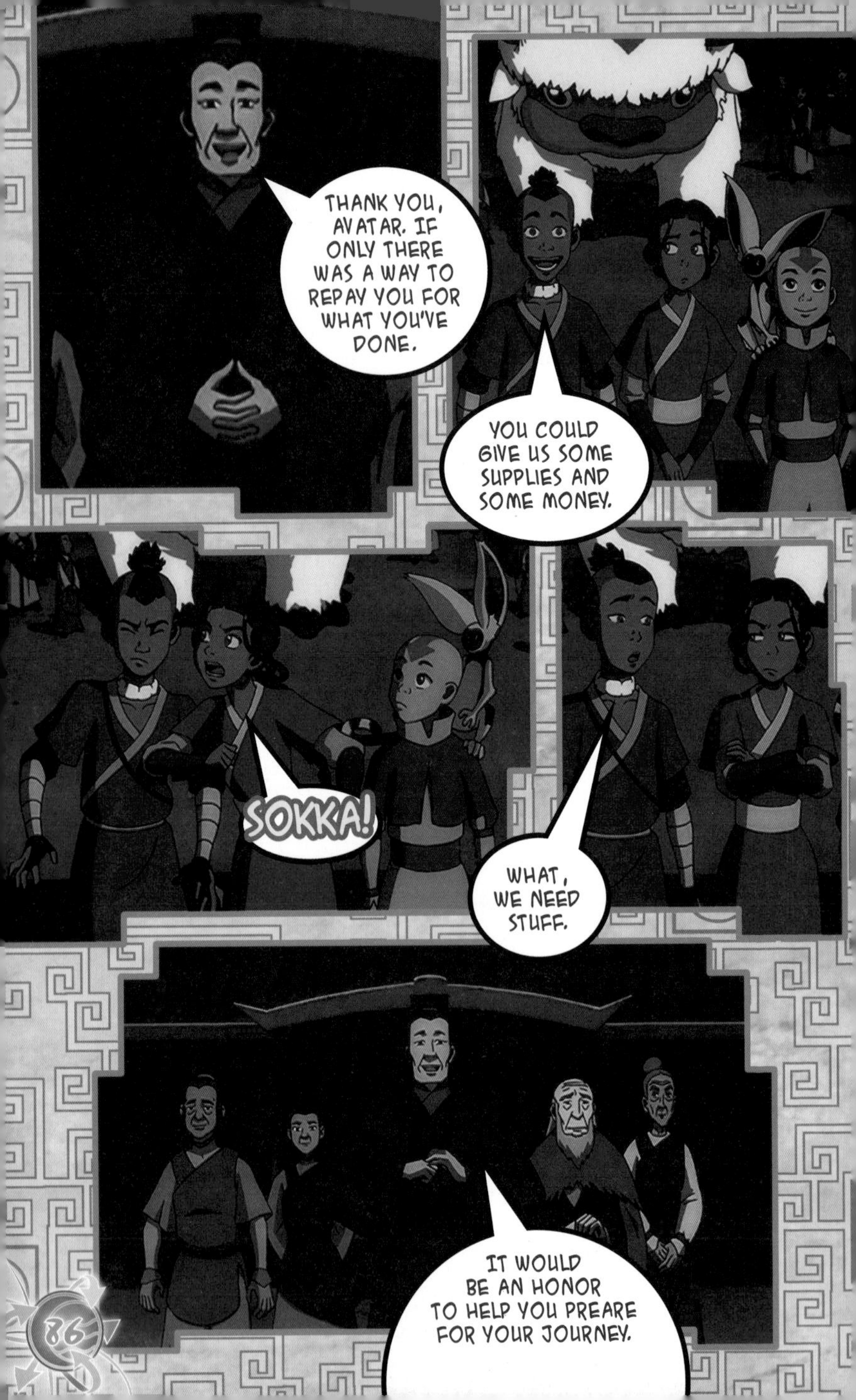
THANK YOU, AVATAR. IF ONLY THERE WAS A WAY TO REPAY YOU FOR WHAT YOU'VE DONE.
YOU COULD GIVE US SOME SUPPLIES AND SOME MONEY.
SOKKA!
WHAT, WE NEED STUFF.
IT WOULD BE AN HONOR TO HELP YOU PREARE FOR YOUR JOURNEY.

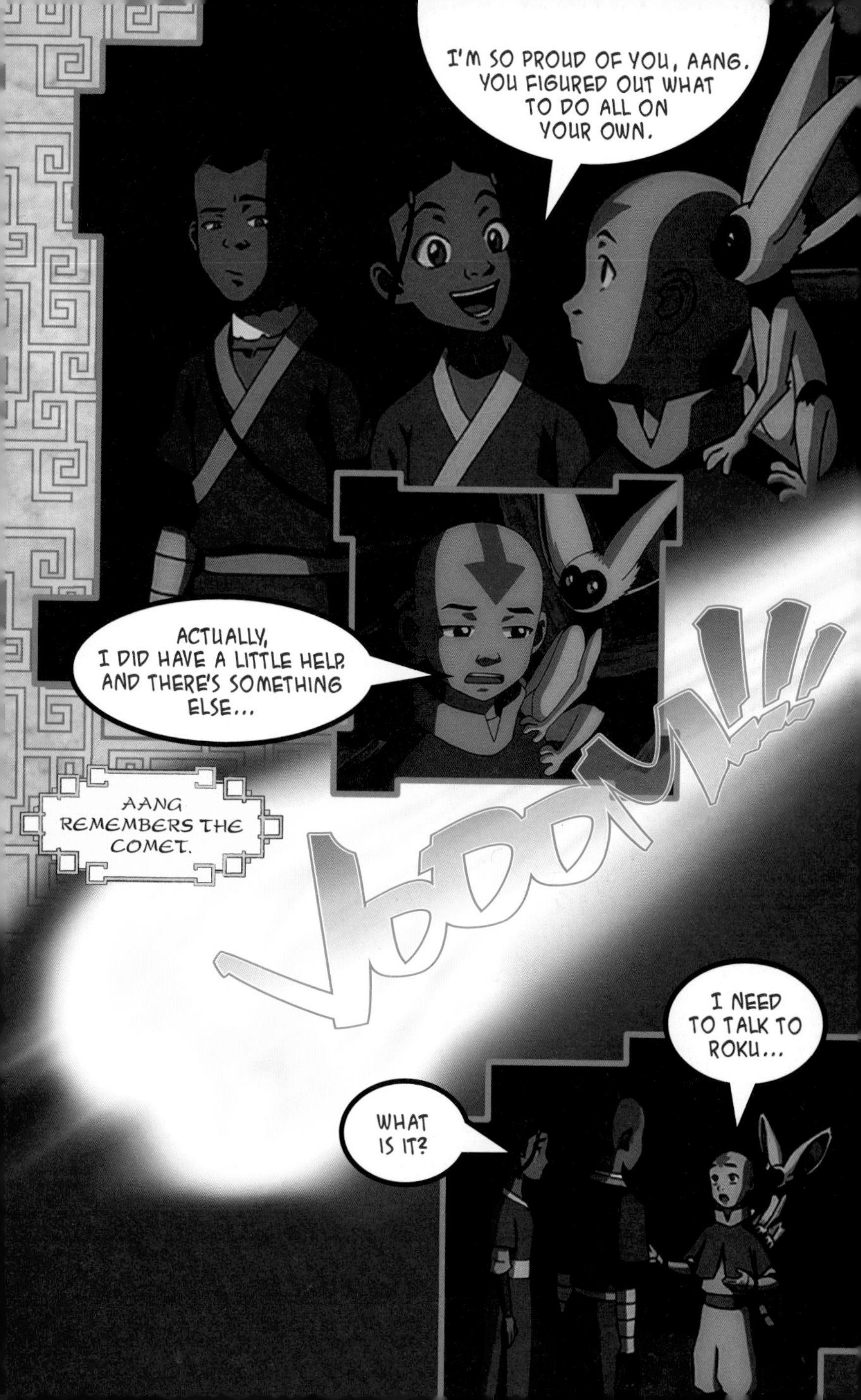
I'M SO PROUD OF YOU, AANG. YOU FIGURED OUT WHAT TO DO ALL ON YOUR OWN.
ACTUALLY, I DID HAVE A LITTLE HELP. AND THERE'S SOMETHING ELSE...
AANG REMEMBERS THE COMET.
VOOOM!!!
WHAT IS IT?
I NEED TO TALK TO ROKU...

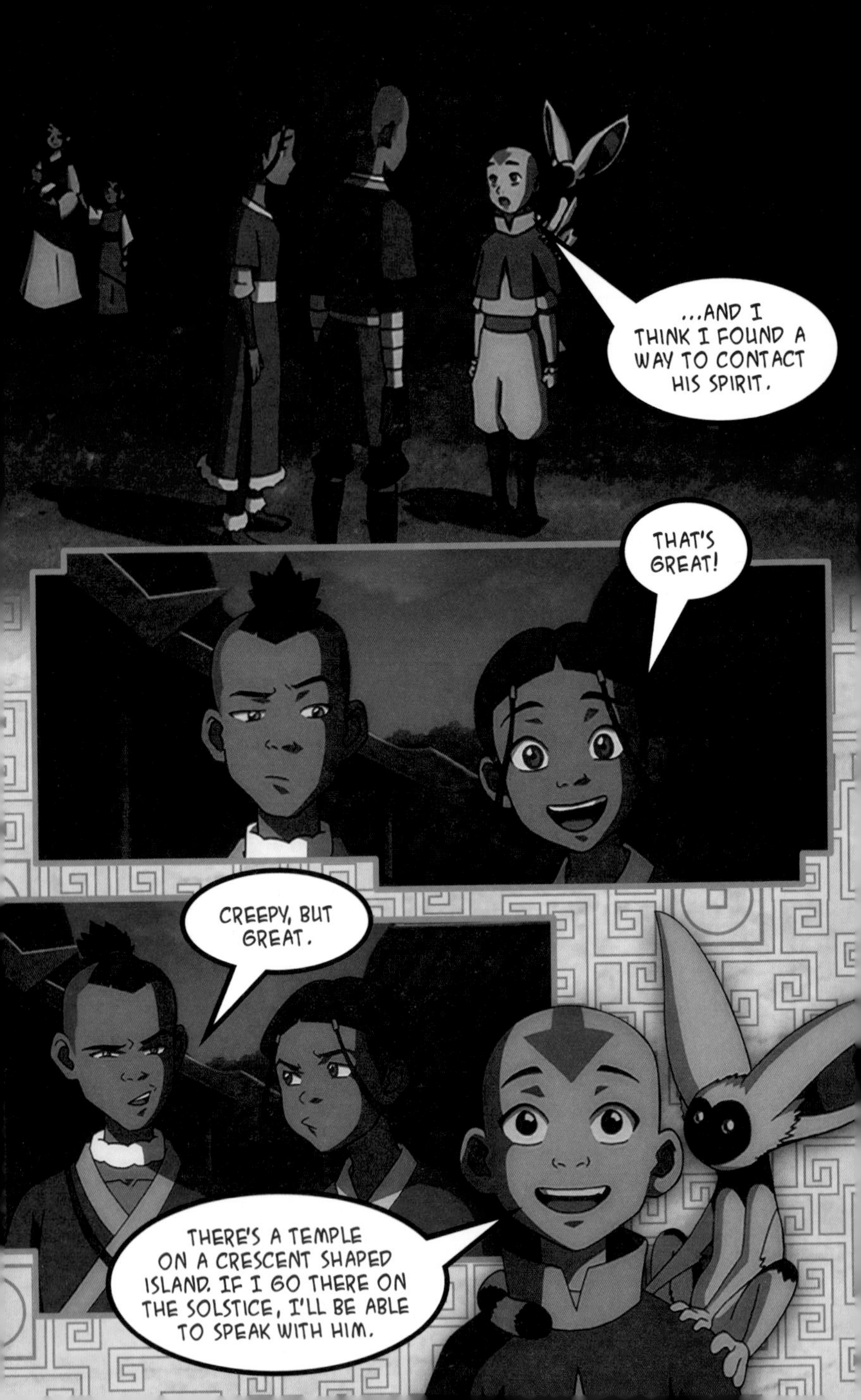
...AND I THINK I FOUND A WAY TO CONTACT HIS SPIRIT.
THAT'S GREAT!
CREEPY, BUT GREAT.
THERE'S A TEMPLE ON A CRESCENT SHAPED ISLAND. IF I GO THERE ON THE SOLSTICE, I'LL BE ABLE TO SPEAK WITH HIM.

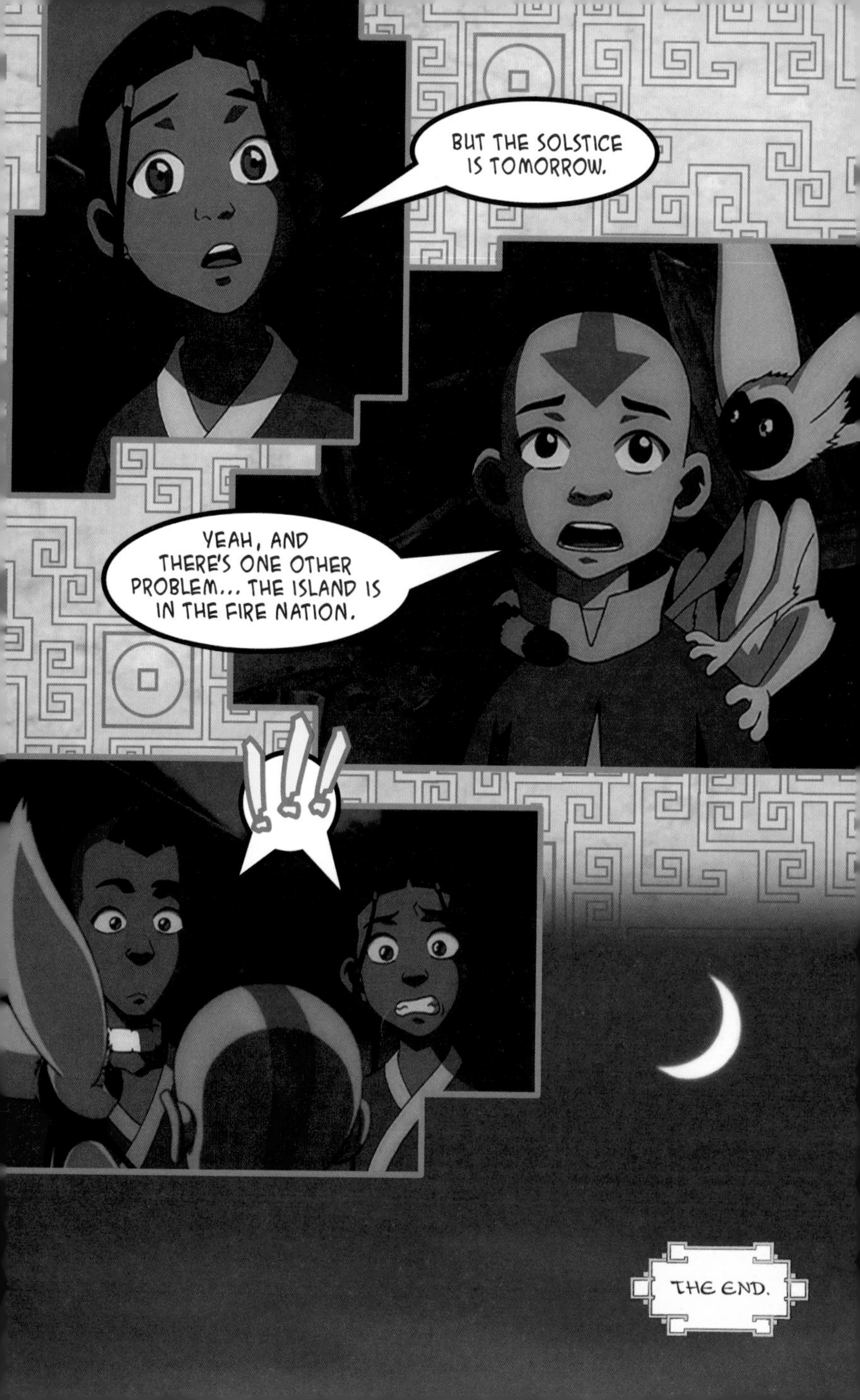
BUT THE SOLSTICE IS TOMORROW.
YEAH, AND THERE'S ONE OTHER PROBLEM... THE ISLAND IS IN THE FIRE NATION.
!!!
THE END.

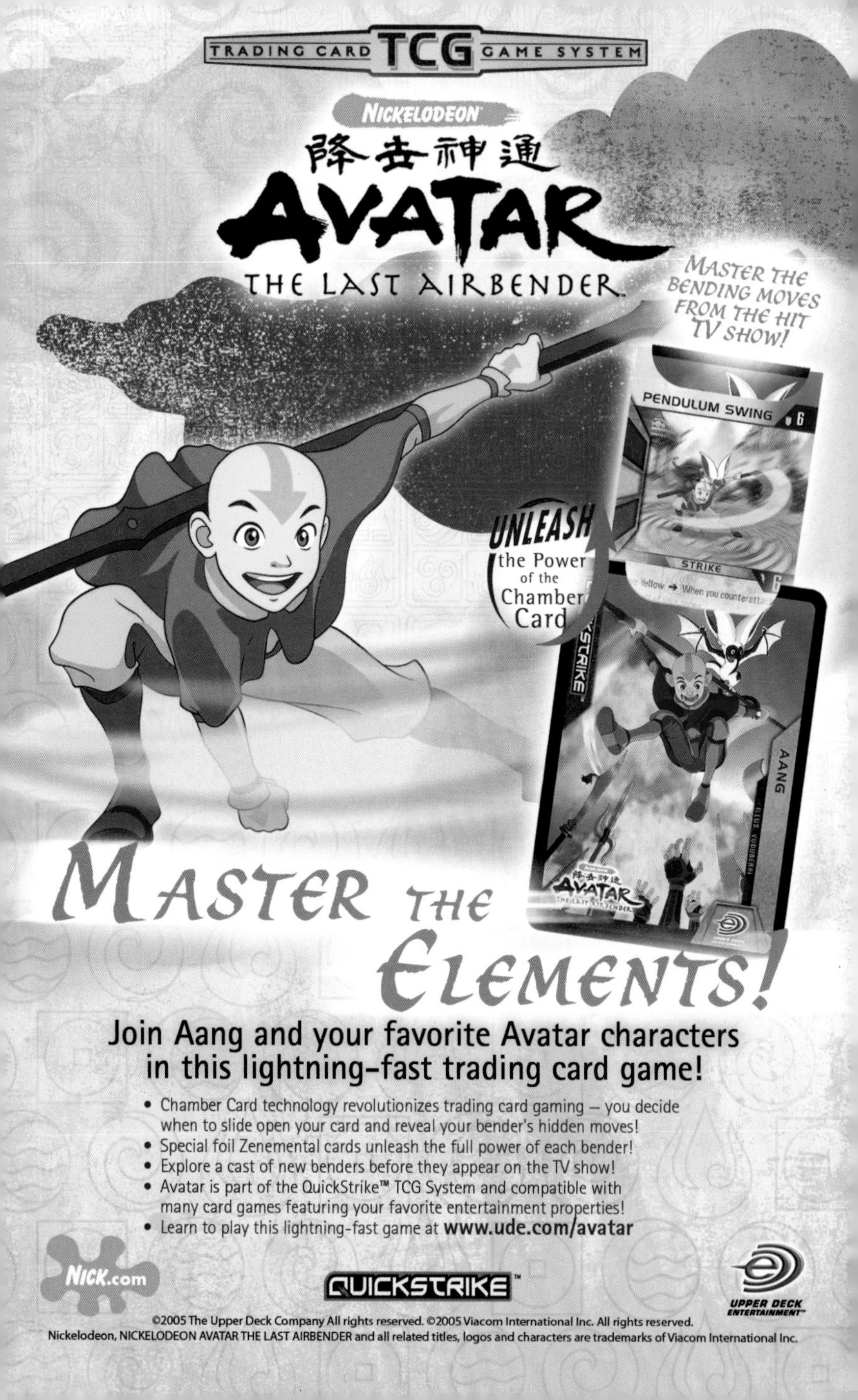
TRADING CARD TCG GAME SYSTEM
NICKELODEON
降去神通
AVATAR
THE LAST AIRBENDER
MASTER THE BENDING MOVES FROM THE HIT TV SHOW!
PENDULUM SWING
6
STRIKE
UNLEASH the Power of the Chamber Card
QUICKSTRIKE
AANG
MASTER THE ELEMENTS!
Join Aang and your favorite Avatar characters in this lightning-fast trading card game!
• Chamber Card technology revolutionizes trading card gaming – you decide when to slide open your card and reveal your bender's hidden moves!
• Special foil Zenemental cards unleash the full power of each bender!
• Explore a cast of new benders before they appear on the TV show!
• Avatar is part of the QuickStrike™ TCG System and compatible with many card games featuring your favorite entertainment properties!
• Learn to play this lightning-fast game at www.ude.com/avatar
NICK.com
QUICKSTRIKE™
UPPER DECK ENTERTAINMENT™
©2005 The Upper Deck Company All rights reserved. ©2005 Viacom International Inc. All rights reserved.
Nickelodeon, NICKELODEON AVATAR THE LAST AIRBENDER and all related titles, logos and characters are trademarks of Viacom International Inc.

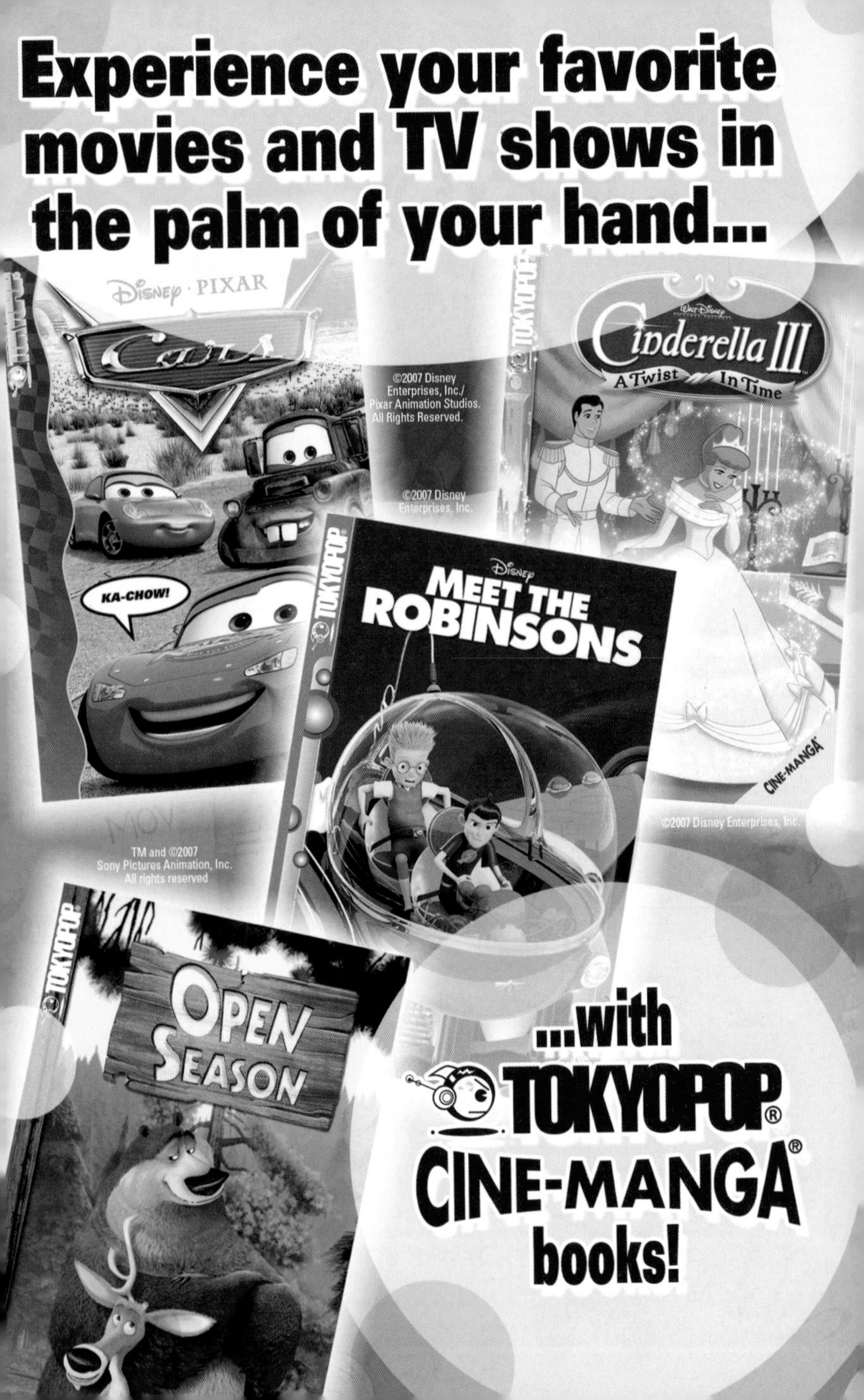
Experience your favorite movies and TV shows in the palm of your hand...
DISNEY · PIXAR
Cars
KA-CHOW!
©2007 Disney Enterprises, Inc./ Pixar Animation Studios. All Rights Reserved.
©2007 Disney Enterprises, Inc.
TOKYOPOP
Walt Disney
Cinderella III
A Twist In Time
CINE-MANGA
©2007 Disney Enterprises, Inc.
Disney
MEET THE ROBINSONS
TM and ©2007 Sony Pictures Animation, Inc. All rights reserved
OPEN SEASON
...with
TOKYOPOP®
CINE-MANGA®
books!

- Aladdin
- All Grown Up
- The Amanda Show
- Avatar
- Bambi
- Barbie™ as the Princess and the Pauper
- Barbie™ Fairytopia
- Barbie™ of Swan Lake
- Cars
- Chicken Little
- Cinderella
- Cinderella III
- Drake & Josh
- Duel Masters
- The Fairly OddParents
- Finding Nemo
- Future Greatest Stars of the NBA

- G.I. Joe Spy Troops
- Greatest Stars of the NBA: Dynamic Duos
- Greatest Stars of the NBA: Greatest Dunks
- Greatest Stars of the NBA: Kobe Bryant
- Greatest Stars of the NBA: Tim Duncan
- Happy Feet
- International Greatest Stars of the NBA
- The Incredibles
- The Adventures of Jimmy Neutron: Boy Genius
- Kim Possible
- Lilo & Stitch: The Series
- Lizzie McGuire
- Meet the Robinsons
- Madagascar
- Mucha Lucha!
- Open Season
- Pirates of the Caribbean: Dead Man's Chest
- Pooh's Heffalump Movie

- The Princess Diaries 2
- Romeo!
- Shrek 2
- SpongeBob SquarePants
- SpongeBob SquarePants Movie
- Spy Kids 2
- Spy Kids 3-D: Game Over
- That's So Raven
- Totally Spies
- Transformers

COLLECT THEM ALL!

Now available
wherever books are sold or at
www.TOKYOPOP.com/shop

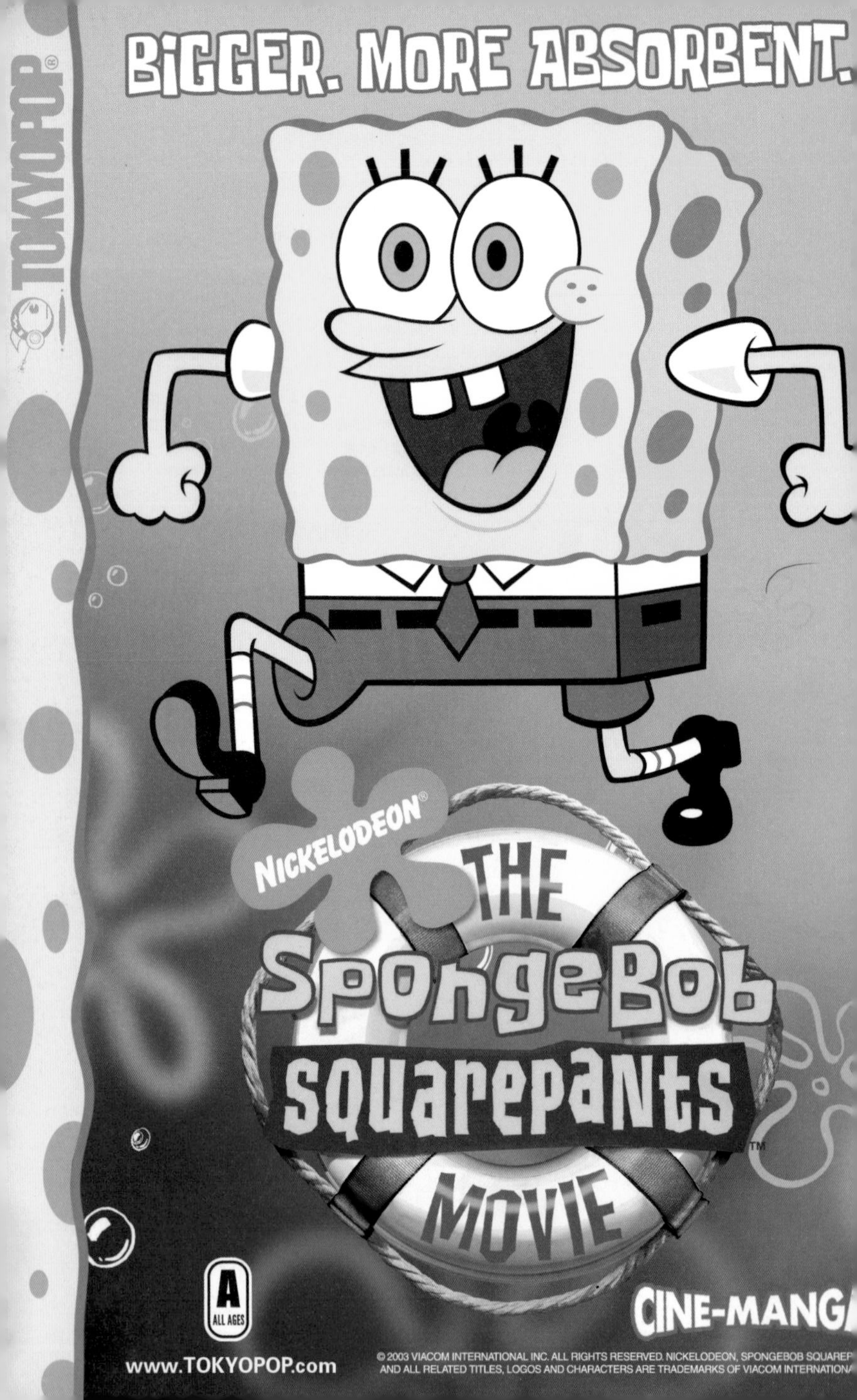
TOKYOPOP®
BIGGER. MORE ABSORBENT.
NICKELODEON®
THE SpongeBob squarepants™ MOVIE
A ALL AGES
CINE-MANGA
www.TOKYOPOP.com
© 2003 VIACOM INTERNATIONAL INC. ALL RIGHTS RESERVED. NICKELODEON, SPONGEBOB SQUAREP
AND ALL RELATED TITLES, LOGOS AND CHARACTERS ARE TRADEMARKS OF VIACOM INTERNATIONA

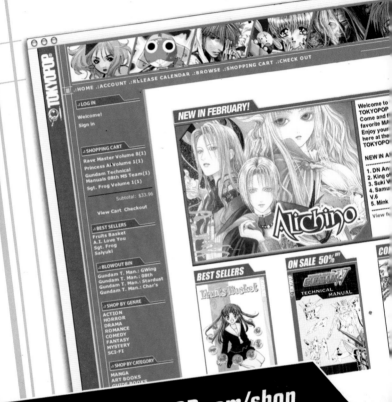